# Kate
## The Women of Valley View

SHARON SROCK

# THE WOMEN OF VALLEY VIEW SERIES

Callie
Terri
Pam
Samantha
Kate
Karla (coming 2016)

# DEDICATION

To my pastors Fred and Gloria Owens. You've led us by example, and you've taught us truth. But most of all you've been a blessing!

# ACKNOWLEDGMENTS

Writing a book is hard work. Having good people, Christian friends, in your corner makes the job a little easier.

Lacy Williams, thanks so much for taking my darkest moment and shining a new light on it.

Robin Patchen, Critique partner, editor, and lover of all things Valley View. I'm still asking God what I did to deserve you. Whatever it was, I hope He never changes his mind!

Marian Merritt, Your thoughtful insight and critique made Kate's story stronger. I'm looking forward to working with you in the future.

Jeff Salter, USAF Col, retired, Your input regarding military life and the facts and fictions involved in a friendly fire accident gave me just the touch of realism the story needed.

As always, my readers and prayer partners, Kaye Whiteman, Sandy Patten, Teresa Talbott, Wanda Peters, Lynn Beck, Carol Vansickle, Barbara Elis, Lisa Walker. If I had one wish to bestow on the women of the world, it would be for each of them to have the same friendships God has blessed me with in you.

My husband, Larry. He hasn't read a single word of a single story, but he thinks what I'm doing is pretty cool.

My daughters Amber and Tammi, you two support me in so many little ways. You make me proud, I hope I can return the favor.

# CHAPTER ONE

Nicolas Ethan Black heard his buddy returning long before he saw him. C.W.'s off-key whistle did no justice to the old hymn floating on the hot desert air. He'd never heard *Amazing Grace* butchered quite so effectively. He shrugged. Entertainment was sparse in this godforsaken wasteland. Sometimes you needed to make your own.

Nicolas shaded his eyes against the sun and looked over the barren landscape. Nothing moved in the shimmering desert light. The heat, the sand that worked its way into every sealed container in camp and every sweaty crease of his body, the fleas living in the grit, and the boredom—those things would kill him long before a human enemy did.

C.W. rounded the corner of the compound, desert BDUs rumpled and sweaty, the good-natured grin firmly in place. It never seemed to leave his face. Nicolas raised his eyebrows and the whistle died.

"Serenading the camels?"

C.W.'s grin broadened. "Just lifting up a praise."

"I sure hope God's deaf today."

"Hey."

Nicolas chuckled at his own joke, resettled the strap of the M16 on his shoulder, and nodded to the fence line. The two men continued along the perimeter together for a few yards. Today, they were the first line of defense against any enemy foolish enough to try and breach the inner wall of the compound.

Nicolas stopped long enough to drain his canteen of lukewarm water. He swiped the last drops from his lips with his sleeve. "Man, I need something cold. A tall glass of iced tea and one of those cookies Blondie sent you."

His friend shook his head. "All gone, dude, but mail's due today. Maybe she sent more. More cookies and new pictures of Little Man. She promised a shot of his first tooth just as soon as she could get them developed."

He grinned. "Your son's a cutie. I want one just like him someday." Nicolas removed his hat, swiped his sweaty brow with an arm, and beat the heat-wilted cap against his leg, releasing a small storm of grit. It disappeared into the sand at his feet. "Are you sure this is what we signed up for?"

C.W. laughed. "My recruiting officer promised me adventure in exotic locations. I don't think we were speaking the same language."

Nicolas smacked his friend's arm and pointed at the horizon. "Take a look at that."

C.W. looked, hands on hips, brows pulled low over his blue eyes. "Just a group of herders."

Nicolas took in the handful of scrawny cows topping the dune alongside a few men dressed in rough clothes and boots. He nodded his agreement. "They're coming a little close, don't you think?"

"It's their country, bro. As long as they don't approach the fence, they're fine."

"Maybe so, but let's mosey back to the gate."

The herders stopped a couple hundred feet from the fence, made a small camp, and prepared a meal over an open fire. Nicolas and his buddy lounged by the gate, watching as the five coarsely dressed men ate and laughed. He had no idea what they were cooking, but the rich meaty fragrance made his mouth water. One of the men broke away from the group and approached the fence. He held a platter in his hand, holding it out as if he meant to share some of their food. Nicolas straightened and motioned for the stranger to stop.

"Don't come any closer!"

The man kept coming. Something pricked the nerves at the back of Nicolas's neck. That heavy jacket, zipped up to the herder's chin in the hundred degree heat, didn't make sense. *I don't like the look of this.*

He spoke to his partner without taking his eyes off the approaching stranger. "Get some back up out here." Nicolas raised his weapon. Maybe the M16 would bridge the language barrier. The herder was close enough now for Nicolas to see that he was just a kid, younger than either of the Air Force Security Police officers guarding the gate. He stopped when Nicholas raised his weapon, dropped the platter, and started fumbling with something under his shirt.

Before Nicolas could get out a warning, the earth shook with an explosion. The concussion of the bomb knocked both SPs to the ground.

Nicolas scrambled to his feet, looking for the source of the explosion. All that remained of the herder was a grisly red stain in the sand. Nicolas brought his rifle to bear on the rest of the herders. He yelled through the smoke. "You OK?"

"Yep." C.W. answered. "Reinforcements are on the

way." C.W. stepped though the haze and took his place next to his friend, weapon trained on the threat. Without warning, two of the remaining men charged in their direction. Nicolas and C.W. crouched, aimed, and took their shots. When the next bomb detonated, it knocked the soldiers to the ground a second time. Vehicles screamed to a stop at the gate behind them, loaded with the support C.W. had requested. The last of the insurgents fled in the face of reinforcements.

American troops poured from the gate. Some raced through the sand, giving chase to the enemy. One bent down at Nicolas's side. Nicolas could see his fellow soldiers' mouth moving, but no sound penetrated the cotton in his ears. He frowned. The eerie silence was more terrifying than the explosion. He closed his eyes and gave his head a quick shake. The pressure in his ears released, and the silence gave way to roaring. Words filtered through, as though someone were increasing the world's volume.

"Don't...injured."

Nicolas pushed himself to his knees, brushing grime from the front of his uniform. His hand came away covered in blood and grit. More blood ran into his eyes now that he was upright. He swiped it away, blinking back the blowing sand.

He turned to where C.W. had stood a moment before, trying to find his partner in the chaos.

~ * ~

The baby in Kate Wheeler's arms jerked as the first round of rifle fire split the quiet of the afternoon. She gathered her son close with one arm, his head pressed to her chest, and managed to cover his exposed ear with her free hand before the final two volleys exploded. It didn't help much. Patrick's startled wails rose to provide the perfect counter point to the three-volley salute. His own tribute to a father he'd never know.

Beside her, Kate's mom touched her arm and made a silent offer to take the howling baby. Kate shook her head and held him tighter. He was all she had left.

Patrick continued to cry as the bugle began its slow, mournful rendition of taps. The drawn out notes regenerated Kate's tears. Frightened, heartbroken, confused, they streaked down her cheeks and dripped from her chin. Some of them landed on the baby.

Sorrow mingled with fear.

The new landscape of their future.

Kate followed the military ceremony from a detached distance as the six-man honor guard lifted the flag from Chad's casket and began the tedious exercise of folding it into a perfect triangle. She recalled the chaplain's explanation. Each of the twelve folds held a special meaning, though Kate couldn't remember a single one. She bit her lip as the flag was flipped a final time and a member of the honor guard slipped objects from his pocket into the last tuck. Three of the spent shell casings from the volley, representative of the Father, the Son, and the Holy Spirit.

Patrick's crying faded away, as if he could sense the solemnness of the moment. Kate kissed his head and surrendered him to his grandmother as an officer approached with the flag and knelt at her knees.

"On behalf of the President of the United States, the United States Air Force, and a grateful nation, please accept this flag as a symbol of our appreciation for your loved one's honorable and faithful service."

Kate took the flag, searching the officer's eyes for answers she'd been denied. All she found was sympathy. "Thank you." Her muttered response sounded as empty as her heart.

*Friendly fire.* Kate closed her eyes against a pain that threatened to rip her heart from her chest. How could they call it friendly when it robbed families of their futures? Oh, she understood the concept. Her husband died while serving his country, not felled by the enemy, but by the hand of a fellow countryman. She clenched her teeth. Maybe the how of it shouldn't matter—dead was dead. An enemy's bullet wouldn't have broken her heart any less, but it might have made sense. The truth served no purpose and offered no closure.

Kate rose and stood with the small group gathered at the graveside. She acknowledged whispered words of condolence with polite nods, her thoughts not nearly so well-mannered. "So sorry for your loss." *Let's hold your heart over an open flame and see how sorry you are.*

"He's in a better place." *Says who?*

"Try not to worry, God has a plan." *Sure wish He'd share.*

*Can't they all just go away and leave me alone?* She glanced at her mom and dad, who were standing on either side of her, and realized that tomorrow when they flew back to Kansas City, she'd get her wish. She'd finally be alone, alone like she'd never been in her whole life. Her breathing hitched even as her knees threatened to turn to mush.

Dad slipped an arm around her waist. "Kate?"

"I'm OK. Would you and Mom take Patrick back to

the apartment for me?"

"We should all go."

She leaned into him and shook her head. "I can't leave just yet. I need to..." Her voice broke, forcing her to swallow before she could continue. "I need to say goodbye, and I can't with all these people milling around. Go back to the house, give Patrick his dinner. I promise I won't be late."

Once her parents left, Kate pulled a chair out from under the funeral awning, situated it under a tree a few feet from the open grave, and waited. People drifted away in twos and threes. The staff from the cemetery packed away their chairs and the tacky artificial turf. The back hoe covered Chad's grave with dirt. A lone caretaker made a half-hearted attempt to organize the floral arrangements before he took his leave.

As the sun slipped low on the western horizon, painting the sky with the soft, pearly pastels of a sea shell, she approached the pile of flowers and removed a single red rose. She retreated to her chair and carefully eased the final fold of the flag apart, tucking the flower inside with the spent shell casings. *The Father, the Son, the Holy Spirit, and my heart.* Her hands trembled as she worked the flap back into place. She lifted her tear-streaked face to the final rays of sunlight. Kate was alone.

# CHAPTER TWO

*Twenty years later*

"Are you insane?" Kate Wheeler Archer stood at the edge of the porch and pushed long blonde hair out of her face. She frowned down at the man floundering in a puddle of late January slush, and swiped at her mouth with the sleeve of her coat. "This was a business meeting, you troll, not a date."

"But—"

She cut him off with a sharp downward slash of her hand. "Don't speak, just leave."

Kate turned her back while the man continued to sputter.

*Seal the deal, seriously?* She looked over her shoulder. "And just FYI...we won't be doing any business together." She opened the front door of her home, swept inside, and slammed the door behind her. "Seal the deal...of all the nerve." What deal? Since when did business dinners end in a tonsil-diving lip lock? Since when did one meeting equal a deal to seal?

*I really wanted that building.* She raised her eyes to the ceiling and muttered a quick prayer. "I know You have the perfect location for me, and the perfect partner." Despite the prayer, Kate's shoulders slumped as she crossed another lost cause off her mental list. "I'd appreciate some direction."

The sound of nails scrabbling on the tiled floor of the entry alerted her to an additional presence in the otherwise quiet house. Kate pushed away from the door and stooped to scoop up the one-year-old black cocker spaniel. She tucked him under her chin. The pup grew still against her heart. "You're my best guy, aren't you, Merlin?" The sound of a car door slamming in the driveway filtered through the door, immediately followed by the racing of an engine and the squealing of tires on pavement. *Good riddance!* She snuggled the pup closer for a second, finding comfort in the warm, silky fur and the faithful heart. "And the only man I need in my life."

She hung her bag on a hook by the door, set Merlin back on the floor, and shed her coat. "You won't believe what just happened." Merlin planted his hindquarters on the tile and tilted his head. Adoring brown eyes gave her his full attention.

"Woof."

Kate grinned in response to the soft bark. Knowing when to use his *inside* voice was just one of Merlin's tricks. She crossed through the living room and turned toward the kitchen. After filling the teapot with water for her favorite bedtime brew, a decaffeinated chamomile tea that would soothe her ruffled feathers and help her sleep, she reached back into the pantry for a box of dog treats. Merlin knew the drill. He sat without being told, his eyes glued to the box, his stubby tail wagging double time.

The pup pulled his lips back into a toothy doggie grin while his back legs quivered with excitement. His antics took Kate's temper down a few degrees and yanked an unexpected chuckle from her throat.

She launched into their nightly ritual. "Is there a good dog in this house?"

"Woof."

"Where?" Kate looked around the room

"Woof, woof."

"Oh, there you are." She tossed the snack in a high arch. Merlin jumped, caught the biscuit in midair, made a perfect four-paw landing, crunched twice, and sat for another.

Kate obliged. "If I could find a man half as adorable as you, I might be tempted to try for number three." The memory of uninvited lips pressed against hers sent a shiver of contempt up her spine. "As it is, I'm more inclined to have a heart with a line slashed through it tattooed on my forehead."

The old-fashioned pot erupted in a shrill whistle. Kate poured the boiling water into a heavy mug and added the tea, inhaling the fragrance as she stirred in a spoonful of sugar and a splash of cream. The routine moved her from irritated to resigned and eased the rest of the tension between her shoulders. *Tonight didn't turn out the way I'd hoped, but tomorrow is another day.*

Kate carried her steaming beverage to her home office and sank into her desk chair. After setting the cup to one side, she opened the lone folder resting next to the keyboard and fed the contents to the shredder. It was hard not to be disappointed as the machine chewed the paper up and spit it into the bag below. *One more promising lead down the drain.* There weren't a lot of options left if she wanted to remain within the comfortable driving radius she'd determined for herself. Merlin bumped her leg, looking for some cuddle time. Kate sat back and allowed the pup to scramble into her lap. He made a half circle and settled with a huff of contented doggie breath. She stroked his head and sipped her tea, her gaze coming to rest on the two pictures sitting side-by-side on the back of her desk. Chad Wheeler and Alan Archer smiled back at her. Her two dead husbands.

The first love of her life, Chad Wheeler, was the embodiment of the tall, dark, and handsome cliché. Factor in his intense blue eyes and gentle smile, and you had a masculine package guaranteed to send the average female heart into overdrive. Determined to serve his country, Chad had wanted nothing more than to make the world a better, safer place for their infant son. His death during Desert Storm put an end to his dreams...and Kate's. *Friendly fire.* Kate closed her eyes against a pain that never quite went away. She gave a halfhearted shrug, not even sure why it should matter after all these years. She reached out and traced the medal hanging from the corner of the picture frame. A Purple Heart...cold metal and cold comfort. Their nineteen months of marriage had been much shorter than the lifetime she'd envisioned on their wedding day. But he'd given her Patrick. For that reason alone, Kate would love him forever.

Alan Archer had come along almost two decades later, and just in the nick of time, rescuing Kate from the empty nest created when Patrick went away to pursue his law degree. So many plans and dreams rekindled by the love of a second wonderful man. So many plans and dreams dumped in the trash pile when that second wonderful man died just short of their first anniversary. Kate's sigh filled the empty room. She glanced at the front door and thought of the man she'd pushed off the porch. *You may be cold and wet, but believe it or not, I did you a favor. Men die when they get involved with me.*

She blew fragrant steam away from her cup and sank back into her memories. Chad's death left her with a child to raise, a paltry life insurance policy, and too many unanswered questions. Alan's death left her with too many regrets and too much money. The funds at her disposal were obscene. But Alan's money would allow Kate to build a legacy to both of the men she'd loved and lost.

The thought of her dream brought a smile to her face. The foundation she wanted to build would offer military widows the support she hadn't received— scissors to cut through the never-ending red tape of military bureaucracy, legal advisors to pursue the benefits deserved and often overlooked out of grief or ignorance, education grants for the widows and children, emergency funds to keep body and soul together in those first few weeks of shock. Counselors, pastors, a shoulder to cry on, and a hand to hold. This was her passion, but even with an obscene amount of money, she couldn't do it alone. *I need property, a business partner, investors—people I can trust and depend on. Not—*her mind returned to the front porch—*uninvited romantic advances.*

She shook her head in frustration, and the amethyst hoops, Alan's wedding gift to her, brushed against her neck. *Romance?* God had given her two good men to love. Looking for a third would be greedy. The only romance on her horizon was Patrick's summer wedding to Samantha Evans. She'd focus her future on building her foundation and loving Sam's daughter, Bobbie, and the other grandchildren Samantha and Patrick were bound to provide. Surely, those things would be enough to fill the gaping hole in her heart.

~ * ~

"Mom, you're killing me." Nicolas Black pushed his half-eaten dessert to the center of the table, leaned back in his chair, and stretched his legs. The wide black utility belt of his police uniform bit into his waist as he shifted in the seat.

"You gonna waste that?" His father reached across the table and forked up a bite of Nicolas's discarded coconut cream pie. "I'm half-starved with the tiny little sliver your mother doled out to me. She used to save the big slices for me, until you came home."

Nicolas shook his head. "Help yourself, Pop. If Mom keeps feeding me like this, I'll be buying new uniforms in a month. I hate to admit it, but keeping fit is a lot harder at forty-something than it was at twenty."

His mother passed behind him, stopping at his side to fill his coffee cup. "Enjoy it while you can, Nicolas. The new will wear off your homecoming soon enough." She crossed to her chair, sat, and cut into her own dessert. "I put a piece aside for Tyler. That partner of yours is too skinny. Hard to believe his wife owns a bakery."

"See what I mean?" Pop asked. "She'll have the whole thing given away, and I'll be left with nothing but crumbs." He looked at his wife of forty plus years. "You're a cold, cold woman, Karla Black."

Mom glared across the table. "And you're a silly old coot. There's half a pie left in the kitchen. I'd hardly call that crumbs."

Nicolas chuckled. Would nothing ever change between his folks? *It really is good to be home.* The random thought caught Nicolas by surprise. It had been his decision to leave and stay gone for most of the last twenty-two years. A career in the Air Force had given him plenty of legitimate excuses to be absent, and he'd exercised them freely. But the truth remained the truth. Guilt kept him gone, always deployed as far from home as possible, constantly on the move, living the solitary life of a confirmed bachelor, forfeiting all dreams for a family of his own as the hours, days, and minutes of his life ticked by. *Nothing less than due penance.* How could he enjoy his own family when he'd destroyed someone else's?

The loop in his brain jumped into overdrive at the reminder, inundating him with the acrid smell of smoke too thick to see through, the noise of running feet, screams, and gunfire, the taste of his own blood in his mouth... A life-changing event reduced to a two-second flash of memory.

Nicolas Ethan Black, USAF Col, retired, jerked himself out of the past by sheer force of will. He gave himself a mental shake and searched for the thread of the conversation. *Oh yeah, pie or the lack there of.* He picked up his cup and raised it to his father in a silent salute. "I think we've been told."

The look of concern on his dad's face was there and gone so quickly Nicolas almost managed to convince himself that he'd imagined it. That Pop hadn't noticed his lack of attention, that the pain of old memories was invisible to everyone standing on the outside of his skin.

Almost.

Nicolas held his breath. *Just let it go, Dad.*

As if reading his mind, his father turned from him and sent a sly wink in his mom's direction. "She's always been a bit of a tigress."

Nicolas hid a grin behind his cup. The low growl that followed the wink had him laughing until he choked. Once the coughing fit passed, he studied his parents. Both over sixty and retired, but the spark of romance that still smoldered between them was as tangible as the cup in his hand.

"Do I need to leave you two kids alone?"

"Yes," his dad said.

"No," his mother answered at the same time. "If you stick around, maybe our old married behavior will put ideas into your head and you'll go forth, find a wife, and multiply as the good Lord intended."

"Here she goes." His father chuckled and slumped in his seat.

Nicolas crossed his arms and met his mother's gaze. Mom's campaign to marry him off never took a holiday. "Mom, I can quote this script by heart." He stuck out his chin and tapped it with his finger. "But go ahead, give me your best shot."

Mom narrowed her eyes at him. "You've been home for almost four months. How's Ida's house working out for you?"

He tilted his head and studied his mother. This wasn't the approach he'd expected for her weekly you-need-to-get-married-and-settle-down lecture. Nicolas shrugged, grateful for the reprieve. "Gran's house is great. I appreciate you guys letting me use it."

"The timing worked out. It was empty, and you

were coming home. Have you been to see her lately?"

Nicolas nodded, still confused by her direction, treading lightly with his answers. "I try to get out to the care center at least once a week. I stop and get an extra burger or something, and we eat lunch in her room and play cards. Sometimes, I drag Tyler along with me. Grandma seems to get a kick out of our uniforms and guns. Invites everyone that comes down the hall into her room to meet her 'bodyguards.'"

His mother nodded. "Ida missed you all the years you were away. Your grandmother thinks it's a well-kept secret, but everyone knows that you were her first grandchild and as such, always just a little special." Karla paused to sip her coffee. "I know she still talks about moving back home on occasion, but deep down I think she knows that won't happen. She seems to be happier since you moved into her house, knowing what she cared for all those years is still a source of comfort to someone she loves." She leaned forward, placed her elbow on the table and propped her chin in her hand. "You are comfortable there, right? You have everything you need...plenty of room?"

Nicolas laughed. "Mom, the house has three bedrooms. More than enough space for a lonely old bachelor accustomed to living in sparse military housing."

His father groaned and lowered his face into his hands. "Walked right in to her trap."

He glanced at his father and returned his gaze to his mother just in time to catch the tail end of a triumphant smile.

"Speaking of lonely bachelor's—"

"Karla..."

His mother kept her eyes locked on Nicolas's face as she pushed his unfinished pie across the table to her husband. "Eat this."

"Mom—"

"You're the one who used the word *lonely*. I just want you to know that I have plenty of friends with daughters, nieces, and co-workers. I could speak—"

"Don't you dare."

Karla sputtered to a stop.

"The match-making skills of you and your cronies"—his mother gasped at the word—"may be legendary, but you need to take me off your radar."

"While you were gallivanting all over the globe, I could understand your...reluctance to drag a family along in your wake. But that's irrelevant now that you've retired. It's time you settled down. You need someone to share the rest of your life with, and I need a grandchild."

"You have seven."

"Eight, and none of them belong to you."

Nicolas didn't hesitate to burst her bubble. "May I remind you that I'm almost forty-four years old? If I got married tomorrow, it's highly unlikely that my *bride* would be willing to have babies. If I were in the market for a wife, which I'm not, I'd be looking for someone my own age, not some twenty-something looking to start a family." He took a final sip of his coffee and struggled to keep his words respectful. *She doesn't...can't...understand.* He needed to leave before the conversation took any more unexpected turns. "Dinner was great, but it's time for me to head home."

Mom sat back, shoulders slumped, eyes downcast. She reached across the table. Nicolas let her sweat for a couple of seconds before he clasped her hand in his own.

"I'm sorry, son. I wasn't trying to upset you." She rubbed her thumb along his knuckles, tugging until he raised his gaze to hers. "Don't go. Four or forty-four, you're still my baby. I just want you to be happy."

"Who says I'm not happy?"

"I haven't seen you completely happy in more than twenty years. There's always something just below the surface. I can see it in your eyes. If it isn't loneliness..."

Her words filled his nostrils with the smell of long-dissipated smoke. *If you only knew what your* baby *had done*. Nicolas wrestled with the urge to come clean with the two people who loved him most in the whole world. The thought died under the weight of twenty-two years of guilt. The word *murderer* made a brief appearance, and he squashed it. "Can we please change the subject?"

His mother nodded, squeezed his hand before releasing it, and turned to his father. "Did I tell you Kate called yesterday? She was just bubbling with enthusiasm." She looked back to Nicolas. "You remember Kate Archer, don't you?"

"Mom."

"No...no." She waved a hand in his direction. "Yes, Kate is one of my single friends, but I really am trying to change the subject."

He searched his mother's face for any lingering sign of maternal meddling. "Yes, I remember Kate Archer. Blonde, fortyish, petite, green eyes." The description came in the dry, clipped style of police officers around the world. "Hard not to. The kidnapping of Terri's granddaughter was an intense couple of days. I'm still amazed by the outcome."

"The grace of God," his mother said.

Nicolas closed his eyes. *Please don't go there, either. I don't need the you-should-come-back-to-church lecture stacked on top of the other one.* He really would go home. Between Christian parents he loved and respected and a Christian partner who looked for every opportunity to shove God in his face, it was getting harder and harder to ignore the sorry state of his heart. He shored up his defenses with bricks built of bitterness and blame. A relationship with a cold-blooded God was no longer a part of his life.

"Well?" his mom asked.

He opened his eyes, prepared to make an excuse to leave. A small sigh of relief chased the idea from his mind. She was facing his dad, her question aimed at him.

"I don't think you mentioned it," Dad said. "What had her so excited?"

"She thinks she found the perfect location for her project. It's a rental, but she's having dinner with the building owner tonight to discuss the terms of buying it outright." Mom looked at her watch. "In fact she's probably home by now, maybe she'll have good news to share tomorrow."

"That's great. Did she say—?"

"What sort of project does she need a building for?" Nicolas asked, eager to keep his mother focused on any topic that didn't include wedding bells or prayer.

She turned back to Nicolas. "Sorry, sweetheart, sometimes I lose track of what you know and what you don't. Kate's husband died last year and left her a boatload of money. She's using part of it to start a resource center for military widows. Finding the location is the first step in getting her dream off the ground."

Nicolas tuned out his mother's chatter, drawn to Kate's idea like metal shavings to a magnet. *I just might need to reach out to Kate Archer after all.* His gaze cut back to his mother. Not, he assured himself, for the romantic reasons she would no doubt encourage, but for professional ones.

He mulled the idea while his parents chatted on about their day. This was something he definitely wanted to explore. Nicolas took a final sip of his coffee and scooted his chair away from the table. His action brought his parent's conversation to a halt.

"Leaving us?" Dad asked.

Nicolas nodded. "I'm beat. Tyler and I have been putting in some serious hours lately. My bed is calling me so loud, I'm surprised you two can't hear it."

His dad chuckled. "Not just your diet that changes after forty, is it?" He stood and circled the table. "Go get Tyler's pie. I'll walk you out."

Something in his dad's tone put Nicolas on alert. *I wish there weren't secrets and silent disagreements between us.* He stepped out the door and zipped up his jacket, waiting while his father did the same. What could be important enough to drag Dad out into the late January air? *Maybe it has nothing to do with me.* He glanced sideways. The sight of his father's nervous lip chewing drove that hope from his mind.

Nicolas unlocked the door of the Camaro. Maybe he could make a quick getaway. "Tell Mom I said thanks for dinner." He reached for the handle.

"Where do you go?"

Nicolas looked up. "What?"

His dad jammed his hands into his pockets and met his gaze eye-to-eye. "When your eyes get glassy and you zone out of the conversation. Where do you go?"

Nicolas lowered his eyes and tucked his chin into the neck of his jacket. *Come clean.* He shook the thought away, afraid to damage the only real relationships he still had. "I...nowhere, really."

"That's a load of horse hockey, son, and we both know it." He cocked his head and studied Nicolas. "I won't harass you like your mom does, but we both know you've got something locked away," he poked a finger into Nicolas's chest—"right here. It's been eatin' at you for years. You need to let it go."

"Pop—"

"End of lecture. I just want you to remember that your mom and I are here for you." He pulled Nicolas into a gruff hug. "I'm going in now, because I'm old and it's freezing out here, but you remember what I said."

Nicolas couldn't speak around the lump of emotion lodged in his throat. He nodded and pulled the door open. How long was too long to keep secrets from the people you loved?

~ * ~

Melanie Mason paced, anger building with each step she took. The already overwhelming pressure in her chest tripled every time she glanced at the clock.

*Inconsiderate, self-centered, self-involved...* "Jerk!"

How could Tyler forget about tonight and their plans? If he hadn't forgotten, how could he just blow them off without a word to her?

Her path took her back to the clock. *Midnight.* "This is the last time." And hadn't she said that before? Hadn't *he* said that before? Fairness forced her to give a little credit. Things had been better the last few months, but somewhere deep in her heart, she'd known it was just a matter of time before things went back to normal. *I won't go back to being last on his list. I should be more to him than an afterthought.*

Melanie stomped across the room to the coat closet in the entry hall and yanked the door open. She fished in the pocket of her coat and withdrew a small box wrapped in silver and tied with pink and blue ribbons.

It wasn't just dinner for her thirty-third birthday he'd ruined. She'd planned to share the most important and unexpected news of their twelve year marriage with him this evening. Just one more time his self-centered attitude spoiled something special. *Why am I even surprised?*

"I'm"—she rested her free hand on her stomach—"we're not worthy of his time." Oh, that thought stung. Melanie ripped the package open. The ribbons fluttered to the floor. With the box open in her hands, she stared at the used pregnancy test and the bright blue X visible in the little window. She shoved the package back into the pocket of her coat, retreated to the couch, and gave way to tears.

# CHAPTER THREE

Tyler Mason juggled his keys and a bouquet of colorful hot-house daisies. He unlocked the front door, stepped into the living room, and tilted his head, listening for signs of life. It was early. If Melanie were still asleep, maybe he could get a nice breakfast fixed. He'd prefer to use the flowers as a centerpiece instead of an apology. His position as one of two detectives in Garfield's little police department was a job Tyler took seriously, and he always gave it his best. An occasional all-nighter was just part of that job. It made his wife crazy, but...

The truth ground his train of thought to a halt. *Be honest, bud. Last night's pointless vigil was all your idea.* He shrugged the facts aside. Maybe, but as long as there was a drug dealer running loose in their little town, the job took priority. If Melanie hadn't learned to accept his schedule after twelve years of marriage then someone needed to try harder, and it wasn't him.

Muffled thumps and muttered words from down the hall drew his attention. A deep breath of resolve filled his lungs. Tyler shelved the breakfast plans and followed the noise to the door of the master bedroom. *Time to pay the piper.*

"I'm done. Just done."

Tyler watched as Melanie slammed a drawer shut

25

and dumped an armload of clothing into an already overflowing suitcase that lay open on the bed.

"What are you doing?"

Melanie straightened, put her hands on her hips, and turned to face him. He took in her red, swollen eyes, and the smudges of black mascara, high on her cheekbones, that looked like bruises. Tyler took a step forward, hand outstretched.

"Sweetheart, what's wrong? What's happened?"

Melanie took a step away from him and looked at him as if she didn't understand the question. "What's wrong?"

"You've been crying, you're packing... Oh sweetheart, is it your dad again? Has he had another stroke?"

She shook her head, turned away from him, and bent to refold some of the items sticking out of the bag. "Dad's fine, at least he was when we talked last week."

"Then what...?"

Her breath hiccupped into the room as her hands stilled. When she looked up at him, the desolation in her eyes cut him to the bone. "You don't have a clue, do you?"

Tyler stared at his wife. *This is about more than a late night.* He waited, better to let her explain than for him to wade into the unknown.

"I didn't think so." Melanie bent back over the bag. "I'm leaving, Tyler. I can't do this anymore."

Her forlorn response sliced a dull knife through his heart and left him fumbling to process her words. *Leaving...but...*

Melanie stared at him over the open suitcase, fresh

tears in her eyes. "Do you have any idea what yesterday was?"

Tyler sat on the edge of the mattress and scrubbed a hand down the length of his face. Neglected whisker stubble scraped at his palm. Apparently he hesitated too long.

"Figures." Her eyes and hands went back to the suitcase. "It was my birthday."

His gaze came to rest on the flowers in his other hand. How could he have forgotten...again? Flowers meant as an apology for working all night morphed into a shabby excuse for a birthday bouquet. He held them up with a silent prayer. "I brought you flowers."

Melanie ignored the vibrant blooms. "Fresh from a last minute stop at the grocery store, no doubt."

She lowered the lid of the suitcase and snapped it shut. Her head remained bowed, and he saw a tear drip from her chin to puddle on the vinyl.

"I don't know what's worse, that you forgot...again, or that you thought a handful of flowers would make your neglect acceptable." Her eyes met his. "I waited for you all night, even after I sent Tiffany and Jason back to their hotel."

His head fell back on his shoulders with a groan. Dinner with Tiffany and Jason...he'd forgotten more than her birthday.

"I waited," she whispered.

"Why didn't you remind me?" He struggled to keep frustration out of his voice. *How am I supposed to remember every date in her appointment book?* "I called to tell you I was hung up, you never said a word about dinner."

Melanie glared at him, eyes narrowed and mouth

tight. "Don't you dare try to turn this around to make it my fault. There are some things I shouldn't have to remind you of. If I have to beg for your attention, I don't need it."

"Melanie, I'm a jerk, OK, but we can fix this." He silently kissed his Super Bowl plans goodbye and prepared to grovel. "I got a call on the way home this morning. Church is cancelled because of the ice and snow. We can spend the whole day together. A lazy Sunday morning. We can fix breakfast, and I'll clean the kitchen. After I grab a couple of hours sleep, I'll even call Tiff and Jason and tell them I'm an idiot. We'll go to dinner today instead, any restaurant you want."

"Because church is cancelled?"

He nodded.

"Now that your precious job is done with you for a bit, and church is cancelled, you have time for me?"

"That's not what I meant."

"But that's what it boils down to, and whether you meant it that way or not, I'm still last on your list of priorities, just like always. I'm tired of it. I'm not doing it anymore."

*She's serious.* The realization accelerated his heart rate and had his pulse pounding in his ears. "Mel, don't make a decision like this when you're angry. Think about—"

"I'm not angry." Melanie went to the closet and returned with the white shoes she wore when she worked. She shook out a recycled plastic shopping bag, wrapped up the shoes, and stuffed them into the zippered compartment on the front of the bag. "I was angry the first two times, hurt the times after that. Now? I'm just resigned and tired."

Melanie slid the suitcase off the bed, extended the telescoping handle, and situated a second, smaller bag on top of the larger. She tilted both, detoured around him, and maneuvered down the short hallway to the front door. After grabbing her jacket from the closet, she paused on the threshold.

Tyler laid a hand on her shoulder. "Melanie, you're overreacting. You know I love you. It's cold and nasty outside. Do you even know where you're going once you walk out that door?"

"Someplace better than here." The sadness on his wife's face belied the flippant answer, but it ramped up his temper none the less.

"Fine. I don't want you to go." Tyler swept a hand across the threshold. "But I not going to beg you to stay."

Melanie shrugged. "That's good." Her voice cracked, and she pulled in a deep, shuddering breath. "Because right now, I wouldn't stay if you begged."

~ * ~

The ringing of the phone shattered Kate's beauty sleep long before her alarm had its scheduled chance to intrude on her Sunday morning. She kept her eyes squeezed shut as her hand groped across the top of the nightstand. She connected the call and brought the instrument to her ear.

"Hmm?"

"Mom?"

Her son's voice got a smidgeon more of her attention. She took a deep breath and pushed herself up in the bed. "Hey, sweetheart. What's up?"

"Not you," Patrick joked.

She squinted at the clock, always a blur before her contacts went in. "My alarm was set for eight."

"Well turn it off and go back to sleep. I just got off the phone with Sisko. They dismissed church today. The roads are pretty clear, but the parking lots at Valley View are still slick with ice and snow. I wanted to make sure you got the message before you ventured out."

"Thanks, baby." She took a deep breath. The cobwebs of sleep began to dissipate, allowing her to remember what day it was. Kate doubted that all of the school kids in the world, combined, had never offered up as many prayers of gratitude for a snow day as the men in Garfield were offering today. "No service tonight works out nicely for you, doesn't it?"

Patrick's laugh rumbled through the phone.

Kate smiled. He sounded so much like his father. Nostalgia tugged at her heart. *How is it even possible for her baby boy to be living in his own home, planning a wedding and a family?* She shook the maudlin thoughts away as he continued.

"I'll admit that the fact that church is cancelled on Super Bowl Sunday is a rare opportunity. I can say with all honesty that I did *not* pray for another six inches of snow this week."

Kate's response was a muffled yawn.

"Anyway, go back to sleep. I'll talk to you later."

A second yawn slurred her response. "'K. Bye." She dropped the phone and pulled a pillow over her head to block the rapidly increasing light filtering into the room. The phone rang again.

Kate rolled over and snatched it up. "How can I go back to sleep if you keep calling?"

"Do what? Why are you still asleep?" Karla asked.

Kate rubbed at her grainy eyes. "Why are you up so early on a morning when church is cancelled? Didn't you get the message?"

"Early? It's almost ten."

Kate rolled over, grabbed the clock, and held it in front of her face, frowning when she saw that it was, indeed, almost ten. She'd slept for three hours since Patrick's call. *Being pawed the night before must have taken more out of me than I realized.* She sat up and swung her feet to the floor, doing her best to force a little enthusiasm into her voice. "Okay, I'm up. What's going on?"

"It's Super Bowl Sunday. While our men didn't expect to be at home this evening, there are obviously no plans to neglect this opportunity to watch the big game, live, start to finish. Some of us are organizing a no kids, no men, Super Bowl alternative party. Are you game?"

"Cute. What's the plan?"

"Chili Mac's, one o'clock. That should put us between the lunch crowd and the game day revelers. Callie, Pam, and Terri have already said yes. Sam said no. She and Bobbie are going over to the new house to spend the day with Patrick. You're my last call."

"Karla, the high today is only predicted to be twenty-five—"

"Yes, and all the men will be planted in front of the television with every snack they can beg, borrow, or steal. I for one don't care who wins Super Bowl six hundred and ninety-two blah, blah, blah. My time is much better spent at the mall."

"I don't know—"

"Southwest eggrolls," Karla wheedled. "Chips with chili cheese dip."

Kate groaned. "That's below the belt. I haven't had breakfast yet."

"All's fair." A second yawn forced Kate's eyes shut. *Why am I hesitating? It's not like I have anything better to do.* "OK, sounds good." *Oh, shoot, Melanie!* "I might have a friend with me."

"The more, the merrier. Who?"

"Melanie Mason. I met her through Sam and Patrick's wedding planner. She's doing their cake. I've been talking to her about coming to church, and I was supposed to call her later. Since service is cancelled, she might enjoy meeting some of you over lunch."

"I know Melanie," Karla said. "Her husband Tyler is Nicolas's partner. The little bakery she owns has become a weekly stop on my Friday morning round of errands. That free cookie Friday thing she does is more than a little addictive. You've met Tyler haven't you? He's been attending services pretty regularly for a few months now."

"Wait a minute." Kate closed her eyes and pictured Valley View's large sanctuary. "Tall, skinny guy with salt and pepper hair, always by himself on the back pew?"

"That's Tyler. He's a sweetheart and getting very involved in the men's ministry. He's organized a few father-son outings, and he's taken over the bi-weekly men's Bible study. If he's keeping half the schedule Nicolas does, I don't know how he does it."

"I've seen him in the back a few times," Kate said, "but I haven't met him yet. He's always gone before I get back there."

"I'll make sure you meet him. He'll be thrilled to

know you're talking with Melanie about church. I know it breaks his heart that she won't attend services with him."

"That's got to be a tough situation. I'll be praying for both of them now. In the meantime I'll give her a call about this afternoon. I'll see you there for sure."

Kate replaced the phone and poked at the small mound under the covers. "Come on, lazy. If I have to get up, so do you." She waited a few seconds before lifting the bedclothes and peering into the gloom at the foot of the bed. "Merlin." The light filtering through the window shades provided enough illumination for her to see his ears flinch at her voice. "Merlin, we both know you aren't asleep. You want to go outside?"

The O-word worked magic on the somnolent dog. He scrambled from beneath the covers, jumped off the bed, and hit the floor running. Kate laughed as his joyful barks echoed through the house and faded as he pushed through his doggie door and out into the fenced back yard. "Works every time."

~ * ~

Nicolas stumbled into his house, kicked off his shoes, concealed his Glock in the nightstand drawer, and collapsed on top of the comforter, clothes and all.

The call from his partner had come just as he was leaving his parents' house last night. There might be an important break in their case, and he needed to come join the party. Now, after a pointless all-nighter staked out at the trailer park they suspected of housing a meth lab, Nicolas was more than beat.

Exhaustion yanked him beyond dreams and

dropped him into a place where colors, sounds, and feelings coalesced into a familiar nightmare. On some level of consciousness his brain struggled against the dream, fighting against invisible forces to wake up before his memory could play back that moment in time that he couldn't forget, awake or asleep.

*Nicolas walked the line of barbed wire with his buddy.*

This wouldn't end well, and he couldn't stop it now any more than he could have stopped it then. The dream skipped to the moment of the second explosion. Smoke and screams filled his head just as they had twenty years ago. *Look out!*

Nicolas rolled from the bed, slicked with sweat and gulping for air. Eyes closed, he stumbled into the bathroom, turned on the faucet, and splashed cold water on his face. Deep breaths rumbled in his chest as he straightened and fought to bring the present into focus. When he finally opened his eyes and looked into the mirror over the sink, he could almost see the shrapnel cuts on his cheeks, bleeding into the dirt that once caked his face. Those physical wounds had healed years ago with hardly a scar. The nightmare ripped the scabs off emotional wounds that weren't so lucky.

He spoke to his reflection. "We were kids on an adventure. Wet behind the ears despite our training. We thought we were invincible." The realities of that day slammed into his chest and threatened to turn his knees to water. "It wasn't a game C.W., it was war...a war I came home from, and you didn't." Nicolas bowed his head, suddenly ashamed to look into the face of the man he'd lived to become. "There's not a day that goes by that I don't wish I could tell you how sorry I am."

Kate was late. She was always late. It was a genetic defect. Both of her husbands had teased her without mercy, to no lasting avail. They learned quickly that if they wanted Kate to be somewhere at two, they needed to tell her one-thirty.

She hurried up the walk, stopping when she caught sight of her friends, already seated at a table near the window. Kate took the chance to study them while they visited without her. They were a diverse group of women. Callie Stillman, short, blonde, on the high side of her weight curve. With the holidays just fading from everyone's rear-view mirror, she'd be on her spring diet soon. Karla Black, her hair a stunning silver, shorter and heavier than Callie—and comfortable in her own skin. At sixty-three Karla, was the oldest of the group and took it upon herself to mother them all equally. Terri Evans was tall and slender. She'd recently cut her shaggy brown hair even shorter to accommodate her busy schedule born of running a business while keeping up with a couple of toddlers, a husband, two stepdaughters, a granddaughter, and a dog, all while planning her step-daughter Samantha's wedding.

*Just the thought makes me tired!*

Samantha Evans, her soon to be daughter-in-law, sat next to Terri. Kate grinned at the pleasant surprise—*I thought she was spending the day with Patrick*—and wondered how much of the game Patrick would see, since he was probably babysitting Bobbie, Sam's four-year-old daughter.

Her eyes traveled on to the last lady at the table, Pam Lake. If ever there were two women least likely to become friends, it would be Kate and Pam. They were the same age, same religious background...and they'd shared a husband. Well, not at the same time, but Pam had been married to Alan Archer years ago. That she and Pam had become friends had taken both women by surprise.

A diverse group, one that had welcomed Kate with open arms in the wake of Alan's death. They'd offered her friendship just when she needed it most. Kate watched them laugh together for a few more seconds. Her shoulder muscles bunched under her jacket in an unfamiliar wave of emotion. Disconcerted, she searched for its source, confused to find small kernels of envy and loneliness at the core.

In preparation for marriage and fatherhood, Patrick had moved into his own house two weeks ago, leaving Kate to deal with the solitude of an empty nest for the second time in her life. She'd join her friends today for a few hours of girl talk and laughter, maybe a little shopping before the mall closed. Once their afternoon was over, they'd all go home to houses full of children and husbands. They'd make disgusted noises about the game, but they'd fix snacks for their men and likely sit with them through the final play.

Kate would go home to Merlin and, as much as she loved the pup, he wasn't much of a conversationalist. She straightened. *What's wrong with you? You've still got the best end of the deal. Your house stays clean, you cook or go out as you please, you can read without interruption, you can watch TV without having to wrestle a man for control of the remote. Snap out of it and count your blessings.*

Kate caught a movement through the glass. Her friends motioned her in out of the cold. She waved in return, hitched the strap of her purse back up on her shoulder, and turned for the entrance. When she pulled the door open, a wall of noise almost blasted her back outside. Chili Mac's was doing its best to live up to the designation of *sports grill*. Four hours ahead of game time, the bar area was already packed with rowdy fans, and the flat screen televisions all blared with every tidbit of pregame trivia and game day stats the news crews could dredge up.

The youngster at the hostess desk grabbed a menu and smiled in Kate's direction. "Welcome to Chili Mac's. Table for one?"

Kate shook her head and motioned toward her friends. "I'm with them."

"Great, follow me." He led Kate through the maze of diners, then laid a menu at one of the two empty spaces at the table. "What can I get you to drink?"

She shrugged out of her coat, hung her bag on the chair, and took her seat. "Diet cola, please."

"I'll send it right out."

Kate surveyed the table. "Sorry I'm late."

Karla smirked. "I said one and it's only one-fifteen. That's early on Kate time, isn't it?" She stopped and looked back to the door. "I thought you were bringing Melanie."

"I couldn't reach her. Her phone kept going straight to voice mail. I left a message and told her where we'd be. Maybe she's a closet football fan and decided to stay home with her husband. Trust me, now that I know about her free cookie Fridays, I'll see her before the week is out." She turned her attention to Samantha. "I thought you and Bobbie were spending the afternoon with Patrick."

Samantha tossed her long brown hair over her shoulder. "We were, but I cut a deal with your son. I promised him homemade salsa and cheese dip to snack on during the game if he'd watch Bobbie so I could have lunch with you guys. He couldn't get me out of the house fast enough." She glanced at her watch. "I figure they're both down for an afternoon nap by now. I stopped at the grocery store before I came here, but I still need to pick up a blender and a crock-pot and be home before kickoff." Her eyebrows drew together over a wrinkled nose. "I don't get it. He's been in the house for two weeks, and he still hasn't stocked the kitchen. How do guys live like that?"

Kate smiled. "He'd consider that women's work."

Sam's response was a smug smile of her own. She cracked her knuckles, dug into a pocket, and held up a rectangle of plastic. "Yeah well, I have his debit card and a list. I'm about to show him how expensive *women's work* can be. He better be glad he has a hefty chunk of that trust fund deposit left. Besides the blender and crock-pot, there are a few other kitchen essentials I've decided he can no longer live without."

Terri leaned forward. "I helped her with the list. We're going shopping when we're done here. You want to join us?"

Kate shrugged. "Sure." She grinned at her future daughter-in-law. "I might even think of some things you missed. Is everyone going?"

Pam shook her head. "I've got to get back home before game mania hits. If I give Harrison and the kids unsupervised access to my kitchen, I won't be able to find the sink by halftime."

"Same here," Karla said. "Nicolas and Benton are coming to the house to watch the game with Mitch. I'm going straight home while Callie makes our snack run."

Kate focused on each of her friends in turn. "So...you're all telling me that our alternative game-day party has to end in time for everyone to be home for the game?"

Laughter erupted around the table.

Karla snatched the napkin from her lap and used it to wipe her streaming eyes. "I guess it does." She tilted her head and studied Kate for a second. "If you want to come by the house after you finish bankrupting Patrick, feel free. We'll have plenty of food, and I'm sure Nicolas would love to see you again."

Kate narrowed her eyes at her matchmaking friend, prepared to sidestep another well-meaning but transparent effort to put Kate in her son's path. "Thanks, Karla, but I think I'll take in a movie while you guys are enduring the game." She fluffed her hair and struggled to ignore the lonely ache in her heart. *A movie by myself? Boring!* She forced a note of flippancy into her voice. "Just one of the many benefits of being single."

# CHAPTER FOUR

Something large and noisy rattled down the road in front of the motel. The windows in the old place vibrated with the force of its passing and jerked Melanie out of a fitful sleep bright and early Monday morning. Before she had the chance to ignore the street noise, the alarm began its morning symphony. She rolled over in the hard-as-a-rock motel bed and, in her attempt to shut off the noise, knocked the clock to the floor. The fall did not silence the persistent beeping. She groaned and stretched an arm to the floor, yanked the noisy offender into the bed with her, and pressed the snooze button. The movement awakened the nausea that had been her morning companion for the last two weeks. Melanie lay still, sucking in deep gulps of air. If she had to choose between a late start to her day or the joys of puking the remnants of last night's hamburger into the toilet, she'd bake later. *Beep...beep...beep.*

She punched the button a second time, waiting for her stomach to make the call. The few extra minutes in bed would cost her, but she had a great assistant. Staci could get things started on her own in a pinch. Melanie eased up, swung her legs to the floor, and rested on the side of the bed. The nausea receded. Looked like the morning was a go. That was a good thing, since a baker's day started early—three am-early—the bad news of her chosen profession, bad news made worse when she was sick. The good news was that when she locked the door of her little shop at one pm, the rest of the day belonged to her. *Yeah, and I can come back to this tiny rented room, stare at four unadorned beige walls, and think about my ruined marriage and how to manage my life and my business as a single mom.* It was enough to bring back the nausea. "You're in a fine mess, girlfriend." Melanie stood, one thought sustaining her resolve. *Whatever I decide to do from this moment on, it'll be because I want to do it.*

Right now, she'd better get a move on. She crossed to her open suitcase and yanked out a pair of jeans and a sweatshirt. A bit of riffling produced a T-shirt as well. She'd wear the sweatshirt, but take the lighter shirt for later. Once the bakery ovens kicked into high gear, the heat in the small building would be stifling.

Melanie took everything to the bathroom where her toiletries awaited, lined up on the sparse countertop. She leaned against the counter and spoke to her reflection. "Today is the first day of the rest of your life." *Trite but true.* "You have a business you love, and after years of fruitless expense and effort, you have a baby on the way. Get out there, get to work, and get a plan." She picked up her hair brush and pulled it through her sleep-tangled natural curls.

"I wouldn't need a plan if Tyler had loved me enough to make our marriage a priority." Emotion clouded the reflection of her eyes. Melanie's hands squeezed the edge of the sink until her knuckles were white with determination. "Stop right there, don't you dare cry. It's done, it's over."

No more waiting for a man who might not show up.

No more hours of her precious time off cooking meals that languished in the microwave. No more trips, vacations, holidays, and special occasions forgotten, rescheduled, or endured on her own while she made excuses for an absent spouse. Annoyance welled up inside of her. Too many years, too many things, too many excuses. She was done, and if she had her way, the precious child she carried would never be the victim of Tyler's neglect.

Anger replaced annoyance, and she released the sink. Her hand shook as she squeezed toothpaste onto her toothbrush. "Tyler's neglect made you independent, and it's time to exercise that." Blue eyes narrowed in the mirror. "You've got seven months before you have to settle in to motherhood. What does Melanie Kaye Mason want to do next?" Her expression brightened as a long-abandoned dream coalesced in her mind. *Australia.*

Melanie dressed for the day, locked up the rented room, and headed for the bakery only twenty minutes late. All while that single word tumbled over and over in her mind, refusing to give place to the more pressing thoughts of a pregnant woman who'd just walked out on her husband. *Australia.* Could she?

The back door to the little shop slammed behind her when she entered. Staci turned from the counter, her flour-dusted hand clutched at her throat.

"Merciful heavens, you scared me to death!"

"Sorry." Melanie shrugged out of her coat. "And sorry I'm a little late. I wasn't feeling well this morning."

"Hey, you're the boss, but that's two or three times in the last couple of weeks. Have you been to the doctor?"

Melanie turned to retrieve her apron from the hook next to the door, hanging her coat in its place. She sucked in a breath and rested her hand on her flat stomach for a second. *Time to change the subject.*

She faced her assistant, hands on her hips, and a forced grin on her lips. "I'm sure it's nothing, just laziness. You're so good at this, you've got me spoiled and depending on you." Her fingers worked behind her back, securing the apron strings. "Speaking of depending...is that granddaughter you've been begging me to hire still looking for a part-time job?"

Staci's eyebrows rose in surprise. "I think so, but when I mentioned it last month, you said you wanted to wait a while."

Melanie shook her head. "No time like the present. Business is better than I ever hoped, and I never wanted to be a workaholic." The word reminded her of Tyler, and she paused to swallow back bitter emotion. "Can you get her in here for a visit?"

"Can you wait two weeks? She left Saturday on a cruise with some friends. Sort of a belated Christmas present from her parents."

Melanie arranged ingredients for a batch of sugar cookies on the counter. "Not a problem. Bring her in just as soon as she gets home. I've got some vacation plans of my own, and I can't make that happen until we have some more help."

Staci studied her. "Where are you planning to go?"

"Australia."

"Tyler finally—"

"Nope, just me. Just as soon as we can get some more help trained and you tell me you're comfortable running the place without me for a couple of weeks." Melanie shrugged. "That's the plan, anyway." She glanced at the clock. "We better get busy." With her back turned, she focused on the recipe, hoping the task would drown out the little voice whispering *buts* in her head. *But the trouble with that plan is that I still love my self-absorbed, stupid jerk of a husband. A husband who doesn't know that he's about to be a father.* She buried her hands in the dough and hoped that Staci wouldn't see the tears she couldn't hold back any longer.

~ * ~

Kate sat in her car and squinted through the windshield. The ad had described the property as a diamond in the rough. It resembled a diamond about as much as a lumberjack resembled a French model. The continuing failures drove frustration and doubt straight to her heart.

She leaned her head against the headrest, her gaze boring a hole through the roof of the car. "Did I get it wrong? I *thought* You placed this dream in my heart all those years ago. Back then, I didn't have the resources or the time to make it a reality. Now I have all the time in the world and plenty of resources, and I can't take a single step that feels useful." She closed her eyes and found the ever-present doubt dancing around the corners of her heart. "I was so certain this dream came from You, but maybe it's just Satan's way of distracting me from Your real plan for my life. There are plenty of government and private agencies dedicated to helping military widows. Will one more really make a difference? Maybe I should just scrap all this nonsense and send a nice donation to an established organization. I—"

*Follow the plan.*

The words snatched Kate up from her slouched pose. "We have a plan? I don't suppose You'd like to share it?" The silence echoed with her sarcasm. *Good one, Kate. Let's get snarky with God.* "Sorry, Father."

Another glance at the dilapidated storefront clenched her stomach. She reached for the key dangling from the ignition, determined to make her escape before the owner arrived. She'd call him from the road and offer her apologies. Claiming an upset stomach wouldn't be stretching the truth by much.

Before she could start the car, a beat up pickup swung into the space beside her. A loud backfire issued from the tail pipe of the tricolored wreck. Kate cringed when the driver stepped out of the cab. Smarmy was the best word she could come up with. As round as he was tall, he wore a dingy shirt, the buttons straining to contain his girth. His black hair, weeks past due for a cut, was slicked back from his face and bore an oily sheen. The mustache over his upper lip was equally distasteful. He stared at her expectantly. Out of options, she picked up her cell phone, held up a finger to let him know she'd be just a second, and dialed Patrick's number.

"Hey, Mom."

"Hi, sweetheart. Are you at lunch?"

"Yeah, for a few more minutes."

"Can you call me in ten minutes?"

"Another stinker, huh? That's like...four in a row now."

"They were mansions compared to this. Ten

minutes, OK?" She disconnected the call and climbed out of her car.

"You Ms. Archer?"

Kate pasted a smile on her face. "That's me."

He held out a hand. "Nice to meet ya. I'm Willie Cranford. I own this little jewel."

Kate stared at the grimy hand. *Suck it up, girlfriend, you raised a boy. It's not the first filthy thing you've touched.* She forced herself to take his hand in hers. "Thanks for meeting me on such short notice."

"No problemo." He dug a set of keys out of his pocket. "Let me show you around."

She trailed behind him, not the least bit enthused to see what lay behind the door. As low as her expectations were, the reality was worse. Dirt and trash littered the floor. The walls, probably white when new, were gray with age. The acoustic ceiling tiles were water-stained, and several of those were missing. Insulation dangled, swaying in the breeze from the open door.

"The place has real potential, don't you think?"

Kate swallowed. *How much of that ten minutes is left?* She nodded in response to his question and continued her perusal of the room. The toe of her shoe brushed against a pile of discarded paper. She glanced down and caught the glow of beady eyes.

Kate took a step back, her eyes locked on those of the rodent. The beady eyes stared at Kate, long whiskers twitched in indignation. Kate wasn't even sure if the squeal that cut through the air came from her or the rat. She was in the car and five miles down the road before Patrick's call came through.

Her hands were still shaking when she connected

the call. "Thanks, baby."

"Not a big deal, but I've got to get to class. Bye."

Kate tucked the phone away and looked at the sky through the windshield of her car. "Um, God. About that plan..."

~ * ~

"Hey, Black. What happened to your boys last night?"

Nicolas fed coins into the vending machine, offering a grin and a headshake in answer to the question. He took his can of soda back to his desk while the good-natured banter continued.

"That was some game."

"Boy, that California team was on fire last night."

Nicolas ignored the comments while the rest of the uniforms in the office shared a laugh at his expense. It was part of the squad room fellowship. Had the game gone differently, he'd be dishing out some abuse of his own. For the first time in two decades, he'd been home to watch the big game, and he'd chosen the underdog. His team had not only suffered defeat, they'd had their butts handed to them in their own helmets. Forty-eight to six. He'd be the brunt of their morning jokes. It would only get worse when his partner arrived. They'd made a personal side bet on the game. Loser washed the winner's car every Monday morning for a month. Tyler would not hand over his keys without making Nicolas relive every scoring play. Across the street, the clock atop the city hall building gonged the top of the hour. Tyler was late, and that wasn't like him.

Nicolas searched for a clean spot on his littered desk

to set the soda can. A new stack of paperwork caught his eye. Nicolas opened the folder. Transfer orders for Chick Malone. A formality, since the kidnapping case closed weeks ago. Wouldn't even be a trial, since the perp pled guilty. Mr. Malone was on his way from his temporary home in the county jail to a more permanent spot in the Oklahoma prison system. This notification was just a courtesy to him as the arresting officer. Now, he could file the case folder away for good. He tapped the papers into a neat stack, retrieved his official folder from his desk drawer, and prepared to do just that. A phone number on a green sticky note caught his eye. The name written below the number had him pausing. Kate Archer.

He remembered the blonde in much greater detail than the abbreviated description he'd rattled off to his mother a few nights ago. Hard not to. She was a looker with an internal strength he'd admired during the difficult hours when young Bobbie Evans had been missing. *You liked this woman.*

Nicolas shrugged. So what? He was a man, he had a pulse, and he liked a lot of women. Didn't change the fact that he had no intention of becoming involved with any particular one. And this one was especially off limits for two very good reasons. One, she was his mother's friend, and despite protests to the contrary, he knew Kate Archer was the focus of Mom's latest let's-get-Nicolas-married campaign. Two, there had been a definite spark of attraction—on his part—even during the stress of the kidnapping. His memory retained every detail of her heartbroken green eyes, bright with tears, and the feel of her soft hand in his when they'd finally gotten around to introducing themselves. A hand he'd hesitated to surrender.

But still. Nicolas stared at the number. According to his mother, Kate Archer was getting involved in a cause he cared a great deal about. He'd like to be involved with those plans, if not the woman.

He'd spent the last day and a half trying to figure out how to contact Kate without going through his mom or one of her buddies. Asking Mom for the number was a one way ticket down a dead end road. Nothing he could have said would have kept her from going off the deep end in a romance-induced tizzy. Nicolas peeled the note from the paperwork and stuck it in his desk drawer. *Problem solved!*

He prepared the Malone file for the archives, mulling his options while he worked. From his mother he knew that Kate Archer was a two-time widow. Common sense told him that she was probably looking for husband number three. He wanted to get to know her on a business level while keeping the personal off limits. *Dangerous ground there.* He could almost picture a *quicksand ahead* sign hanging from the creamy skin of the woman's slender neck.

Creamy? Slender? *Seriously?* Nicolas coughed and shook himself free of whatever daydream he was wondering around in. He glanced at the closed drawer. He had the number, so he just needed to figure out the best way to put it to use. Folder in hand, Nicolas pushed away from his desk and headed for the bank of filing cabinets on the far wall. Before he had a chance to cross the room, the outer door opened, and Tyler stepped inside.

The expression on Tyler's face halted Nicolas in his tracks. His normally upbeat partner slouched into the room, not only late, but grim-faced and red-eyed. He passed Nicolas without a word, dropped into his desk chair, and bowed his head over a large cup of takeout coffee.

*I bet he went back to that trailer park last night. I swear the man is like a dog with a bone.* Nicolas filed his paperwork and crossed back to his desk. He cuffed Tyler on the shoulder as he passed. "Bud, you look like crap. You've got to chill. We'll catch the break we need on this case sooner or later, and we'll nail this creep's hide to the wall of his own meth lab." When Tyler didn't respond, Nicolas held out his hand. "Give me your keys. I'll run your car over to the Jiffy Wash."

Tyler raised his head. "What?"

"Your keys. Our Super Bowl bet. You won, I lost. I owe you a car wash."

His partner continued to stare at him with empty, bloodshot eyes. Nicolas reconsidered his earlier conclusion. He'd seen that look on too many faces over his years of military service. Not fatigue from too many late nights on the job, but soul deep defeat. "Tyler?"

Tyler slumped down in his seat and allowed his head to rest on the tall, padded back. "Melanie left me."

# CHAPTER FIVE

Age definitely had its perks. Kate settled in at Karla's table once Monday night's Bible study was over. The youngsters, those under the age of thirty with little ones to tuck in, said their goodbyes and hurried home, leaving Karla's leftover cherry chocolate cheesecake to the four founders of the group and her.

She'd seen the same group of women at Chili Mac's yesterday, but Kate was still grateful for their company tonight. Despite her efforts to shake it off, the morning's melancholy mood continued to weigh her spirit down. The laughter and noise gave her something else to think about, and if the cool, creamy texture of the cheesecake failed to soothe her soul... Kate lifted another bite to her mouth and allowed the confection to melt on her tongue...she probably needed to be buried, 'cause she'd been dead for at least a week. Fully alive, she scooped up a second bite with a shrug. *It's a girl thing.*

Callie sat across the table with her own plate of dessert, and, if the look of ecstasy on her friend's face was any indication, Kate wasn't alone in her assessment. "Absolutely sinful, huh?"

"More like illegal." Callie waited until Karla joined them at the table. "Karla, we've been playing with cheesecake recipes for almost four years. Where have you been hiding this one?"

Karla reached across the table for a package of sweetener for her coffee. "I found it when I was looking for a new dessert recipe for Christmas." She ripped the small yellow package open, dumped it into her cup, and stirred. "It sounded yummy, but I knew most of my family wouldn't touch it, either because of the cherries or the nuts, so I saved it for us."

Pam lifted a bite to eye-level and studied it. "I don't think I've ever had a cheesecake with nuts in the filling. I love the crunch." She chewed. "Almonds, right?"

Karla nodded.

Pam shook her head. "I can't believe your family would pass this up."

Terri ran a finger through the remnants of chocolate on her plate, stuck it in her mouth, and sucked it clean. "Totally their loss."

Chuckles circled around the table. Terri shook back her short brown hair. "What?"

"We don't call you the baby of the group for nothing." Karla turned her attention back to Kate. "I forgot to ask you about it yesterday. How was your business meeting on Saturday night? Did you get the deal you wanted?"

Kate snorted. "Business meeting, my great aunt Liddie's garters."

"Oh, that sounds ugly," Pam said. "What happened?"

"He kissed me...or he tried. I shoved him into a slush puddle."

"Whoa!" Pam sat back and crossed her arms. "That bad?"

Kate sputtered. "I didn't ask him to put his mouth

on me!"

Callie raised her cup to her lips. "Well, that's certainly the least romantic description of a kiss I've ever heard."

Kate ground her teeth, struggling to keep the heat of her Irish temper from boiling over on her friends. "Read my lips. I. Am. Not. Looking. For. Romance." She enunciated each word clearly and separately before scooting her chair from the table and pacing away a step or two. She needed to calm down. "Look, guys, I know you mean well, but please, I'm off the marriage market permanently."

"What makes you think that we think otherwise?" Karla asked.

Kate stopped in her tracks, tilted her head, and regarded the older woman. "I'll admit the attempts have been subtle, but they've been there. Just like yesterday's invitation to join your Super Bowl party because"—she changed her voice and mimicked Karla—"Nicolas would love to see you again." Her voice went back to normal. "I'm not interested in another man."

Karla dismissed Kate's protests with a wave of her hand. "You're a beautiful woman with half of your life ahead of you. You can't mean to live it alone."

"That's exactly what I mean to do." Kate looked at each woman in turn until she was certain she had their attention. "I love you guys, but you need to respect my wishes on this. I—" Her cell phone rang and she hurried back to where her bag hung from the back of her chair. She dug it out and glanced at the screen. Nicolas Black's name flashed on the display. She held it up. "Karla..."

"What?"

She closed her eyes and tapped the phone against her forehead. "It's your son. Why is Nicolas calling me? Please tell me you didn't—"

Karla raised her hands. "I didn't tell him to call, and he didn't get your number from me."

Kate narrowed her eyes as the call went to voice mail.

Karla drew an X over her heart. "Cross my heart. Whatever he wants, he's calling on his own."

Kate shook her head and dropped the phone back into her purse. "OK. But, Karla, I'm serious about this."

"I heard you." Karla lifted her cup, pausing before she drank, speculation clear on her face. "But I do have one question for you?"

Kate raised her eyebrows.

"If you're so set on avoiding men in general and Nicolas in particular, why do you have his number saved in your phone?" Her smile turned hopeful. "Were you thinking about calling him?"

Terri leaned forward. "I can answer that question, Karla. He gave all of us his personal number back in December." Her swallow was audible. "When Bobbie was missing. He—"

Kate finished Terri's sentence. "We all programed his personal number into our phones. He said we needed to be able to reach him in case we were contacted by the kidnapper. Perfectly innocent, Karla, so pack away your schemes. There is no romance in my future with your son or anyone else."

~ * ~

The call went to Kate's voice mail. Nicolas disconnected without leaving a message. He wanted to talk to her, but he couldn't work up a lot of regret at not reaching her this evening. He'd spent his day with a sullen partner who refused all his efforts at both consolation and fact finding. Tyler attacked the day with the enthusiasm of a robot. Answering with grunts when spoken to, operating on some internal auto pilot when the job called for more than a surface response. Melanie and Tyler had split. Nicolas didn't know why. His brain was worn slick from trying to figure out a way to help.

He forced his attention back to Kate. *Probably a good sign that she didn't answer.* If an attractive woman like Kate couldn't take his call this late on a weeknight, she was likely out on a date. And if she was out on a date, that meant she had a guy in her sights. And if she had a guy in her sights, Nicolas wouldn't have to worry about his intentions being misread. Their relationship, if they ended up having one, would remain strictly business.

He tossed the phone aside, restarted his movie, and turned up the surround sound on the television. The windows vibrated with the sound of helicopter blades beating close to the ground as men jumped from the open door. Tonight was a prime example of the benefits of living alone, no one to complain about the *noise*.

The screen filled with a black and white close-up of the Duke leading a charge up a mountain side while shells and grenades exploded around him and his men. Nicolas leaned forward in his recliner, silently urging the stragglers to get to cover before the enemy overran their location. He'd watched this movie and others like it with his dad. The young man he'd been then was enamored of the uniform and the glory of battle, where men died a bloodless death, the hero always got the best-looking girl, and the good guys always came home victorious. He shook his head at the screen. That was Hollywood's idea of war. Even today's not-so-bloodless renditions never got it quite right. In real wars, too often the good guys lost and too many good men never made it home to the girls awaiting their return.

Nicolas aimed the remote at the TV and turned it off. Not a good entertainment choice just now. He couldn't be sure what had triggered the nightmares he'd suffered through the last two evenings, but they wouldn't be helped by watching a war movie. Nicolas kicked up the footrest of his chair and reached for the novel on the side table. His attention quickly sank into the crime drama, blood and guts of another kind, but procedures and rules that made sense to his cop's mind. This author had his admiration. Halfway through the five hundred pages, and Nicolas still hadn't fingered the perp.

Nicolas read with half his brain, the other half sifting through stingy clues, visualizing the murder board the story detailed, considering and dismissing suspects. The chime of an incoming voice mail pulled him out of the fictional mayhem. He grabbed the phone and fumbled with the buttons when Kate Archer's number flashed on the screen.

"Nicolas, Kate Archer here, returning your call. I hope I haven't called too late. Please feel free to call me back any time tomorrow."

Nicolas tapped the connection open. "Kate?"

"Oh, there you are. I'm sorry, did I wake you?"

He cleared his throat. "No, I wasn't sleeping, just engrossed in a new book. I didn't even hear the phone ring."

"That's got to be some book to have you so involved. Share the title? I love books like that."

"It's a keeper. *The Midnight Stalker* by Randy Ansohn."

"I've never read anything of his, but I'm making a note. If it's good enough to keep a cop's attention, it must be good."

Silence stretched between them for a beat or two.

"I called you about—"

"I was returning—" They both stopped, and Kate's laughter filtered across the connection. "You called me, so you go first."

The rich, feminine laughter did strange things to his heartbeat. "Um, I wanted...I mean..." He swallowed hard, his thoughts stumbling over his words. *Get a grip Black!* "I hope my call didn't interrupt anything important."

"Just a second piece of your mom's amazing cheesecake."

He grinned. *Not a date.* Why did that make him smile? Nicolas coughed. "Oh yeah, Monday night Bible study. I forgot. Anyway, I had dinner with the folks the other night, and Mom mentioned that you were in the early stages of a new business venture, something aimed at helping Military widows." C.W.'s image flashed into his mind, forcing him to stop and pull in a couple of deep breaths. "That sounds like something I'd like to be involved in, if you're still looking for some help."

~ * ~

Kate's heart kicked up a notch, and it had nothing to do with the pleasing timbre of the voice on the other end of the phone or the handsome man attached to it. This could be the answer to her morning prayer. But she couldn't deny the appealing quality of the voice.

*I don't remember that cop voice being so sexy.* Kate swallowed wrong and started to cough. "Hang on just a minute," she gasped into the speaker. She lowered the phone and struggled to clear her windpipe. *Where did that come from? You aren't interested in finding another man, remember?* "Sorry."

"You OK?"

Kate took a deep breath as Nicolas's voice continued to play havoc with her senses. "Yes...I just...swallowed wrong." She coughed a final time and ordered her unruly sub-conscience to behave. "What sort of help did you have in mind?"

"Well...I...umm."

Kate laughed into the phone. "I didn't mean to catch you by surprise."

"Not surprise, it's just...well, Mom didn't share a lot of the details about what you're trying to do. But what she did say appealed to me, and since I have plenty of experience with the military—"

"According to your mom, you signed up at birth," she joked. His answering chuckle sent goose bumps dancing up her spine.

"Yeah well, that's my mom. Anyway, I saw more than my share of good men..."

Silence stretched for several seconds, wrinkling Kate's brow.

"...die. I can only imagine what the families must go through in cases like that. Your idea struck a real chord with me. If there's anything I can do, any part of the project that could use a pair of willing hands, I'd like to be involved. Maybe we could sit down together, talk about it?"

Was he asking her out? Her face heated at the thought. *Karla, I'm going to kill you!*

Nicolas continued before she had the chance to answer. "I hope you won't take that invitation the wrong way. If you know my mother, then you know...I mean...in spite of what she might have led you to believe, I'm not looking for any sort of romantic involvement with you."

"Excuse me?"

His sigh filled her ear. "Sorry, that came out wrong. My mother has been trying to marry me off for years. Her efforts have intensified since I retired. She's been waving every available female she can find in my face for the last four months. I didn't want you to think that I'd taken the bait. I mean, not that you're bait. You're an attractive women, but I'm just not interested..."

"In women?"

"Yes...I mean no. Of course I'm interested in women, just not you..."

Kate couldn't control her laughter for another second. "You're just full of tact tonight, aren't you?"

A muffled response came through the phone. "The noise you just heard was me pulling both feet out of my mouth. May I start over?"

"Let me make this easy on you," Kate said

"Oh, please do."

"I understand exactly what you're trying to say.

Karla has dangled your name in front of me a few dozen times, but I've had two husbands, and I'm not looking for a third. I'd love to have lunch, or dinner with you, on a purely business basis, to discuss my ideas and see if you're interested in helping." She stopped and bit her lip to keep the smile out of her voice. "I'm not interested in you, either."

"You aren't going to let me live this conversation down, are you?"

A giggle broke through despite her efforts. "Maybe someday, but not tonight."

"Good enough. May I call you later in the week? I need to see what my schedule is like at work before we decide on a time to get together."

Kate leaned her elbow on the kitchen counter, and twisted a strand of hair around a finger. *That voice is just...* She jerked upright. *Focus Kate!* "That's fine. In the meantime, I've got some information I've been sharing with people on my contact list. I could send that over to you, if you're interested in taking a look."

"Absolutely. I'll text you my email address just as soon as we hang up."

"Perfect. I'll talk to you later in the week." Kate disconnected the call. A text message from Nicolas came through thirty seconds later. She smiled. She'd enjoyed their teasing, but their time together would be strictly business. Two people who were not the least bit interested in the other.

# CHAPTER SIX

A bell tinkled over Kate's head as she entered Sweet Moments Bakery. Melanie Mason, her curly red hair bundled into a ponytail high on her head, stood behind the counter bagging sweets for a customer. Three more people waited in line for her friend's attention. Kate returned Melanie's smile with a small wave and moved to examine the array of treats arranged on trays behind the glass of the big display cases. From what Kate could see, cookies weren't the only specialty in this establishment. Cupcakes, muffins, brownies, and pastries vied for her attention, along with the promised cookies. Her eyes nearly crossed at the selection. She'd just stepped into dessert heaven. How in the world could she choose just one?

Kate pulled the tantalizing scents of warmed sugar, chocolate, and spices into her lungs. The aroma alone was enough to add five pounds to her weight, and the visual temptation... Her mouth began to water. Nope, forget a single anything—there was a box of goodies in her future. She leaned against the case and waited for Melanie to send her final customer on his way.

Melanie handed a large pink box across the counter. "Here you go, Max. I hope your wife enjoys the cookies."

"I'm sure she will. It's her fiftieth birthday. I'm

stopping by her office with these." He tapped the top of the box. "Her coworkers have her area all decorated with black balloons and streamers." He pulled his phone from his pocket, tapped up a picture, and handed it across the counter. "It's going to be a little surprise party to start the day." He leaned forward. "I have a dozen roses scheduled for delivery this afternoon."

Melanie nodded at the picture. "Oh...look at the sign on her filing cabinet. *Slow moving traffic ahead.* That's so mean...and sweet."

Kate frowned at the emotional catch in her friend's voice."Tell her happy birthday for me," Melanie handed the phone back to its owner.

"Will do. See you next Friday." The bell sounded as the man left the shop with his box of goodies. Kate straightened when Melanie turned her way.

"You've been holding out on me."

Melanie tilted her head with a small frown. "You knew I owned the bakery."

"I did, and it's totally my fault for not stopping in sooner, but I didn't know about free cookies on Fridays. How could I not know that?"

Russet brows arched over Melanie's emerald eyes. "I kept it from you out of respect for your waistline."

Kate grinned. "Good answer." She turned back to the sinful selection of baked goods. "Doesn't matter. I'm here, I'm hungry, better give me the details."

Melanie motioned to the drink section of her menu board. "Buy a drink, get a cookie."

"You don't go in much for the hard sell, do you?"

"My cookies sell themselves." She smoothed a wrinkle out of the bib of her hot pink apron. "Eat one for free, leave with a dozen in a nice shiny paid for box."

"You sound pretty confident."

"World cookie domination plan 101."

"Whatever, it's brilliant."

"Can't take the credit. It was Staci's idea."

"Staci?"

"My helper. She comes in early to help with the baking and goes home at nine. Come in earlier someday, and I'll introduce you."

"Will do." Kate's gaze went back to the drink choices. "I'll have a medium coffee." She took a step back and pointed to a tray. "And give me one of those."

"Oh...the almond joy cookie. Great choice." Melanie picked up the cookie with a square of thin waxed paper. "Moist, dark chocolate with mini chocolate chips, coconut, and chopped almonds. It's more brownie than cookie." She placed the cookie on a pink paper plate and slid it and the coffee across the counter. "Enjoy."

Kate dug for her wallet. "How much do I owe you?"

"Pay me when you get ready to leave." Melanie turned away from Kate as the bell signaled the arrival of a new customer. "No sense in ringing you up twice."

Kate turned her back on her confident and industrious friend. The small shop held six round tables, each surrounded by four wrought iron chairs. With its white walls and the bright pink accents, it reminded Kate of the ice cream parlor her grandfather took her to when she was younger. She placed the cookie on the closest of the tables and crossed to the coffee station to doctor her drink. A normally simple task made challenging by the selection of flavored creamers. Deciding to keep it simple in deference to the cookie, she stirred plain creamer into her cup and returned to the table.

She broke off a bite of cookie and popped it into her mouth while Melanie continued her conversation with her new customer. "Oh my..." Kate's groan of delight had Melanie looking up from behind the counter. Kate simply stared at her friend and allowed her shoulders to slump in total surrender to the parade of flavors doing the Texas Two-Step across her taste buds. Melanie sent her a shrug and an I-told-you-so smirk.

From her vantage point, Kate enjoyed her snack and watched Melanie interact with her customers. She seemed to be on a first-name basis with most of the people who came into the shop. While two young women with several small children in tow hesitated over the selection, Melanie produced a cookie jar from beneath the counter and treated the youngsters to a sugar cookie. Kate figured that cookie jar earned new friends for Melanie every day.

Once the shop cleared, Melanie poured herself a cup of coffee and joined Kate at the small table. "My poor feet need a break."

"Business is good."

Melanie looked around the shop, unmistakable pride on her face. "I couldn't ask for much better." She sipped her coffee, closed her eyes, and rolled her head on her shoulders. A couple of loud pops echoed. "Oh, that's better." She straightened in her chair. "So tell me, Kate. Other than a free cookie, what brings you into my shop for the first time? Do the kids need to change something on their wedding cake order?"

Kate popped the last bite of cookie into her mouth. "First time, but not the last." She leaned forward and shook her head. "No, plans for the cake are fine as far as I know. I just hadn't talked to you this week. I wanted to renew my invitation to church on Sunday and let you know that we missed you at Chili Mac's last week. Speaking of church...you've been holding out on me on more than just free cookies. Why didn't you tell me that your husband already attends Valley View?" She frowned when her friend's eyes brightened with the sheen of tears. "Melanie?"

Melanie grabbed a napkin from the dispenser in the center of the table and blotted her eyes. "Did he send you in here?"

"What? Who, your husband? No, I haven't even met him. Karla Black mentioned that he comes, that her son Nicolas and your Tyler are partners."

"He's not *my* Tyler anymore. I'm beginning to accept that he never was."

*Oh, goodness, what have I stepped into?* Kate hesitated to get involved. She had plenty on her plate right now and less than three total years of marital experience to draw from, but the look of pain on Melanie's face tipped her over the line. She reached across the table and laid a gentle hand on Melanie's arm. "Hey, we haven't been friends very long, but if you want to talk about it, I'm a good listener."

~ * ~

"No, I appreciate the offer, but I..." Melanie looked into Kate's sympathetic eyes and a week's worth of tears battered at her resolve. Getting the shop up and running, in combination with the weird hours it required, had kept her from socializing much in the months since they'd moved to Garfield. She knew lots of people from the bakery traffic, but none that she could really call friend. Her best friends, Tiffany and Jason, made the ninety-minute drive in when they could, but it would be nice to have someone close to talk to. *Not about the baby, that's my secret for now.* She slid out of her chair, crossed to the door, and turned the open sign to closed. When she turned, she leaned against the door and allowed her eyes to roam the neat little shop. The shiny glass of the display counters, spotless this morning, now bore smudges from the fingerprints of her youngest customers. The white walls bordered in her signature pink. The dainty wrought iron tables and chairs. *My bakery, my dream.* Her gaze shifted to meet Kate's. "I thought things would be different when we moved to Garfield."

Kate tilted her head. "In what way?"

"I've been married to Tyler for almost twelve years. No kids, just us. We wanted kids, just never could make that a reality." *Careful.* Melanie bit her lip as her explanation brushed too close to her secret for comfort. "He spent the first four years of our marriage in the military, away more than he was home. I didn't complain." She shrugged. "I knew it was temporary, and I could deal with the loneliness for a little while." Melanie moved back to the table and took a sip of her coffee. "I guess maybe I was young and foolish when we married. I thought Tyler was the Prince Charming of all my fairy tale dreams. We were destined to live a long life, happily-ever-after." Her short chuckle was mirthless. "I certainly never envisioned spending all of our years of married life alone."

Kate tilted her head. "I'm not sure I understand what you mean."

"No, I don't suppose you would." Melanie took her seat and stared into the distance. "Alone together. It's an interesting phrase, seems like a contradiction, but it describes my relationship with Tyler to a T. We live in the same house, we breathe the same air, we share meals, and we have sex a couple of times a week, but we aren't a part of each other's lives, not really." She rubbed at her forehead. "I'm not even sure who's at fault anymore, him or me. I just know that I've had all I want."

When Melanie looked up, two fat tears streaked down her cheeks. She closed her eyes, her thoughts turned inward, searching for a bright spot in the gloom of failure. She shrugged. "We don't talk. So much of what he does is police business and confidential. I quit asking him to talk about his day a long time ago. I don't think he's ever once asked me about mine. He comes home, eats dinner, and turns on the TV, or he buries himself in whatever hobby is in current favor. Diving, fishing, poker, hunting, and now this church thing he's all wrapped up in." Her shoulders lifted a second time. "I know his job is stressful, and he needs to unwind at the end of a long day." She focused her gaze on the street outside the large plate glass window, unable to meet Kate's eyes. "But I'm the one sending him off to do that dangerous job every day. I'll admit that I worry less since we moved from Joplin. Garfield isn't exactly the crime capital of Oklahoma, but I've been a cop's wife long enough to know that the unexpected can happen. I need a little de-stressing at the end of the day too, and I need to do it with him."

"Girlfriend, you need to kidnap that man, bundle him into the car, and steal him away for a long weekend, just the two of you."

"He won't budge. We both have family out of state. In the last twelve years I can count on the fingers of one hand, with fingers left over, the times he's accompanied me on visits." She shook her head. "We haven't been on a vacation together in five years. I thought it would be different when we moved to a smaller town. A chance for him to slow down." She motioned at the building around them. "A chance for me to finally have my own dream." Melanie paused to wipe her eyes and rolled the spent napkin into a ball. "Do you know where he was on the morning of my grand opening?"

Kate shook her head.

"At work."

"Oh."

Melanie sipped at her cooling coffee. "He's always at work...and now, when he isn't at work, he's at some church thing. We just pass each other headed out the door, and I can't live that way anymore."

"You could come to church with him—"

She shook her head. "You don't get it. This whole religion thing is just his latest hobby. I'll get involved, and then he'll move on to the next big thing, and I'll be left on my own again. I learned to dive, I learned to fish, I even bought books on poker and studied up on games and rules, all to spend time with my husband. He got bored with all those things and left them...and me...behind. Tagging along behind him on another fad just makes me feel like a pitiful imposition in his life. I won't be that anymore."

Kate reached across the table a second time. "I'm so sorry you guys are going through this. I hope Tyler's church attendance goes deeper than you think, but even if it doesn't, I promise you that if you come to church with me and get involved at Valley View, you'll never be an imposition or alone." She squeezed her hand. "I don't feel qualified to offer you any marital advice, but would you let me pray with you?"

Melanie blew her nose, nodded wordlessly, and bowed her head over their joined hands.

"Father, touch Melanie's heart right now. Soothe her hurts and fill up those empty spots with Your love and comfort. Lord, speak to Tyler today. He's given his heart to You. Help him understand that Melanie needs more than just a warm body at home. Please grant them both wisdom right now to find Your will for their marriage."

The door knob rattled and both women looked up to find a young girl peering through the glass through her cupped hands. Melanie scooted her chair back. "Thanks for the shoulder. I've got to get back to work."

Kate pushed her chair back as well. "I'm going to be praying for both of you. I expect you to call me if you need to talk."

Melanie nodded as she crossed to the door and turned the latch. "Thanks, I will."

Kate paused at the register and dug her wallet out of her purse. "I need to pay for my snack, and I think you were right about needing more than the freebie. I have an appointment with Nicolas Black later this afternoon. Why don't you box up a dozen of those cookies for me? Can you divide them up into two boxes? Six for me, six for him."

Melanie moved back behind the counter and motioned to a tray of fat chocolate chip cookies. "If you're meeting Nicolas, these are his favorite."

"Great, six of those for him and six of the others for me."

Melanie assembled two small pink boxes and stacked cookies inside. "Nicolas Black, huh? Late lunch date?"

~ * ~

Kate juggled a half-full cup, a purse, and a wallet, her mind already on her meeting. She'd given Nicolas such a hard time a few nights ago, the cookies would be a nice way to let him know that she knew it was all in fun. Melanie's question caught her off guard. Her answer tumbled from her lips without thought. "You never know."

Melanie handed a receipt across the counter with a wink and a smile. Kate closed her eyes. *Where did that come from, and whatever processed me to say it out loud?* She opened her mouth to set the record straight and knew from the speculative look on Melanie's face that a denial would only make the situation worse. Instead, she picked up her cookies, thanked her friend, and headed for the door.

*Stupid, stupid, stupid!* She crossed the street to her car, flung the door wide, and tossed the boxed treats into the passenger seat. *What's wrong with me? I'm not some hormonal teenager mooning over the senior quarterback. I need a business partner...period.* Kate slid behind the wheel and took a few deep breaths. She studied the boxes. Instead of giving them to Nicolas, she'd make a detour by Patrick's new house on her way home. He liked cookies, and she couldn't afford for Nicolas, or anyone else, to misunderstand her motives.

~ * ~

Nicolas stood in front of his open closet. Fresh from an early afternoon shower, water beaded on the ends of his hair, dropped to his neck, and traced little rivulets down his bare back and shoulders. One hand held a towel cinched around his waist, the other hand shoved through clothes hanging with years of ingrained military precision. He pushed his uniforms aside. Beyond those he confronted a half dozen pair of blue jeans and a handful of button-down shirts in various stripes and plaids. At the very back hung a single black suit, which he wore on the rare occasion when he was forced to dress up. His head shook in disgust. He was scheduled to meet Kate Archer in forty-five minutes, and he had nothing suitable to wear to an afternoon business meeting. *I need to take the time to buy a sports jacket and a couple of ties.* Adding that chore to his mental list of things to do didn't accomplish a thing for today's appointment.

Nicolas yanked jeans and a shirt free of their hangers, frustration bubbling up in a growl. "Get a grip, Black, you're acting like some fussy woman." *If she doesn't like me in jeans, the woman can take a hike.* But that wasn't what he wanted. Nicolas needed Kate Archer to like him enough to include him in her plans.

He returned to the bathroom with his clothes

bundled in his arms. His reflection in the mirror over the sink caught his eye. He frowned at the slight two o'clock shadow barely fuzzing his cheeks. Maybe he should shave. "Maybe I should check my man card at the front door on my way out."

He shook his head as the words echoed in the empty house. This was getting out-of-hand. He was walking dangerously close to the path his mother had laid out for him. Yes, it would be nice if he and Kate could like each other if they agreed to work together. It made things easier on everyone. But he'd be hanged if he'd go out of his way to impress Kate Archer. He'd be hanged twice if he allowed his mother's manipulation to influence his behavior. His phone conversation with Kate a few nights ago might have ended up in teasing banter and laughter, but he was serious about his ban on any romantic intentions. Kate had sounded just as adamant.

Nicolas took a deep breath, glad to have the issue settled in his mind once and for all. He dressed, took a few extra seconds to get his normally wavy hair to behave, and shaved, because, hey, it was a business meeting, and he needed to make a good impression. Last of all, he slapped on some of his favorite aftershave. He studied his reflection with a critical eye, finally nodded in satisfaction. *What she saw was what she got.* "Bring on the business."

~ * ~

Kate parked her car in the lot of the coffee shop and looked around for the vehicle Nicolas had described as his. The shiny red Camaro sat in the spot furthest from the door. It was in two spots actually, at a diagonal. He obviously worried that someone would park close enough to ding his paint.

Nicolas Black was clearly a person who appreciated what he had, which meant he would probably work a bit harder to make their business a success. Kate added this fact to the mental list she'd been compiling over the last few days. Twenty years of service to his country proved him to be loyal and disciplined. Making his post retirement home close to his family meant, to her mind anyway, that he held family values high on his list of priorities. That he'd chosen to continue his career in law enforcement as a civilian spoke of his sense of duty and justice. Kate remembered their few days of close contact when Bobbie went missing right before Christmas. The memory sent waves of creepy crawlers up her back, and she paused to offer thanks to the God who'd brought Bobbie home safe. Nicolas had been both gentle with Samantha and tougher than nails with the miscreants involved in the kidnapping. Everything Kate knew about Nicolas added up to a very attractive package, *figuratively speaking*. She had a feeling she could work with someone like that.

Kate turned off the ignition and reached for her bag. Her eyes fell on the boxes of cookies. She could still leave them for Patrick on her way home, but maybe Nicolas... Indecision gnawed at her. Was she being ridiculous? It was a box of cookies, not a piece of wedding cake, for mercy's sake. "Oh good grief!" she whispered. Why did something so simple have to be shrouded in double meanings? *I'll leave them here and see how the meeting goes.*

She stepped through the door of Garfield's coffee

shop just in time to hear the hiss of steam from the cutesy clock displayed above the door of the shop. She looked up, drawn by the coffee fragrance embedded in the steam. The clock, in the shape of a grinning coffee mug, smiled down at her. *Too cute!*

Garfield's little main street was enjoying a small renaissance. Besides the new coffee shop and Melanie's lovely bakery, there was a new outlet of a popular gym and a new bookstore.

Rumor had it that the old newspaper office was being remodeled as a five-room bed-and-breakfast. Kate did a mental finger snap and conjured the narrowest distance she could imagine between her thumb and index finger. *Missed it by this much!* The old building sold two weeks before Kate inquired about it. Talk about the perfect building for her project.

The door closed behind her, and Kate paused to let her eyes adjust from the bright winter sunlight. Her attention shifted at the sound of metal chair legs scraping on the tiled floor, and there was Nicolas. He rose at her approach. Her eyes traveled up denim clad thighs, passed a trim waist, skimmed across broad shoulders, and landed on a boyish face that wouldn't ever look old. Today his expression greeted her with a beaming smile of welcome. She'd seen that expression harden into the no nonsense lines of a seasoned cop last December. *Wow! Hunk city either way!* Kate swallowed the sudden lump in her throat and schooled her face into a neutral smile. Oh my... *All business, all business, all business.* Nicolas Black cleaned up *real* nice.

# CHAPTER SEVEN

Nicolas pulled out a chair as Kate approached the table. He got a whiff of something fruity and elusive when he bent to push it in for her. It took all of his resolve not to lean in for a closer sniff.

"Thanks." Kate shifted, shrugging her jacket off of her shoulders and onto the back of the seat.

"You're welcome." Nicolas reclaimed his spot. "Thank you for making time for me today. I have to admit that I'm just a little disappointed though."

Kate shoved blonde hair out of her face and tilted her head. The light reflecting off the purple stones in her earrings paled in comparison to the vivid green stare she directed at him.

"How so?"

"When I told my mom that we were meeting today —"

Kate held up a hand. "Wait. You told Karla we were having coffee?" The question was half groan.

Nicolas grinned at the alarm in her voice. Did she know that her eyes got two shades darker when she's anxious? *Oh, get a grip, Black!* He swallowed past the thought. "I told her we were having a business meeting."

"And you think she's going to buy that?"

"It's the truth, and after giving it some thought, I

decided it was better to be straight with her from the get-go. What do you think she'd do if she thought we were meeting on the sly?"

Kate's perfectly arched brows climbed. "Oh, right. Good thinking. That wouldn't be a good thing." Her smile returned. "But why disappointed?"

"Mom cautioned me not to worry if you were a little late. She said that you're always late. I had a whole list of late jokes I was going to use on you to get our conversation started." He raised his arm to look at his watch. "And here you are, right on time." He motioned to a steaming cup of coffee sitting on her side of the table. "Your coffee didn't even have a chance to cool down."

Kate grinned. "Oh well, don't get used to it. Lateness is an art form with me." She picked up her cup, held it under her nose, and inhaled deeply. "Mocha, how did you know?"

Nicolas shrugged. "I have my sources."

"Yeah, and I'll bet her initials are K.B."

"I plead the fifth."

"Um hmm. Anyway, I had some properties to look at this morning, and was running behind, but the last address was so dismal on the outside, I didn't even look at the inside. I'm beginning to think that finding a piece of real estate anywhere within a twenty mile radius of Garfield is a hopeless task. I could find what I want in the city, but making that drive every day doesn't appeal to me."

Nicolas studied Kate's face. He had some thoughts about a location and wondered if she'd find him presumptuous or industrious. "I'm sure something suitable will turn up." He settled back in his chair. "I read through everything you sent me earlier in the week. I have to say, I'm impressed with the scope of your proposal. I get the feeling that this is more than a business undertaking for you. Am I right?"

Kate took a second sip of her coffee and looked at him over the rim of her cup. "You do dive right in, don't you?"

"Sorry, it's a military cut-to-the-chase thing."

Kate set her cup aside. "No need to apologize." She laced her fingers together on top of the table and met his gaze. "You're right. This is much more than business to me. You said your mom mentioned my plans to you. Has she told you anything about how or why I want to take on this project?"

"She said something about an inheritance from your second husband. May I assume that's the how?"

Kate nodded, her eyes, which had been bright with good humor a second before, took on a misty glow that Nicolas recognized as suppressed tears.

"My second husband died a little over a year ago." Her voice caught. "Sorry, I don't mean to get weepy on you, but it's still difficult to talk about." She pulled a napkin from the dispenser and blotted her eyes.

Nicolas watched her, helpless and missing the smile she'd worn seconds before. "We can save the explanations for another day if you'd like."

She shook her head. "No, it's important. If we're going to work together you need to know what fuels my passions." Kate clutched the balled-up napkin in her hand and continued. "Anyway, once the details of Alan's estate were settled..."

Nicolas breathed a small sigh of relief when a thoughtful expression replaced the tears.

"I'm starting my explanation in the wrong place. I need to begin with my first husband." She drew a deep breath and squared her shoulders. "My first husband and I dated all through high school. We knew we wanted to get married just as soon as we graduated, but he didn't want to take that step before he was sure he could support me."

"Reasonable and smart."

Kate nodded. "He was always the more levelheaded of the two of us. I was ready to find a preacher the instant we tossed our caps into the air. We didn't need a plan, we had love." Her slender shoulders lifted in a shrug. "As you can see by the proposal I sent to you, I've grown up a lot since then."

He raised his cup to her. "Haven't we all."

Kate picked up her cup and tapped it against his. "Anyway, no one with a decent job opening wanted to hire a kid fresh out of high school, so he joined the Air Force. At first it was just a steady paycheck, but he fell in love with the discipline and the organization. We got married between basic training and tech school."

Nicolas dipped his head. After twenty years in the service, this was a story he'd heard countless times.

She leaned forward to brace her chin on her fist. "When I look back at how naïve we were, I'm amazed we managed to find the courthouse on our own. Despite his steps to plan for our future, we were just kids, idealistic and green. He was going to save the world, and I was going to stay home and care for our family." Her eyes shifted back to his face. "He died during his first overseas deployment."

"I'm sorry."

"I don't talk about it much."

"I don't need the details."

"I know, but the history will help you understand my dream for the future."

Nicolas nodded his understanding.

"When the news came, I was devastated." Kate sniffed and dabbed at her eyes. "He left me with a toddler to raise, a baby boy who would never know his father, and a measly $100,000.00 dollar life insurance policy to provide for the both of us."

Nicolas cleared his throat. "It's more now."

"Well, that's something at least, but even back then, $100,000 didn't go very far. I searched, for a while, for programs and aid, but this was just before the Internet took over the world, so my resources were limited. I found a program or two willing to help with my school and daycare for the baby, but mostly, I was on my own with a purple heart to keep me warm at night. It was not the life I envisioned when I married and left home. I was forced to move back to Kansas City with my parents for a couple of years while I went to school. If I was going to provide for Patrick, I needed a good job, if I was going to find that good job, I needed to go back to school. It was a vicious circle." Kate paused, wadded up the tattered napkin, and shoved it into the pocket of her jacket. "Sorry, it's been more than twenty years and it still frustrates me."

"I can understand why. That's got to be a tough situation to be in."

She nodded. "I remember the night I called my mom to ask about moving back home. I was sitting at the kitchen table in our Texas apartment surrounded by forms for this thing or that thing. Fill this out, sign on the dotted line, mail, stand on one foot, and wait.

*Maybe*, if I held my mouth just right, I'd get an answer before Patrick graduated from high school. If I hadn't been so desperate, the whole thing might have been funny."

Kate at back in her chair. "The ten seconds between my asking to move home and Mom's answer were the longest, scariest of my life. That's when I knew there had to be a better way."

"There are options—"

She interrupted him with a bitter laugh. "I know that now, but even with today's technology, when you're in that first rush of grief or swallowed up by a life that won't hold still while you mourn, those programs aren't always easy to find, and too often they're wrapped up in so much red tape they're impossible to navigate." Kate pulled her cup towards her, making a face when the chilled liquid touched her lips.

"Would you like another?"

She pushed it away and shook her head. "I was lucky, or determined, or blessed. I'll let you decide which. I made it. I got my business degree, and Patrick and I had a good life together, despite our losses. But it was always my dream to work with others not so blessed or lucky. I never had the time or the money to get my ideas off the ground."

Nicolas finally saw where her story was headed. "Your second husband, Alan, right? He changed that?"

"He wanted to. We talked about my ideas, and he wanted to help me, but once his doctors diagnosed his heart disease, our focus changed. There were personal things he needed to accomplish and a limited amount of time. We sold the house and business in Kansas City and moved back here."

Her eyes brightened with moisture a second time. Nicolas fought an almost unbearable urge to wipe the tears from her face. *Quicksand, bud, remember the quicksand!* He handed her a second napkin instead.

"We didn't even have a year together, but he left me in a financial position to make my dream a reality. I intend to build a legacy to both men."

~ * ~

The sympathy Kate saw in Nicolas's eyes threatened to derail her train of thought. *Way to impress a potential partner, Kate. You were a mess in December, and here you are crying on him again.* She pressed the napkin to her eyes. "Sorry. I promise I'm not normally so weepy during business meetings."

He shrugged. "Trust me, I understand the pain of old wounds. So, if you have the money to finally do what you want, why are you looking for a partner?"

Kate sat up, squared her shoulders and focused on the reason for their meeting. "Money is not nearly so much a consideration as a second brain and a second pair of hands. This is a huge undertaking, and I was raised to believe that two heads are better than one. The Bible bears that out as well." She sat back, tears gone as she warmed to her subject. "I want to offer a range of services from a central hub—grief counselors for both adults and children, help in securing education grants and scholarships, financial counseling, investment planning, assistance wading through state and federal aid programs, free legal advice, and for those who need it, a shoulder to cry on."

"You want to build a high-rise in the middle of

downtown Garfield?"

She laughed. "No, computers will allow most of the services to be outsourced to providers around the country, which is good, because I don't think there are a lot of military widows in Garfield. But I need a central office to work out of and a second opinion to keep me on track with sound decisions and..." Her voice dwindled away when Nicolas's blue eyes met hers. Her pulse fluttered even as her heartbeat pounded in her ears. There was such a steadiness about him, something that made her believe he could be the helper she'd been looking and praying for. She licked dry lips and forced her mind to function. "Does it sound like something you'd like to be a part of?"

He lowered his head but not before Kate caught the small frown gathering between his brows. She hastened to explain. "It's not something you'd have to devote every day to. I know you have a new job that you enjoy." Words failed her a second time, and she stumbled to a stop. *Great first impression, Kate.*

Nicolas held his hand out. "I'm ready to shake on it." He pulled back a bit when Kate reached toward him. "With one condition."

Kate frowned at his answer. *Condition? What sort of condition could he possibly have?* "OK."

"Fifty-fifty deal, or no deal."

"You'd quit the force?"

"No, not equal time. You're right about my job. I enjoy it too much to give it up, and its time demands are unpredictable." He laid his outstretched hand flat on the table and smiled across the small space that separated them. "I'm talking monetary investment. I want an equal partnership there."

"Nicolas, that isn't necessary, I have more than enough money to fund the operation."

"And so do I. I spent twenty years in the Air Force. I lived a solitary, frugal life that allowed me to invest and build more of a retirement nest egg than I would have dreamed possible when I started. On top of that, I have my military retirement and my salary from the police force, more than what I need to live on."

He paused for a couple of heartbeats. Kate studied his face. *Why such a pained expression?*

"For reasons I won't go into, this is an issue that's as dear to me as it is to you, something I've needed to do for a long time." Nicolas lifted his hand and stretched it back across the table. "If we do this together, we do it as equal partners. Deal?"

*Equal in everything except sharing our motives.* Kate held his gaze while she considered.

"Kate?"

*Something to explore on another day.* Kate took his hand and, despite the unanswered questions, warmth tingled its way up her arm when his fingers closed around hers. She struggled to ignore it.

"Deal." Her fingers trailed against his as she slid her hand free. "I'll have my lawyer draw up some initial paperwork for your approval. We can hammer out the details from there." She grinned. "You'd better let your mom know what we're doing. My lawyer is Pam's husband, and Pam works in his office. She'd never break a confidence, but the fact that we're working together? Karla will have the bare facts in less than twenty-four hours."

Nicolas nodded. "I'll take care of my matchmaking mother. I love her to death, but we're gonna have our work cut out for us convincing her that this is just a business arrangement."

She grinned. "Maybe we should make that stipulation a part of our contract."

Nicolas didn't respond to her joke. He sat back and crossed his arms. "Now that our partnership is official, I have some news for you. I might have a lead on the perfect location for us."

Everything inside Kate's body warmed at his use of the word 'us'. "Really? Where?"

"Right on Main Street."

"Here? In town?" When he nodded, Kate narrowed her eyes and mirrored his arms-crossed pose. "Not possible. I've looked at every available property in town. Nada."

"You know the old newspaper office?"

The question set her heart pounding in her ears. "The one they're turning into a bed and breakfast?"

"The bed and breakfast deal fell through. I have it on good authority that the property will be back on the market early next week. They're continuing with the interior renovations, but if you're interested in taking a look—"

"Yes!"

Nicolas laughed at her response. "Well, OK. My contact says the owner will be back in town on Tuesday to check out the construction progress. I can set up a meeting if you're free."

"Oh, I'll be free, even if I have to burn my appointment book." Kate closed her eyes and whispered, "Thank you, Father."

"What?"

"Just giving thanks where thanks are due. This

meeting with you. Your information about the property. This whole day has been one big answer to prayer. Four days ago, I was ready to throw in the towel. I was so tired of every door slamming shut in my face. I told God I was ready to give up on the whole project. He told me to follow the plan, but I never dreamed His plan would end up here, in less than four days."

She stopped and tilted her head as she studied Nicolas's expression. It seemed as if every word of praise that left her mouth etched another degree of sadness onto his face. For the second time that day, Kate found herself following her heart. She didn't stop to think, she simply reached across the table, her hand settling lightly on his arm. "Nicolas, I hope you won't think I'm being forward, but we're going to be partners...and friends...I hope?"

He nodded.

"I don't know anything about the pain you're carrying around on the inside, but I can only imagine how Karla and Mitch raised you. I know that you know that just like God had the answers to my hopes and dreams, and pain, he has the answers to yours as well." She felt the muscles in his arm stiffen under her hand.

"I don't—"

"Shhh. I don't want to end our successful meeting with arguing or preaching. Just think about what I'm saying. OK?"

Nicolas nodded, and Kate could almost see him pigeon-holing the pain and her suggestion for later consideration. The clock on the wall hissed out its top-of-the-hour steam.

Nick glanced up. "Four o'clock. I can't believe we've

talked for two hours. Can I have a bit more of your time?"

Kate smiled, grateful her words of testimony hadn't sent him flying out the door and out of her life. *Oh, I really shouldn't, but that smile.* "What did you have in mind?"

"An early dinner to celebrate our partnership."

"Oh, you do like to walk a dangerous line, don't you? If your mother gets wind that we spent the whole afternoon together, she'll never buy the business story."

Nicolas stood up, and Kate followed suit. He helped her with her jacket, his solution simple. "We just won't tell her."

# CHAPTER EIGHT

Late winter dusk stained the sky gray by the time Kate and Nicolas drove back into Garfield after dinner. Old fashioned streetlights illuminated the sidewalks with a soft glow. A few cars took up spaces directly in front of the open restaurants, but by seven on a weeknight, even that activity had pretty much run its course for the evening.

Kate caught a smile on Nicolas's face. "What's funny?"

"Oh nothing. I guess I'm still readjusting to a place that goes to sleep for the night so early. I know I spent the first eighteen years of my life here, but..."

Kate nodded. "I know what you mean. Alan and I lived in Kansas City before he decided he needed to come back here. Not a sprawling metropolis by any means, but a gigantic step up from this." Her contented sigh filled the car. "I'm so glad I'm not there anymore."

"Country girl, Kate?"

"Who knew, right?"

The coffee shop where she'd left her car was dark. Nicolas maneuvered his vehicle into the parking spot next to it. If she were any judge, he'd left just enough space between their two vehicles for his passenger door and her driver's side door to be open at the same time.

Kate smiled. All she had to do was scoot from one

car to the other. Considerate, since the mild temperatures of the afternoon had given way to a brisk evening wind.

"You're good," she said.

"No sense in freezing." Nicolas shifted the standard transmission into neutral and allowed the tires to kiss the curb. "Give me your keys. I'll go start your car, and we can visit for a few more minutes while it warms up."

Kate dug in her bag. "Not tired of me yet?"

"Oh, I think I can probably stand ten more minutes before I have to kick you to the curb."

His fingers brushed hers as he took the keys, and a tingle of something almost forgotten, and certainly unwelcomed, brushed against Kate's heart. As he darted from his car to hers in the dim light, Kate was at a loss to explain the sudden and urgent attraction she fought every time he came close.

A wave of cold air nipped at her ankles when Nicolas opened the door and returned to his seat. He boosted the heater to the next notch and angled toward her. "Thank you."

"Why are you thanking me?" Kate asked. "You drove, you insisted on paying for our meal, a very nice meal in a very nice restaurant. And you didn't complain when I said no to dessert. If anyone should be saying thanks, it's me."

"Any time someone rescues me from solitary take-out or reheated leftovers, they get my thanks." His grin flashed a row of perfect white teeth, his gaze holding hers in the soft glow of the dash and street lights.

Tiny goose bumps paraded up her arms a second time.

"Trust me, dessert or not, tonight, you're my hero."

Her throat went dry and her heartbeat thundered in her ears. She searched for something, anything to break the tension she hoped he couldn't feel. *Say goodnight and leave.*

"Um...glad to be of service." Kate cringed at the strangled sound of her voice. She shoved her arms into the sleeves of her jacket and lifted her hair out from under her collar. "I'll have Harrison contact you with the paperwork..."

Nicolas leaned forward, bringing his face closer to hers. She shoved him away. *Oh please, not another tonsil diver.* "What are you doing?"

"Just hold still for a second." He held her chin in one hand and reached for the dome light with the other. He turned her head from side to side in the dim glow. "One of your earrings is missing."

Kate's hands flew to her ears. "Oh no!" She patted herself down from neck to waist. "Oh no," she repeated, shifting to look in the floor, running her hands along the seat beside her. "It can't be gone. Do you have a flashlight? We have to find it!"

"Settle down." He opened the glove box, pulled out a heavy metal flashlight, and flipped the switch. "Let me take a look." He trailed the light from her collar to her shoes. "I'm not seeing it. Lean forward and let me look behind you."

She inched forward, her foot tapping on the floor mat, her voice a whisper. "Please...please...please."

The search came up empty. Nicolas turned off the light. "I don't see it anywhere."

Kate lowered her face into her hands. *No...no...no...*

"I'm going to guess those were more than just your favorite earrings."

Her head bobbed. "Alan gave them to me on our wedding day. I know I should have put them away for safekeeping, but wearing them made him feel close." Kate lifted her head. She swiped tears from her cheeks with the back of her hand. "I've been out all day. There's no way to tell where I lost it."

"You had them both when you came into the coffee shop this afternoon. Describe them for me."

Kate glared at Nicolas, her frustration threatening to bubble over onto him. She yanked the flashlight from his hand, shook back her hair, and aimed the beam of light at the remaining earring.

He shrugged and pulled out his phone, flipped through a few screens, and punched a button. "OK, we'll let the restaurant know we lost a purple earring."

"Amethyst."

"I'm a guy, sweetheart, and detective or not, if you want more than round and purple, ya gotta work with me."

Kate pulled a breath deep into her lungs. There wasn't any need to be snippy with someone trying to help her. "I'm sorry. It's a small, white gold hoop, with amethysts all around. The post is threaded."

He nodded and held up a finger. "I'd like to speak to the manager, please."

Kate listened as he relayed the description of her earring, along with the approximate location of their table to the person on the other end of the phone. He nodded a few times, thanked the person for their time, and disconnected the call.

"Do you really think they might find it?"

His shoulders lifted. "I have no idea, but at least they're looking. That's better than giving up and calling it lost forever."

"Yes, you're right. I just panicked for a second." Kate pulled her wallet out of her purse, removed the remaining earring, and dropped it inside one of the zippered pouches. She looked at the darkened storefront. "First thing in the morning, I'll get a call in to the coffee shop and ask them to look for it as well."

Nicolas patted her shoulder. "That's the spirit. As soon as I get up in the morning, I'll comb through the car. Unless you dropped it on the street somewhere, the odds are good that we'll find it."

"I hope so. I'm going to pray really hard tonight." She stopped when his mouth hardened into a straight line, the tug in her heart unmistakable. "Nicolas, I'm still not going to preach to you, but I'd have to be blind not to see the pain on your face every time I mention anything to do with my Christian beliefs. I've lost two husbands. You're looking at an old hand when it comes to second-guessing God—and the bitterness that comes with it. But God sustained me through everything. Whatever has your heart so tangled up, He'll do the same for you."

He lowered his head, but not before she saw the pain in his expression transition into something that hardened his boyish looks.

"No preaching," she repeated, "but I am going to invite you to church on Sunday. I'll even save you a seat."

His response was a noncommittal noise.

Kate reached for the door. "I enjoyed dinner, and I'm looking forward to working with you. Something tells me that we'll make a great team. I...oh, my goodness. Wait right here for just a second."

Kate slid out of his car, opened hers, and leaned over to the passenger seat. When she turned back around, she held the small box of cookies she'd purchased earlier. "Melanie tells me these are your favorite. If the cookie I had earlier is any indication of her overall ability, these should take the sting out of missing dessert." She turned back to her own car before he could respond, waving in his direction as she backed from the parking spot and headed for home.

~ * ~

Nicolas dunked his sixth cookie in the remains of his milk and brooded. He watched as chocolate bled from the cookie and stained the milk a light shade of brown. The muddy color in his glass matched his mood.

Kate's words about hidden pain and godly solutions rang in his ears. Why would God bother to fix a pain He hadn't done anything to prevent? Nicolas replayed the final seconds of C.W.'s life in his head.

He flinched at the memory of the first explosion. They'd both snapped into a battle-ready posture, their training taking over where experience lacked. The second explosion knocked Nicolas off his feet. The fall discharged his weapon. The bullet killed his buddy. Nothing he could have expected, changed, or prevented. The incident had been ruled accidental by his superiors.

Nicolas had carried the guilt of C.W.'s death in his heart for more than twenty years. Guilt, but not blame. He knew it was a fine line, but he didn't blame himself, he blamed God.

His parents raised him in the shadow of the church his whole life, schooled him in God's word, love, and provision. He wasn't just taught, he was shown. They lived a life in front of him and his siblings that exemplified the realities of everything they taught. And he'd believed.

He'd taken that belief into the Air Force and out of the country. He'd rejoiced that his first buddy believed in the same things. That common ground led to many late night chats, cementing their friendship and forging a bond that went deeper, in some ways, than the one he shared with his younger brother. Then God let C.W. die, not taken by the enemy, but at his own hand.

Nicolas drowned the last bite of cookie and popped it into his mouth. Mom always said that chocolate was God's gift to women. Must be. It certainly wasn't doing much to calm his troubled thoughts.

~ * ~

A stray tear plopped on the top of her dresser as Kate studied the remaining earring. She'd probably been foolish to wear them so often, but the posts were threaded and the backs screwed on. When she took them off intentionally, it was a challenge. There was no way it could have just fallen out of her ear. *Except it obviously had.* She opened her jewelry box and laid the solitary amethyst hoop in an empty compartment. The brilliant purple stones sparkled at her from the black velvet that lined the box. With her head bowed, her hand lingered on top of the inlayed ivory lid. "Father, I know it's just a thing and unimportant in the grand scheme of the world, but it's dear to me for so many reasons. Please let someone find it and return it to me."

Kate wiggled out of her slacks and pulled her sweater over her head. She tossed both items into the laundry hamper and plucked her robe off the hook on the back of the door. *What a crazy day.* She sat on the stool in front of the old-fashioned vanity and stared into her reflection as she brushed her hair. One hundred strokes. A habit she'd had for as long as she could remember. The day had been a bungee jump of ups and downs. Then there was that moment in the car. For a fleeting second, she'd thought Nicolas intended to kiss her goodnight. Her face heated as realization slammed into her heart. The brush slipped from her fingers and clattered to the top of the vanity. She swiveled on the stool. The squeak she kept meaning to oil brought Merlin's head up. "I wanted him to kiss me," she admitted to the dog and the furnishings. "I batted his hand away, but that was reflex. If he'd been serious...?" Her hand rested on her lips, her eyes wide above them. "I'd have let him," she whispered.

The thought soured her stomach, filling her throat with the burn of acid. "No, no, no...this can't happen! Sweet heaven, Karla will never let me live this down."

The acid churning in her throat stung a bit sharper with every beat of her traitorous heart. She hurried to the kitchen and grabbed the antacid bottle. *Empty?* Her gaze darted around the room and fastened on the pink bakery box. A treat she'd set aside for her son. She crossed to the fridge and poured a tall glass of cold milk. Patrick would have to fend for himself. This was an emergency. The milk would calm her stomach and the chocolate? Kate ripped the lid off the box and ate every crumb.

~ * ~

Nicolas jerked awake. He lay in the dark, trying to isolate what had disturbed his sleep. It wasn't the familiar nightmare. His heart beat calmly and steadily, and when he lifted his hand to his forehead, he felt no sheen of sweat. He rolled from his back to his side, rearranged his pillows, and shifted his feet to find a cooler place between the sheets. *Too many cookies.*

He grinned at the juvenile thought, not able to remember the last time something so innocent as a late night snack had kept him awake. The echo of his sigh filled the room as he burrowed deep into the covers and started to drift. This partnership with Kate would take him in a new and proactive direction. Maybe that was all he needed to find some much-needed peace in his life.

*My peace I give to you.*

His eyes snapped open again. Where had that come from? His brow wrinkled in a frown. Nicolas recognized the words as part of a Bible verse. Probably an old memory verse. He'd been forced to learn more than his share as he grew up. Not forced, he admitted. He'd believed every word at one time, but that was before...

*My peace I give to you.*

Nicolas latched onto the words, struggling to bring the rest of the verse into focus. Something about not being troubled or afraid. He cobbled the words together. *My peace I give to you. Don't let your heart be troubled or afraid.* Not quite right but still a comfort.

*My peace I give to you. Don't let your heart be troubled or afraid.* The words became a mantra as he slipped back into sleep, and somewhere on the edge of consciousness the partial verse became a prayer. *Father, give me peace.*

# CHAPTER NINE

"OK, I appreciate your time. Please let me know if you find it." Kate disconnected the call to the manager of the coffee shop and sprawled on the couch. Someone had to find that earring. Maybe Nicolas was having better luck. Her fingers hovered over the keypad. She reeled in her impatience. *It's only ten. He probably hasn't even had a chance to look. He knows it's important. He'll look, he'll call.* She fumbled the phone when it rang, vibrating in her hand. She stabbed the accept button without looking at the display.

"Tell me you found it."

"What?"

"Who... Oh, Melanie. Sorry. I was hoping you were Nicolas."

"Really..." The single drawn out word held volumes of conjecture. "That's interesting."

"Not as much as you think. I lost an earring while we were out last night—"

"I thought you were meeting him for lunch yesterday afternoon."

"I did."

"And you spent the evening with him too?"

Kate closed her eyes. This was getting much more complicated than it needed to be. "Hold on and let me explain." She shared the whole story for her friend, ending with Nicolas's promise to call once he'd had a chance to look through his car. "So you see, it's all very innocent and strictly business."

"Um hmm."

Kate bounced her head on the back of the sofa.

"Sorry about the earring, though. That stinks."

"Understatement. I'm hopeful, I'm praying."

"That's a big deal to you, isn't it?"

Kate frowned. "Like I said, Alan gave me those earrings on our wedding day, they're—"

"Not the earrings. The praying."

"Of course it's a big deal." Kate said. "God is my Heavenly Father. He cares about the things that are important to me, even the small things like lost earrings." Her heart ached for her friend and the current issues with her marriage. "He cares about relationships as well. I don't want to sound like a broken record, but I wish you'd accept my invitation to church. You might find some answers for your own life."

Silence met Kate's comment. "Look, Melanie that probably sounded pushy. I just—"

"That's why I called."

"What? Good."

Melanie cleared her throat. "I thought about what you said, about finding some lasting friendships, and since I intend to live in Garfield for a long time, I figured that's a good thing. Tyler isn't a part of my life anymore. I don't want you to think that I'm accepting your invitation so I can keep tabs on him. I just figured...you know...if I visit and I like it, I can find someplace he doesn't go to, right?"

"No shortage of churches in Garfield, that's for

sure."

"Can we meet somewhere and go together? It feels strange when I think about going by myself."

"Absolutely. Why don't you come over here? Got a pen?" Kate recited her address into the phone, nodding as it was repeated. "That's it. Just come on over in the morning, and you can ride with me. If you can be here by nine, we can get there in time to have a cup of coffee and a pastry before Sunday school starts."

"Pastries?"

Kate chuckled. "Well, not anything like what you're used to, I'm afraid. Just some prepackaged honey buns and sweet rolls, maybe some donuts if someone is energetic enough to swing by the store. It's more about the fellowship than the food."

"Do you think they'd mind day-old?"

"What did you have in mind?"

"I usually have a few things left at the end of the day. I used to box them up and send them to the station with Tyler, but...well..." Her voice caught, and she sniffed into the phone.

"Girlfriend, if you're about to say what I think you're about to say, you'll be everyone's sweetheart before the morning is over."

Melanie laughed, obviously moving beyond the painful memory. "I just don't want anyone to think I'm trying to drum up business for the bakery."

"Even if you were, there wouldn't be anything wrong with that. You just box up what you want, and I'll help you carry it in. They'll love me by default."

"OK, if you're sure. It'll be an odd assortment. I never know what I'll have left," Melanie said.

While her friend spoke, the doorbell rang. Kate

crossed to the window and peeked through the curtain. A white delivery van with *Millie's Flowers* emblazoned on the side sat at the curb in front of her house. *What's the florist truck doing here?* "Hey, just bring what you have. It'll be a nice surprise for everyone." The doorbell sounded a second time. "Melanie, I have to go. Someone's at the door." She closed the call and opened the door to find Wesley, the retired gentleman who made Millie's deliveries, standing on her porch. He held a beautiful bouquet of spring flowers.

"Morning, Wesley."

Wesley nodded his response and held out the basket of flowers. "Gonna be a good day for you, I'm guessin'."

Kate took the proffered arrangement. Lilies, irises, daisies, and the smallest, daintiest carnations she'd ever seen. The basket overflowed in an explosion of pink, purple, white, and orange. She buried her nose in the fragrant blooms. "Oh, my." She looked up. "Who?"

The delivery man grinned. "Not my surprise to spoil." He handed her a small, white envelope. "But I'm supposed to make sure this gets into your hands and no one else's."

Kate bundled the flowers into her arms and accepted the envelope. "Wait right here for just a second." She set everything down on a small table and went to find her purse. When she returned to the door, she pressed a bill into the old man's hand. "Thanks, Wesley. You have a wonderful weekend."

Wesley touched the bill of his cap, stepped of the porch, and shuffled back to the van. Kate closed the door and stared at the flowers. Her finger traced a line down the velvety petal of one of the irises before reaching for the envelope. She lifted the flap and shook out the card. The card landed in her hand with a surprising weight. Taped inside was her lost earring minus the tiny back. Suddenly weak knees forced her to lean against the table. *Thank you, Father!*

She pried the tape off and read the handwritten message. *I found it in the car this morning. Put it someplace safe. Nicolas.*

Brief, to the point, and not the least bit romantic, if you didn't consider the flowers, which she wouldn't. *Then why is your heart going pitter-patter?* The man was just too smooth. She traced the sloping petals of the iris again. How had he known that purple irises were one of her favorite flowers?

~ * ~

*Stupid, stupid, stupid!* Nicolas circled Tyler's car with the spray wand while hot soapy water gushed from the tip. He hunched deeper into his jacket when the light breeze blew a fine mist back into his face. The water wasn't cold, but the wind was.

Flowers. He'd sent Kate flowers. It had seemed like a good idea at the time, but now? *Serious overkill.* She'd been so vibrant over dinner last night, plans for her...*their*...center, fizzing out of her like bubbles from a champagne bottle. He shook his head at the scope of her plans. She intended to have a lawyer and a psychologist on staff before it was all said and done. That joy had gone flat when her earring came up missing. He remembered Kate's small burst of temper. Hair pushed back, the beam of his flashlight trained on her earlobe. She was a feisty one. And he liked it. *Too much.* Nicolas groaned as the subject of his thoughts came full circle. *Flowers.* He'd wanted to put a smile back on her face. *Returning the earring would have done that just fine, you imbecile.*

He concentrated the spray on a particularly resistant patch of bug guts, determined to put Kate, the flowers, and her smiles—absent or present—out of his mind.

"You missed a spot."

Nicolas turned, aiming the pressurized spray of water at his partner's feet with just enough precision to make Tyler take a quick step back. "And this matters to you how? I don't think this car has seen soap and water for at least a year."

Tyler shrugged, picking his way around the sudsy puddles to a spot just next to the coin-operated wash selector. He placed a couple of sodas on top of the box, leaned against the wall, and crossed his arms. "What can I say? I'm a failure as a vehicle owner." He turned his head and stared into the distance. "Looks like failure is my middle name these days."

The comment was low, but Nicolas heard the gloomy words above the rush of the water. No need to ask what was on his partner's mind. He circled the car and switched the water to the rinse cycle. Some of the noise died with the change in water pressure, enough to have a conversation. Maybe Tyler was ready to get some things off his chest. "Have you talked to her this week?"

Tyler shook his head and reached for one of the sodas. He twisted off the cap and took a long swallow. "She won't take my calls. I don't even know where she's staying."

The last quarter's worth of water trickled to a stop.

Nicolas slid the wand back into the holder. "Did you bring something to dry this off with?"

"Backseat."

Nicolas retrieved a couple of threadbare beach towels. "Garfield's not that big. You could find her if you tried." He buffed the hood. "I'm surprised you haven't tried."

"It's not about finding her. I could find her any day of the week at the bakery. In fact, I've driven by there every morning on my way to work, just to make sure her car's there, make sure she's safe. I haven't gone in. I wanted to give her some time to cool off." Nicolas opened the back door and dumped a wet towel into the back floorboard. "It's been five days, partner. You might want to rethink that cooling-off thing and just go get her."

Tyler took a step away from the wall, shoved his hands into his pockets, and turned his back on Nicolas. "Not happening. I told her that I wouldn't beg her to stay, and I'm not going crawling to get her to come home."

Nicolas stared at Tyler's back and studied his posture. Legs spread, shoulders slumped, head bowed. Not a portrait of happiness.

Tyler continued. "I've given her almost twelve years. She knows I love her. If that's not enough, it's out of my hands. I'm praying about it. If God can't work it out, maybe it doesn't need to be worked out."

"You know, my mom has this thing she likes to say. God helps those who help themselves."

"That's a tired old cliché.'"

"Things become cliché because they're true. Just like the one that says if you want something done, you need to do it yourself. Might be time to put some effort into making things better."

Tyler paced away. When he turned around, he faced Nicolas with his hands folded across his chest and grim lines around his mouth. "I'm an idiot, OK? I missed her birthday and loused up her plans for the evening. I apologized for that. But seriously, it's not like we're toddlers dancing around in excitement, waiting for someone to light the candles on our cake. At this stage in my life, I wish people *would* forget my birthday."

Nicolas gave a quick nod of assent as he continued to move the towel over the wet vehicle. "It's obvious she feels differently."

Tyler shrugged. "You're right, but really, if it hadn't been another missed birthday that tossed us over the edge, it would have been something else. Twelve years, and it feels like we've spent most of that time circling each other, looking for a way to lock the pieces of our lives together. We've never quite been able to get it right." He held his hands out in a gesture of surrender.

"She likes to travel, I don't. But I've seen to it that she goes on a nice vacation every year. I've even paid for friends to go with her. She wants to talk about her day when we get home, and all I want to do is unwind with some down time in front of the TV. She likes to read when she has free time, I like to get out and do something physical. Melanie likes to try new recipes, and I just want her to fry a hunk of meat, open a can of corn, fix me a potato, and call it dinner. We tried for years, but we never had kids. Maybe things would be different if we had. Instead, she's wrapped up in our nieces and nephews. I love those kids, too, but I don't need to make a four-hour drive once a month to see them." He stopped to pull in a deep breath. "She says we don't share anything, but I've tried to get her to come to church with me, and she won't budge."

*And you have no idea how lucky you are and what you're throwing away.* Nicolas kept that thought to himself. "Not a lot of common ground there," he said.

"Tell me about it. But through it all, we loved each other. At least I thought we did."

"Then you need to do something a little more proactive than praying about the situation." He held up his hand to silence the objections he could see forming on Tyler's lips. "I've never been married, so I can't offer you much practical advice. I'm not knocking prayer, just suggesting an add-on."

"Like..."

"Have you considered talking to Pastor Gordon? He's got fifty years of marriage behind him. He might be able to point you in a direction you haven't tried."

Tyler crossed his arms. "You're suggesting a religious solution to my problems. You?"

"Surprises the heck out of me too, but talking it out with someone experienced feels like the right thing to do."

Tyler nodded, and Nicolas saw speculation in his partner's eyes.

"That's actually pretty good advice. I'll think about taking it, if you'll think about taking my good advice."

"Which was?"

"That invitation to church is still open."

Nicolas laughed. His partner had been pushing church in his face for months. "Better take your umbrella to church tomorrow," Nicolas advised.

Tyler frowned.

"I'm thinking of taking you up on that invitation. When the roof of Valley View starts to crumble, I wouldn't want you to get hurt."

Tyler's expression went from confused to surprised. "I'll save you a seat."

Nicolas laughed. "Don't bother. If I decide to come, I've got someone a lot more attractive than you to sit with." He stood back to admire his handiwork, then opened the back door of Tyler's car and dropped the second wet towel on top of the first. Something sticking out from under the floor mat caught his attention. He stooped to pick it up and flipped the soggy manila envelope to Tyler. "I cleaned the outside, the inside is up to you."

Tyler snagged it out of the air with a frown. "I cleaned the inside last night because I knew you were planning to wash it today." He turned it over in his hands, and his eyebrows arched high on his forehead. "This isn't mine, and it wasn't in the car last night." He met his partner's gaze and shifted, holding the envelope now by a single corner with the front facing out so Nicolas could see the single word printed in large capital letters.

PIG

"You don't lock your car at night?"

Tyler shrugged. "It's Garfield." He laid the package on the hood of the car. "It's almost soaked through from the towel, should we try to open it."

Nicolas joined him at the front of the car. "We're the detectives. If someone on patrol found it, they'd bring it to us. Just try to get whatever it is out in one piece. I doubt there's a print left on it, but I wish we had gloves."

Tyler nodded and fished a small knife from his pocket. "Hold the back corners down." He worked the blade under the seal. It didn't take much to break the waterlogged bond. Inch by tedious inch, he worked a single sheet of paper free. He held it up, and they read the mismatched, glued on words together.

WHAT HAPPENS WHEN THE WATCHERS ARE THE WATCHED

# CHAPTER TEN

Melanie balanced a large cake box in one hand and reached for the bakery door with the other, careful to keep the weight evenly distributed. She was halfway through the opening when she saw Tyler's car turn the corner and head in her direction. Her abrupt about face shifted the cake and sent her into a dance to get it righted before it hit the floor. A rarely-used swear word echoed through the shop. "Why can't he leave me alone?" Irritated, she turned back to the window and watched his car turn right at the intersection. If he followed the same pattern as he had every other day this week, he wouldn't be back. Why did he feel the need to check up on her? *And why would he drive by on a Sunday?*

Hadn't she been making it pretty much on her own all these years while he ignored her existence? Why should that change now?

She steadied herself and the box. With a deep breath, she forced the aggravation away. She had an appointment with a lawyer next week. Once she made the split between them official, maybe she'd have some peace. The thought blurred her vision. *Don't be such a baby!* Her chest tightened. And what about the baby?

Melanie straightened her shoulders and marched to the car. She situated the final box in her back seat and checked her dress for stray smudges of frosting. Finding nothing out of place, she tapped Kate's number into her phone, chewing on a nail as it rang on the other end.

The baby was a constant thought. That was probably normal, but the thoughts should be of a life as a family, not life as a single parent and how to keep the baby a secret until divorce papers were signed. Tyler would never...

"Good morning. Sorry I almost missed you. I was just getting out of the shower. Please don't tell me you're calling to back out of coming with me this morning."

"Not exactly, but I think we might need to revise our plan a bit."

"How so?" Kate asked.

"I'm thinking we need to take my car. And I'm thinking that you need to call whoever you need to call and tell them to put a hold on the snacks 'til we get there."

"What did you do?"

Melanie slammed the car door shut, turned, and leaned against it. "It's not what I did, it's what a customer did. I only do cakes by special order, and I had two scheduled for pick-up yesterday afternoon. They never showed, and I couldn't reach them. So, I've got a whole chocolate marble cake with buttercream frosting and a carrot cake with cream cheese frosting loaded in the backseat of my car, along with four or five dozen assorted cookies and a box of cupcakes."

"Wow."

"Yeah, my missing customer won't be happy when they see a charge on their credit card for these cakes, but it's part of the contract." She pushed away from the car and went to lock up the bakery. "That's a mess I'll deal with later."

"You call it a mess, I call it divine providence. I'll call over to Valley View's kitchen and have someone stow the honey buns and break out some plates and forks. You're about to be everyone's Sunday favorite."

Melanie looked up as a car rounded the corner. *Not Tyler, thank goodness.* "It beats throwing them away, I guess."

"Hey, what's wrong? There's more in your voice than wasted cake."

*I'm pregnant and Tyler doesn't know.* The fingernail returned to Melanie's mouth. "It's nothing."

"Spill it," Kate demanded. "If it's got you upset, it isn't nothing."

"I'm just a little worried about seeing Tyler this morning. I've avoided him all week. Just witnessed his daily keep-tabs-on-Melanie drive-by. I don't want him thinking I'm there to return the favor."

"We talked about this. Tyler doesn't come for the pre-service fellowship, and I've never seen him during Sunday school. That's one reason why I haven't met him yet. It'll be fine, I promise."

~ * ~

Tyler lifted a hand from the steering wheel to rub at grainy eyes. Another morning, another patrol of Melanie's Bakery. *It's Sunday.* He pushed the date aside. His wife wouldn't answer the phone, he didn't know where she was staying, so the bakery was the only tangible link he had.

*What happens when the watchers are the watched?* The words unnerved him. Not for himself. It wasn't the first time he'd received a generic threat while working a case. It came with the territory. But what if he wasn't the only member of his family being watched? The world was a messed up place. A threat to him was an indirect threat to Melanie, and it was the first time in twelve years that she had been out from under his direct protection. *And you're reaching.*

He turned the corner and his gazed zeroed in on the unexpected sight of her car parked in front of her shop on the otherwise deserted street. *What's she doing there on a Sunday morning?* He smacked the steering wheel with the heel of his hand. *Idiot! She's right there, go back and ask her. Talk to her. Tell her about the note.* He shook his head. His wife's message had been crystal clear over the last six days. If she was so unhappy that she wouldn't even answer her phone, she'd likely dismiss his caution as an attempt to get her to come back home. Maybe he should just let her go. Tyler sucked in a deep breath and rubbed a shaky hand over a hollow spot in his chest. "But what do I do without her?" The question reverberated in the empty car.

And despite the explanation he'd rattled off to Nicolas yesterday, the other unanswered question was why, or better yet, why now? He wasn't oblivious. He'd never claimed to be a perfect husband. He worked a demanding job that he enjoyed, where he put in more hours than absolutely necessary. Those extra hours sometimes meant he was preoccupied, and preoccupied people forgot things...anniversaries...birthdays...even dinner plans. He cringed in the seat. That didn't mean that he didn't love her, for Pete's sake. For each special occasion he'd forgotten—and it did embarrass him to add them up—hadn't he gone out of his way to make it up to her?

Sure, they didn't get to spend a lot of time together. Her new business didn't help. Running a bakery meant Melanie crawled into bed by eight and rushed out of the house hours before dawn. There were nights he never even saw her. Melanie was great at complaining about his faults. Why couldn't she see what her new schedule was doing to their marriage?

He sighed. It really was just what he'd told Nicolas yesterday. Almost twelve years of circling, and not a lot to show for it. Tyler glanced at his watch at the next stop sign. It was almost nine, and he had absolutely nothing to do. *There you have it!* A Sunday morning I could have spent over a lazy breakfast with Melanie, and where was she? At work. *Fine.* He'd be hanged if he'd go back to that empty house and stare at the walls for the next two hours. This just might be the perfect morning to give Sunday school a try.

~ * ~

Melanie circled the Valley View Parking lot twice. "Wow, this place is packed." She finally pulled into a vacant spot in the lot across the street from the door Kate suggested they use. "Looks like neither of us will need to worry about any extra calories this morning. We're gonna walk them all off just hauling this stuff inside."

Kate grinned and motioned over her shoulder. "Don't worry about it. I called in some reinforcements."

Melanie looked up in time to see Callie Stillman and Pam Lake making their way across the lot. They stopped next to the car and waited for her and Kate to get out.

Callie threw an arm around Melanie's shoulder. "You finally came. I'm so glad!" She glanced into the back seat. "Really glad, because Kate says you brought goodies from the bakery." She took a step back. "Please tell me there's chocolate in one of those boxes."

Melanie laughed. "Yes, there's chocolate."

"You guys all know each other?" Kate asked.

Pam looked at Kate. "Yeah...I get cookies for the break room at least once a week."

"Well, I don't treat myself that often," Callie said. "But my youngest grandson is seriously addicted to that secret cookie jar she keeps stashed behind the counter." She ran a hand across her stomach. "Where do you think part of this winter weight came from?"

"Not taking credit for that." Melanie opened the back door. "Let's get this stuff inside, and we can have a nice visit. I had no idea you both went to the same church Karla and Kate had been inviting me to."

Callie hefted a cake box. "Yep, lifetime members. Terri Evans, too. We were praying about it and waiting for the right time to swoop down on you. Looks like Kate beat us to it."

The four women trooped into the church and spread the boxes out on the bar situated between the kitchen and the fellowship hall. The response was nothing less than what Kate had predicted. Mass-appreciation. Melanie had never seen a crop devoured by a swarm of hungry locust, but she now had a clue about what that might look like.

Melanie was serving a slice of cake to Callie's husband when a familiar male laugh brought her gaze up and across the room. *Tyler!* She cringed when the guys he was talking to nodded at their plates and pointed in her direction. Surprise washed across her husband's face. He frowned and started in her direction. Melanie fled to the kitchen, turning to face him as he pushed through the swinging doors.

Anger bubbled up inside her. "What are you doing here, and why are you following me!"

"Following you? I go to church here, remember? I've been trying to get you to come with me for months. So how does my being here make me guilty of following you?"

"Oh, don't give me that! Kate said you never come this early. I saw you drive by the bakery this morning...and every morning this week." Her voice rose with the anger. "That says *following* to me!"

Tyler made a quick downward slash with his hand. "Lower your voice, will you?" He took her by the arm and pulled her into a corner. "We don't need to advertise our troubles to the world."

She jerked out of his grasp. "Keep your hands off of me," she hissed. "I'm only going to say this one time. Leave me alone. Stop calling me, stop following me, stop driving by the shop. Do it voluntarily, or when I meet with my lawyer this week, I'll have him slap a restraining order on you! How will your boss react to that?"

Tyler took a step back. "A lawyer, Mel, seriously? Have we fallen so far that we can't work this out?" He stopped to clear his throat. "I still love you."

Melanie met her husband's gaze, and the raw

emotion in his eyes clogged her throat as well. *I love you too, you big dumb cop!* She'd give anything to be able to believe him, but she'd heard the promises before, and today, they were too little, too late. Still, they took some of the bite out of her temper.

"Tyler, I think we're beyond talking about it." Her voice sounded tired in her own ears. "I'm not happy. You're not happy—"

"Don't speak for me. How do you know what I am anymore? You're so wrapped up in the bakery—"

"And I'm wrapped up in the bakery because you spent the last twelve years wrapped up in anything that didn't include me. So I can speak for you, because a happily married man doesn't need an excuse to be gone, busy, or otherwise occupied eighteen hours a day."

"Mel..."

The swinging doors to the kitchen creaked open. "Guys?" Kate stepped through. "Everything OK in here?"

"Yes," Tyler answered.

"No," Melanie said at the same time. She moved away from her husband and yanked her coat off the back of a chair. "Kate, I'm sorry, but I can't stay." She slipped her arms into the sleeves. "Will you be able to get a ride home?"

Kate nodded. "Patrick can drop me off." Her gaze shifted from one to the other. She held out a hand to Tyler. "Hi Tyler, I'm Kate Archer. It's nice to finally meet you."

Tyler accepted Kate's hand briefly, but his eyes remained fixed on Melanie's face. "We're sort of having a conversation here."

"Understood. I didn't mean to eavesdrop, but..." She waved a hand at the cavernous room. "Voices tend to echo in here." Kate took one step between the couple and lowered her voice even more. "I don't know either of you well, and you haven't asked for my advice." She leveled her gaze at Melanie. "But I wish you'd reconsider your decision to leave. You might find some answers if you stayed."

Melanie shook her head and turned her back on Tyler. "I appreciate your desire to help, but I don't think I'll find what I'm looking for here, at least not today." She crossed the room, picked up her purse, and tossed a final look at Tyler. "The only thing I've ever wanted was a relationship with someone who understood what makes me, me."

"You're walking out on your best chance to find that," Tyler whispered.

She paused for a second, a frown on her face and her hands buried in her jacket pockets. Melanie swallowed hard when her fingers closed around the small wrapped gift that bore evidence of her secret.

*Tell him. He deserves to know.*

She ignored the thought and swept out of the room.

~ * ~

Seconds ticked by in a counter-beat to the thud of his heart. Nicolas could almost hear both as he sat in his car and stared at the front doors of Valley View Church. So far, the morning had been a gigantic joke. His alarm hadn't gone off, he'd scorched his last toaster pastry, and an unexpected fifteen-minute search for his keys had him running later than he'd intended. He'd been a warrior long enough to recognize opposition when he ran head long into it.

*Thud...tick...thud...tick...thud.* He'd faced live gunfire with less trepidation than this. *And that's just dumb!* I grew up here. I have friends here. My parents practically have their names engraved on their pew. What was it about this morning that had him so conflicted? He sat while two voices waged war in his head.

*What are you doing? You gave up on God a long time ago.*

*I never gave up on you, Nicolas.*

*Going in there is an admission that you've been wrong all these years.*

*Peace, Nicolas. It's time you allowed Me to give you peace.*

*You murdered your buddy! What if they find out?*

"This is ridiculous!" He threw the car door open, planted one foot on the asphalt, and responded to both voices. "I'm going in there. I'm sitting through the sermon. I'm going to look for the promise of peace that woke me up two nights ago. No one's going to find out anything I don't want them to know. And I'm going because it's my choice. You two can just argue on without me." The air seemed to thicken like cold molasses with each step forward. Nicolas set his gaze on the door of the church and ordered his feet to move. *I don't understand any of this.* I've been to church with Mom and Pop a few times over the years—baby dedications, weddings, funerals, Christmas. What makes today different?

*It's time to come home, son. We both know that.*

*Going in there is a mistake. Your life will never be yours again.*

The hand that reached for the door seemed

disconnected from the rest of his body, moving in a slow motion that didn't belong to him. The voices in his head continued to argue, but he ceased to listen to either one, intent on just getting the door open. When it finally swung open, a wall of worship music enveloped him. *Amazing Grace.*

C.W.'s off key whistle filled his head and brought unexpected clarity. The most important thing in his buddy's life had been his relationship with God, beyond family, beyond home, beyond friendship. C.W. would be appalled to know that Nicolas had allowed self-imposed guilt to drive a wedge between him and God.

The freedom of that moment dissipated the molasses, and drowned the voices. All that remained was an almost physical hunger and a soul numbing thirst. He knew just where to find satisfaction for both.

Nicolas walked into the sanctuary, and his vision narrowed to the front. He walked past his partner, past his parents, and past Kate. He found himself in front of the altar as the music flowed around him. He didn't think about disrupting the service. Somewhere in the back of his mind, he knew that his presence before the altar would bring rejoicing, not disruption. His only thought was that it had been too long since he reached out to the God of his youth.

"Twenty years." The thought was more groan than prayer. "Father, forgive me, I've been such a fool." Twenty years of guilt and bitterness lifted from his shoulders. He couldn't stand. Nicolas fell to his knees and allowed himself to be embraced by warmth and peace as he entered into a place of communion with his heavenly Father.

# CHAPTER ELEVEN

The next morning Nicolas shut the car door and settled in behind the steering wheel to wait for his slow-moving partner. He positioned his sunglasses on the bridge of his nose and tapped the wheel in time to the song running through his head. When he stopped to add the words to the tune, he chuckled. It was one of the peppy worship songs from last night's service. *I'm humming gospel.* The realization only broadened his smile.

He knew it was cliché to say that today the sun was brighter, the air smelled sweeter, his breakfast tasted better, and his steps were lighter. But like he'd told Tyler a few days ago, cliché's became cliché's because they were true. And today, experienced through the filter of a brand new salvation, the world truly was glorious. It was shaping up to be a good day for Garfield's lowlifes. They were still going to get their due, but they'd get it with a smile.

His grateful heart tumbled into a prayer. *Thanks again for not giving up on me when I gave up on You. I can already feel You pulling the bits and pieces of my life together.* The spontaneity of the words and the ease of his reclaimed relationship with God took Nicolas pleasantly by surprise. "Yep," he whispered. "It's gonna be a good day."

Movement from the rear of the building caught his

attention. Tyler slammed the back door of the station and trudged to the car. Even fifty feet away, Nicolas could read suppressed anger in his partner's jerky movements and tight expression. *Lord, if there's a solution for Tyler and Melanie, please help them find it.*

Tyler yanked the door open, fell into the seat, and buckled his seat belt. "Let's roll."

Nicolas started the car and weighed his options. Ignore the mood and hope it improved, or confront the hurt and offer what help he could. He shrugged. Tyler hadn't been shy about poking at Nicolas's resistance over the last few months. Maybe it was time to return the favor. He shifted into drive and pulled out onto Main Street.

"Did you get a chance to talk to Melanie this weekend?"

Tyler snorted and stared out the window. "Oh, I got that chance, all right. She wasted no time in informing me that she's got an appointment with a lawyer this week."

Worse than he thought. "Oh man, I am so sorry. But an appointment just means she's exploring her options. If she's talking to you, that has to be a good thing. Did she call you?"

"Nope, I talked to her at church yesterday."

Nicolas thought back on yesterday's service. He didn't remember seeing Melanie, but he'd been a little preoccupied. "Tyler, that's great."

Tyler shoved his reflective shades up into his hair and frowned at Nicolas.

"Not the lawyer thing," Nicolas clarified. "That bites. But the fact she finally accepted your invitation to church. That's huge. That's got to be something you can work with. I can't believe I missed seeing her."

Tyler sat back in his seat, lowered his shades, and crossed his arms. "It wasn't my invitation she accepted, and she didn't stay for the service."

"What—?"

"She came because a friend invited her. She left when I tried to talk to her." Tyler's jaw clenched. "Danged interfering woman! If she'd minded her own business and let me talk some sense into Melanie, things might have turned out differently."

"Who are you talking about?"

"Melanie's friend. Slender, long blonde hair. Kathy...Kim..." He snapped his fingers. "Kate—"

Nicolas felt his eyebrows climb. "Kate Archer?"

"That's the one." Tyler nodded. "Nosey, busybody female. All I wanted was a few seconds to tell Mel that I loved her...to tell her about the note and ask her to be careful. Wait a second..." He narrowed his eyes at his partner. "Kate Archer...how do you know her?"

"She's a friend of my mother's." Nicolas took his eyes off the road for a quick glance at Tyler. "We're about to be business partners."

"Partners?" Tyler sat back in the seat and lowered his sunglasses. "Good luck with that, man. Pushy, overbearing—"

"Hey, take a step back, pal. She's not that bad."

"You got a thing for this woman?"

Nicolas snorted. "Hardly. What did she do to set you off?"

"Interrupted the one chance at a conversation with Melanie I've had this week, then refused to leave, just generally got in the way."

"Oh, you probably took it wrong. You're upset, and

you're spoiling for a fight. I don't think Kate would come between you two intentionally."

Tyler shifted in the seat and stared at Nicolas over the top of his shades. "You *do* have a thing for this woman."

Something off limits scratched at Nicolas's heart. He denied it the light of day. "Don't be an idiot. We're going to be business partners—"

"And that means you can't like her?"

"I do like her."

"No, you *like* her."

"What are you, twelve? Give me a break. Besides, I couldn't *like* her even if I wanted to. Not *liking* Kate has become a matter of principle. My mom already has our names written next to each other in the family Bible. We're going to be business partners...period."

Tyler settled back in his seat. "Um hmm. You just keep telling yourself that."

Nicolas drove in silence. Like Kate. *As if.* There was no woman in his future. He'd given up that dream a long time ago. *Didn't I?* While his head answered yes, for the first time in twenty years his heart wavered. He swallowed when he heard the internal click of another piece of his life snapping into place.

~ * ~

Melanie paced the sidewalk in front of the lawyer's office, trying to work up the nerve to keep her appointment. She kept seeing Tyler's face the way it looked the morning before, sad and repentant, an "I love you" on his lips. The trouble was, she believed him. She loved him right back. Unfortunately, love just didn't seem to be enough. But still, how did you divorce someone you still loved? How did you divorce the father of your unborn child? She stomped her foot in frustration. Why couldn't the man just listen...one time?

Tyler was the most generous person in the world when it came to money and material possessions. He'd share his last dollar and the shirt off his back if someone needed it worse than he did, but when it came to his time, he was a bigger miser than the fabled King Midas. His job, his interests, his hobbies, his church. Melanie stomped toward the corner. Wasn't it better to end the farce of their marriage while there was still an ember of love left between them? If they waited until hatred festered, there wouldn't be anything left of their years together worth salvaging. What good would that do their child? Wouldn't divorced and friendly parents be better than married and miserable?

Maybe if the pressure were off of Tyler to be a husband, maybe he could be the friend she'd always craved and the father their child deserved. She nodded, answering her own question. But how to make this work? The baby wasn't obvious now, but that would change soon. Things needed to be kick-started now, because he'd never sign the divorce papers if he even suspected she might be pregnant.

Determination carried her back to the door of Harrison Lake's law office. Everyone she'd talked to said he was the best man for the job—fair and compassionate. She pulled open the door and stepped into a comforting environment more suited to a family room than an office. Heavy wooden accent pieces flanked an oversized striped sofa and chairs. The pretty blonde behind the reception desk looked up with a smile as Melanie closed the door.

"Come right in. How may we help you today?"

"Hi. I'm Melanie Mason. I have a three o'clock appointment."

"Yes of course. If you'll have a seat, I'll let Mr. Lake know you're here. Can I get you anything? A cup of coffee, a bottle of water?"

"No, I'm fine."

"OK, I'll be right back."

The secretary disappeared down the hall, and Melanie's knees went weak. She looked at the door. *I could leave.* Instead, she sat and wiped sweaty hands on the legs of her jeans. *I'm going through with this. For everyone's sake.* Her nervous hands pressed against her flat belly. The child lay still, too small yet to be felt, but she didn't need a baby to churn up her insides. Her stomach twisted at what she was about to do. She forced herself to settle back into the cushions and take a few deep breaths.

"Ms. Mason?"

Melanie looked up to see a tall, handsome man with a thick head of curly dark hair. He approached with his hand extended and a smile on his face. She scrambled to her feet and took his hand in hers.

"I'm Harrison Lake. If you'll follow me back to my office, we can get acquainted."

He released her hand and turned back down the hall. Melanie followed him on rubbery legs. The tears of regret pressing against her eyes wouldn't be denied any longer and rolled down her cheeks. She tried to calm her nerves with a quick internal pep talk. *I just want to get some information. No one's going to talk me into anything I don't want to do.* It didn't work. She swiped the moisture from her face. The lawyer would think she was a loon.

Mr. Lake opened the door to the last room on the hall and motioned her inside. "Make yourself comfortable." She took the seat on the visitor side of the desk. He closed the door and circled around her to claim the chair behind the desk. He picked up a pen and made a few notes on a yellow legal pad. When he looked up, a compassionate smile twitched at his lips. He slid a box of tissues across the desk.

"I don't bite."

Melanie snatched a tissue and managed a nervous laugh as she blotted her eyes. "Sorry. Nerves."

"I understand." He laid the pen aside and leaned forward on crossed arms. "Seventy-five percent of the people who walk through my front door do so because they're in some sort of trouble." He offered her a reassuring smile. "May I call you Melanie?"

She nodded.

"Good." He sat back and retrieved the pen. "Tell me about your trouble, Melanie."

She took a deep breath, forced herself to dig the words up from the pit of her churning stomach. "I want a divorce." The words seemed to hang in the air, final and ugly. She closed her eyes and gave him the details of twelve years of disappointment and loneliness, false starts and stops. He filled the yellow pad with notes as she talked.

When she paused, the lawyer leaned forward and rested his elbows on the desk. "Do you guys own your house?"

Melanie nodded.

"Is it in his name?"

"Both," she said.

"Do you have assets in joint accounts?"

This got a negative shake from Melanie. "I have a business account for my shop. We have a joint household account, but we don't use it much. My husband prefers to pay the bills from his account. I let him."

"Children?"

Melanie strangled on her own spit at the unexpected question, and found herself struggling for breath in a fit of coughing.

"Do you need some water?" Mr. Lake pushed back from his desk.

She held up her hand and motioned for him to stay put as the coughing eased. "I'm fine, thanks. I just swallowed wrong."

The lawyer stared at her and repeated his question. "Do you and your husband have children?"

Melanie bit her lip at the lawyer's questioning stare. She pasted on a smile and shook her head. "No, just the two of us." She shifted the subject before he could ask any more questions. "Tyler's a good man..." She trailed off when she caught the frown on the lawyer's face. "Did I say something wrong?"

"Tyler Mason?"

"Yes."

"Detective Tyler Mason?"

Melanie shifted in the seat. *Why is it so hot in here all of the sudden?* She fought the urge to fan the air in front of her face, not wanting to draw attention to her sudden nervousness. *I wish I hadn't turned down the water.* She swallowed and nodded. "That's him."

"I go to church with Tyler."

"OK..."

The lawyer pulled a hand down the length of his face. "I'm afraid I can't represent you."

The fragile rapport she'd built with the man across the desk shattered at her feet. *He saw my hesitation, and he knows I'm lying.* Melanie used the tattered tissue in her hand to blot tiny beads of sweat from her forehead. "Why not?"

"I go to church with your husband. Taking your case under those circumstances could be construed as a conflict of interest. Beyond that, I make it a point, where I have a choice, not to take a case that puts a friend in the enemy camp."

"But I'm not looking to make Tyler the enemy." Melanie closed her eyes. *I don't think I can rake up the courage to do this again. Surely I can make him understand.* She met the lawyer's eyes. "I want us to remain friends."

"That's a noble sentiment, but I still can't help you." He raised his hand when she started to object. "Don't worry. I can direct you to someone who can." He stood up, came around the desk, and leaned against it. "May I ask you another question?"

Melanie couldn't meet his eyes for fear of what his next question would be. She stared at the hands folded in her lap and shrugged.

"Do you guys still love each other?"

"I think so, but—"

"Then take it from someone who sees way too much drama from people who've lost that. Swallow your pride and fight for what you have. Our society makes giving up easy. Sticking is hard, and it isn't popular. But even with the trouble piled on top of it, what you guys have can be salvaged if you both put some effort into it." He held out his hand and helped her to her feet. "Let me walk out with you. I'll have Stephanie give you a couple of cards for some colleagues of mine, but I've also got some terrific friends who are counselors. We'll get those cards for you as well."

He led her back down the hall and collected the business cards from his secretary. "Here you go. I'd trust any one of them to represent me."

She accepted the cards and turned to leave. The lawyer followed her to the door, stepping around her to open it for her.

"Good luck."

Melanie nodded and shuffled out the door, surprised when Mr. Lake followed her out and closed the door.

"Melanie."

She looked at him over her shoulder.

He paused while the only other person on the sidewalk veered around them and continued down the street. When he continued his voice was low. "I want you to understand that everything we talked about today is confidential, but if you're hiding what I think your hiding, you need to know that this can't end well—for any of you."

Melanie nodded.

"That said, I'm going to offer you one last piece of advice. Pray about your situation before you take this any further. In all my years of legal practice, I've yet to see a client whose situation couldn't be helped by developing a relationship with Christ. I don't have a card for Him, but that's OK, since you don't have to make an appointment to talk to Him. He's the wisest advocate I know."

~ * ~

Kate buzzed around her house, cleaning where no real mess existed, waiting for the cream cheese to get soft enough to mix. It was her turn to host Bible study, and she was excited to try the new recipe she'd found for salted caramel cheesecake. The gooey treat topped with a sticky caramel sauce, chocolate ganache, and a sprinkle of sea salt was going to be a challenge to make, but it was sure to top Karla's cherry-chocolate offering from last week. She smiled as she ran the duster across the mantle. The recipe hunt really had evolved into a competition, but it was all in good fun. The only casualty was their waistlines.

She moved into her office. Company wouldn't come this far, but the room might as well get a good dusting while she was in the mood. Kate stuck the duster in her back pocket and stooped to pick up the pictures of her two husbands. "Good morning, you two." Kate kissed a fingertip and touched it to Alan's lips. "The plans for the center are finally coming together, thanks to your foresight." She repeated the action with Chad's photo. "I still miss your face." Kate returned the pictures to her desk and ran the feathers over the cluttered wooden surface. Not a deep cleaning, but good enough for today.

Time passed quickly with the mixing, tasting, and baking. She slid the two completed cakes into the oven and set the timer. The phone rang as she turned to look for something else to do.

"Hello."

"Kate?"

Why, oh why did that baritone voice turn her knees to jelly? "Hi, Nicolas, what can I do for you?"

"I wanted you to know that I just got a packet of paperwork from your lawyer. I'm about to sign on the dotted line. Our partnership is about to be official."

"You did take the time to read them, right?"

Husky laughter filled her ears and sent goose bumps across the back of her neck and down her spine. The hand she waved in front of her face had nothing to do with the warmth of the kitchen. *That voice!* "Absolutely. Everything looks to be in order. Hang on, will you?"

Muffled scratching replaced the sound of his breathing for a few seconds, followed by the chime of an incoming text, then he was back. "Check your messages when I hang up. I sent you a picture of me signing my life away."

"Nobody twisted your arm."

"Learn to take a joke, *partner.* It's a done deal. Can we celebrate?"

The thought of some alone time with her new partner brought a quick smile to Kate's face. "What did you have in mind?"

"Dinner?"

"No can do. Bible study at my house in a couple of hours."

"Oh yeah, the Monday night hen party."

"I don't think your mother would appreciate her brain child being dubbed a 'hen party.'"

"She'll have to take that up with Dad. The weekly gathering was her idea, but he christened it. How about lunch tomorrow before we meet with the Realtor and the property owner."

"That, I can do. Can you call me in the morning, and we'll decide where and when."

"Will do. I'll let you get back to your preparations. Don't forget to look at the picture I sent you, and don't forget to save your lonely partner a piece of whatever you have in the oven."

"Salted Caramel cheesecake."

"You're killing me! If you see an ugly woman you don't recognize at the meeting tonight, it absolutely will *not* be me in drag."

Kate laughed. "Goofball. I'll talk to you tomorrow." She disconnected the call and opened her text messages. Her laughter filled the kitchen. It was a shot of Nicolas, in uniform, holding up the signature sheet, pointing to his name and grinning like a lunatic. She kissed the tip of a finger and pressed it to the screen. The realization of what she'd just done sent her looking for a chair.

"No, no, no! This isn't right. Just business, just business."

# CHAPTER TWELVE

Kate spent extra time on her hair, makeup, and clothing selections for her lunchtime meeting with Nicolas Tuesday morning. She wasn't trying to make herself more attractive. No, her goal was to appear *only* as the business partner she was determined to be. She scraped her blonde hair up into a ponytail and twisted it into a fashionable, but stern knot. She applied her makeup with a moderate hand, and she left her contacts out, opting for her glasses instead. Gray slacks, gray pumps, gray pinstriped blazer. Her hand hovered over a white blouse, but her sense of fashion rebelled at the last second. She selected a red-ribbed turtleneck instead.

Toilette complete, Kate surveyed the end product in the mirror. Her eyes closed on a groan of fashion pain as she slumped against the door frame. She looked like her grandmother! *Why am I doing this?* She wasn't worried about enticing Nicolas. It was her attraction to him that had her on edge and acting like a high school freshman.

His broad shoulders and ready smile did strange things to her insides, and that voice... In another time or place, she wouldn't be opposed to spending some social time with Nicolas Black, but her time for those things had passed. She refused to subject another man—and her own heart—to the consequences of a romantic involvement with the original unlucky in love, Kate Wheeler Archer. Add in Karla's not-so-gentle prodding and Nicolas's resistance to his mom, and the man might as well have a big *no trespassing* sign hanging from his neck. Kate rubbed temples that suddenly began to throb. She had to get a grip on this situation, or their partnership was going to be torture.

When the phone rang, she grabbed it like a lifeline, smiling when she saw Patrick's number on the screen.

"Hi, baby!"

"Hey, Mom, how's your day?"

"Better now." She glanced at the clock and frowned at the time. "Why aren't you in class?"

"I'm between actually. But I just got word that the professor for my last hour class is sick today. I wanted to see if I could take my best mom out to dinner this evening."

"Best mom?"

"Well, I can't say best girl anymore, not with a fiancée and a daughter. So I have a best girl, a best daughter, and a best Mom."

Kate laughed. "I see your dilemma. Your best mom would love to have dinner with her favorite son. I'm looking at some property today with my new partner—"

"Partner? Who...? When...?"

Kate grinned. "Nicolas Black. Yesterday."

"Detective Nicolas Black...from back in December?"

"That's the one."

"How?"

"Sweetheart, I thought you outgrew single word questions at the age of two."

"Very funny, Mom. How about some answers to those questions?"

"It all came together pretty quickly. I promise to tell you about it tonight. Can you pick me up at five?"

"Sounds like a plan," Patrick said

"Good. If it looks like the property thing is going to run later than that, I'll call you. If I'm not here when you get here, just come on in. Merlin misses you."

"OK, I've got to run to make class."

"I need to go, too. I'm having lunch with Nicolas."

"What? Lunch too? You're going on a date?"

"Later, son, later."

Kate disconnected the call. She removed her glasses and chewed on the earpiece while she stared down at the gray pumps on her feet. Was it a date? Could it be? And a better question—did she want it to be? She folded the glasses away. What would it hurt if it was? Something had shifted in her heart over the last couple few days, something that was eating away at her determination to avoid another relationship with a man, something that ached at the thought of spending the rest of her life alone. *But is Nicolas Black the answer?*

If she and Nicolas did manage to get together, Karla would never let them live it down, but in the grand scheme of things, the matchmaking didn't really enter into the calculations. *Kate minus two husbands is still an ugly equation.* Kate acknowledged the reality of that thought with a nod. "But maybe not as insurmountable as I've been trying to make it."

Mind made up, she pushed away from the wall and headed back to her bedroom, loosening her very proper hairdo as she walked. She'd need her contacts as well as her new, red pumps. Grandma would not be joining them for lunch today.

~ * ~

"Kate, I know we agreed on a strictly business relationship, but..." Nicolas rolled his eyes at his reflection in the mirror. *That's romantic! Idiot.* "Kate, I really feel like God is telling me to ask you out..." He cringed. Blaming his abrupt change of heart on God probably wasn't the best direction to take either.

"Are you tired, because you've been running through my mind all week." He grinned into the mirror. "That one's actually true, but I'm not twelve." *Not twelve...*

"What are you?" Nicolas laid aside the comb and studied his reflection. His dismal chuckle filled the bathroom. "I'm a forty-four-year-old man who hasn't asked a woman out in more than twenty years." *I don't even know how to start that sort of conversation.* "Maybe I'll just keep my mouth shut." Other than those two frantic days last December, they'd known each other for less than two weeks. Anything he told her about the way he was feeling would be inappropriate after such a short acquaintance, doubly so given their mutual—and adamant—agreement to avoid personal entanglements. But he couldn't ignore his heart and the soul-deep feeling that after twenty plus years of self-recrimination, God was nudging him down a new path, and it seemed that Kate was waiting at the end.

Nicolas turned his back to the mirror and leaned against the sink. *And there's more to it than my knee jerk hesitation.* Kate had been open and honest about the tragedy that had taken the life of her first husband. How would she feel if she knew that his past contained a similar experience, endured from the point of view of the perpetrator instead of the victim? He shook that thought aside. *I'm not going there. The two incidents don't have anything to do with each other.*

He finished in the bathroom and headed into the kitchen, where his freshly ironed shirt hung from the back of a chair.

The shirt was still warm when he slid it on. He looked up at the ceiling while his fingers worked the buttons. "OK, God, You've got my attention. I'd be a fool to ignore a woman like Kate Archer, and I'm not a fool. But I'm not Don Juan either. The best I can do is keep an open mind and watch for You to open a door for me." He considered his earlier thoughts. "If this is Your direction for Kate and me, help us move beyond the obstacles our past experiences have placed in our way."

Nicolas checked his appearance a final time, standing on one foot to buff a smudge from the top of his shoe against the back of his pant leg. Satisfied, he squared his jaw and grabbed his keys. If he were going to dive back into the dating pool, who better to swim with than a woman he'd already committed to spending some serious time with?

~ * ~

"My funniest traffic stop story?"

Kate nodded and pushed her salad aside. "I've heard every cop has one, and I want to hear yours."

"Hmm..." He tapped his fingers on the tabletop.

"Don't forget that most of my law enforcement career was spent in the military. Military cops and detectives don't make a lot of traffic stops."

"You're stalling. I know you can come up with something."

The smile he sent across the table flipped Kate's heart onto its side and sent heat rushing up her neck. She grabbed her glass of tea and took a deep drink while he thought about her request. She was grateful that the conversational ball was in his court, since her ability to speak had temporarily vanished.

Nicolas straightened in his chair. "OK, not really a traffic stop, and more scary than funny." He crossed his arms on the table and leaned forward. "One evening I'm coming home from dinner in the city, and I see flashers on the side of the road. I slow down, and once I get closer, I can see that the car has a flat tire. But beyond that, there's this shirtless guy pacing back and forth on the passenger side of the vehicle. It's getting dark and cold, so I stop to see if I can help. I'm out of my car, yelling at him, because traffic is zipping by so fast, and he can't hear me. He finally moves to where I can see him from the waist down. The guy is buck naked."

Kate covered her mouth with her hand. "On the side of the road?"

Nicolas nodded. "Yep, in all of his birthday-suit glory. So, he comes around the car and he's got his keys clutched in one hand and a nearly empty whiskey bottle in the other. He looks at me without a care in the world and tells me how glad he is that I stopped to help, because he can't get to his spare. He was trying to use the trunk key on the hood."

Kate snorted. "What did you do?"

"I was out of uniform and in my own car, but I hustled him into the back seat with a blanket. When I got him back to the station, his BAC was point-two-six."

"BAC?"

"Blood alcohol concentration," Nicolas explained.

"Oh, and that's a lot?"

Nicolas sat back and picked up his own drink. "DUI for Oklahoma is point-oh-eight. For his body weight...I'd say he'd consumed the whole bottle of liquor in just under an hour."

Kate shivered. "That's horrible."

"Told you. When I look back at the whole incident, I remember thinking God must have poked His finger through that guy's tire Himself. If that stooge had stayed on the road in that condition...it was just a matter of time before he killed himself or someone else."

She leaned across the table. "It's hard to get away from it, isn't it?"

"It?"

"That religious upbringing. Even when we aren't living where we should, it still has moments when it sneaks up on us."

Nicolas nodded. "That's a fact."

"And then when you are living where you should be, there are those confusing moments when you aren't sure how to get to where it seems God wants you to go." Kate paused as something flickered through his eyes. She studied his expression and saw her own uncertainty reflected there.

"Have you ever felt that way, Nicolas? Like God was

holding out the answer to your problems, and it seemed too good to be true, and you couldn't quite work up the courage to reach for it?"

His eyebrows arched and he leaned forward again, his eyes intent on her face. "A lot lately."

Kate's heart pounded at his answer. *Can it be that simple, Father? Ask and receive?*

"Kate—"

"Nicolas—"

Kate swallowed hard and motioned for him to continue. It was several seconds before he spoke again.

"I lied to you."

She tilted her head and waited for him to continue.

"When I said I wasn't interested in you on a personal level. That was a lie. I've been interested since December, but the circumstances then were...inappropriate. I've thought about you a lot, but I guess I'm more stubborn than I am honest. Mom's matchmaking made it imperative that I override my feelings and avoid you at all costs." He grinned at her. "Let that serve as a warning for the future." He stopped to take a deep drink.

Kate studied him from across the table, not sure if she was warmed or frightened by his words. *We have a future?* She would have sworn that she saw a nervous tremor in his hand when he lifted his glass. He returned the glass to the table, taking a few seconds to position it carefully in a ring of moisture. When he looked up, his eyes held a sadness that made her heart ache.

"I've never done anything illegal, but there are things in my past I'm not proud of. Things I may never be able to share with you." He shrugged. "Lots of reasons why I've never seriously pursued a woman...never thought that I deserved to. Even before last weekend, God was trying to show me that I was wrong. That He had better plans for me than I had for myself."

Kate's heart thudded behind her rib cage. The words came from her lips, whispered and unbidden. "'For I know the plans that I have for you...'"

"Yeah." Nicolas held his hand out across the table and waited until Kate slipped hers into it. "I'll understand if this changes things for you as far as our business relationship is concerned, but I'm hoping you'll think about it for a day or two before you make any decisions." He rubbed her fingers with his thumb. "You never know. I might grow on you."

Kate stared at their joined hands, speechless. Every brush of his thumb against her knuckles accelerated her pulse. *Are you granting me a third chance Father?*

"Kate?"

She pulled out of her thoughts and raised her gaze to meet his. "I won't ask you about the past if you won't try to rush the future. I'm feeling a little ambushed." He tried to pull away. "Not by you." She tightened her grip. "By God. When Alan died, I promised myself that I was done with men. Two loves, two funerals, two heartbreaks...that should be enough for any woman."

Kate tilted her head and studied the serious cop eyes across the table. She'd seen those eyes turn steely with determination. Today hope mingled with sadness in their blue depths. "I've felt the same things you have," she admitted, and smiled when relief washed across his face. "I've denied them for some of the same reasons. But I decided this morning that I needed to stop letting my past dictate my future." She held out her free hand

and waited until he took it, delighting in the unhampered jolt of attraction that zipped up her spine at the sight of their hands, joined on the table top.

"Can we make a new promise to each other?" He nodded and she continued. "We've got so much on our plates right now. You have a demanding career, I have a son getting married in a few months, and we have a business to launch. Can we just take things slowly and enjoy each other's company without worrying about the future or the past?"

"That's exactly what I want."

Kate's throat was parched. She slid her left hand free to reach for her glass, and her watch caught her eye. "We're late." She pulled her other hand free and jumped to her feet.

"What?"

She grabbed her blazer from the back of the chair. "We're late for our appointment at the old newspaper office."

Nicolas stood, more calmly than she, and tossed some bills on the table. "Calm down," he told her with a grin.

"But I don't want to lose this opportunity."

"We're not late."

"What? It's after three."

"Kate-time, remember. Mom told me to always give you half an hour. I told you three, but our meeting isn't until three-thirty." He stepped around to help her with her jacket.

She settled it on her shoulders, turned, and swatted at his arm. "That's so not fair."

"But it's effective." He leaned forward, hesitating for just a second before he brushed a light kiss across the wrinkles between her brows.

The touch of his lips on her skin sent a jolt of electricity rocketing across her nerve endings. She was still in a daze when he took her hand and led her out of the building.

"Let's go check this place out, partner."

# CHAPTER THIRTEEN

The well-dressed older man who greeted them was a vast improvement over the building owners Kate had encountered over the last few days. His professional manner and open approach to the business at hand gave her hope that the end of her search might be in sight.

She excused herself to explore the building on her own while Nicolas talked business and studied the list of pending repairs with the owner. She had every intention of being a part of that business, but she wanted a feel for the space before they made any decisions. She wanted some time to walk through the rooms alone to get a vision of what they could be, a chance to listen for God's plans above her own. The old place had a grip on her heart five minutes after she walked through the door.

The high ceilings, the spacious, well-lit rooms, the old fashioned latticed windows that faced the street and etched the floor of a sizable reception area with diamonds of sunlight captured her imagination. They spoke of a stability lacking in some of the newer structures she'd looked at.

Scaffolding lined the walls of the lower-level rooms to accommodate painting and repairs to the plaster moldings. Tarps protected the old wooden floors, real wood that creaked here and there as she continued her inspection. Kate paused in the middle of the larger of the downstairs rooms. She wasn't delusional—she understood that her plans might seem a bit grand for a small town in central Oklahoma. But Oklahoma had its share of military bases, and the surrounding states did as well. And the world? Well, the world was never going to be at peace. There would always be a need for good men to go fight over some godforsaken piece of dirt.

And as long as they fought, there would be families left behind. She intended to serve those families.

Her mind placed furniture around the room, nothing industrial or institutional, but items with deep cushions and soft colors designed to bring calm and comfort to the broken hearts she expected to walk through the door. She mentally partitioned off two substantial areas along the back wall, one to hold toys, a play area for toddlers, and the other to house a television and a couple of computers for adolescents. Nothing she'd seen so far spoke a single negative vibe to her heart.

Kate climbed the stairs, trailing her fingers along the wooden railing worn smooth by so many hands before hers. The five rooms on the upper level offered lower ceilings, multiple windows, and carpeted floors. They would make excellent offices. The building had more space than they would need in the beginning, but she didn't want to start with a facility that offered no room for the growth she planned. The growth she knew God intended.

Satisfied, she descended the stairs. Halfway down, the toe of her shoe hung on something and sent her stumbling for balance. She caught herself before she fell, saving her pride at the final second, but not without gaining Nicolas's attention. He hurried to her side, the building owner following closely, as she stooped down to examine the stairs.

"You OK?" Nicolas asked.

"Yes, just clumsy." She ignored the warmth his concern bred, felt along the risers, and found the culprit, a loose board, invisible from this side, but raised just enough on the opposite side to catch the toe of an unsuspecting traveler. Kate tapped it with a finger and looked up at the owner. "Might want to add this to your list."

"Yes, sorry. I should have warned you. The contractors have determined that the most cost-effective repair for the stairs is carpet. The wood can be replaced, but it will take considerable time and funds. When the bed and breakfast deal fell through, we put a hold on that and some of the other repairs, because we wanted to wait to see what a new buyer might want."

Kate nodded. "I'll need a copy of that list, if you don't mind." She looked at Nicolas. "What do you think?"

Nicolas surveyed the building. He put his hand on Kate's arm and applied a gentle pressure. "I think there's a lot that we could work with here." He faced the owner. "If you could fax our lawyer a list of completed repairs along with the list of pending ones, you can expect to receive a bid from us by the end of the week."

"I can do that," the owner replied. "But I was hoping we could come to some sort of agreement this afternoon. I have appointments to show it to two other perspective buyers tomorrow."

Kate opened her mouth to speak, closing it with a snap when the pressure on her arm grew firmer. Nicolas exchanged a few more words with the owner before he steered Kate out of the building. She fumed, doing her best to remain pleasant until they were out of ear shot of the owner.

She allowed him to pull her down the street to where he'd parked. *How dare he just take over. Oh, he's gonna get an ear full...* She stopped on the curb, halting him as well, and whirled to face him. "What was that?"

"What?"

"That...that show in there. That *you'll hear from us by the end of the week* nonsense. It's perfect. I love it." She turned in her tracks. "I want it, and I'm going back in there to tell him so."

Nicolas hooked her arm and swung her around, releasing her when she batted at his hands. "Hold up there, partner. How does this building at five thousand dollars below the advertised cost sound to you?"

Kate crossed her arms and frowned up at him. "I'm listening."

"You remember my contact that told us it was going back on the market?"

She nodded.

"I got a text message from him while you were upstairs." He pulled out his phone and brought up the screen. "He's connected to the construction company." Nicolas handed her the phone and continued while she scrolled through the message. "The bail-out of the previous buyer really hurt this guy. It's Garfield, Kate. Despite what he says, there aren't a lot of prospects for this type of property, and—"

Kate held up a hand to stop him and read the last of the message aloud. "If he doesn't have a buyer by Friday, he's willing to drop the price by five thousand dollars. Yes!" She shoved the phone back into his hands, pulled him down to her level, and kissed him square on the mouth. When she pulled away, the heat of embarrassment flooded her face. It dissipated when he grinned down at her.

"Sorry."

"I'm not."

She used a thumb to wipe a trace of her lipstick from the corner of his mouth. "There you go, good as new." She patted him on the cheek. He turned his face into her hand to place a quick kiss on her palm. The kiss she'd given him had been giddy impulse, more joy than heat. The touch of his lips against her open palm raised the hairs on her arms and rocked Kate to her toes. She whipped her hand behind her back and closed her fingers over the spot that still tingled.

He raised an eyebrow at her. "Not sorry for that either." He turned away, opened the passenger door of his car, and motioned Kate inside. "Now let's get you home. Your son is probably waiting, and I don't want him to think that he can't trust me with his mother."

~ * ~

Tyler took a deep breath. Pastor Gordon's car, which was sitting in the space closest to the side door of Valley View Church, mocked him. He loved the old pastor, enjoyed his style of ministry, but Tyler was a man and should have control of his household. Admitting that he didn't, seeking advice on his marriage, grated on every masculine nerve he possessed. He slammed out of the car. Might as well get it over with. *Maybe Brother Gordon will be too busy to talk to me right now.* The possibility almost restored his humor. *At least I can say I tried.*

He covered the distance on leaden feet. Between worry over Melanie and the stubborn case Nicolas and he continued to work, Tyler's reserves were depleted. If something positive didn't happen on one of those two fronts soon... He abandoned the thought when he reached for the door.

The hallway was dark except for the light shining from the open doorway of the pastor's office. Tyler approached, stopping to rap the wooden door frame with his knuckles.

The pastor looked up from a desktop littered with notes and books. His smile was welcoming, but his eyes glowed with mischief. The older man raised his hands into the air. "I'm innocent, Detective. Whatever they say I did, the devil made me do it."

Their laughter echoed through the deserted hallway. When it faded, it took a part of Tyler's tension with it. He stepped into the office and took the chair the pastor indicated with a nod. But words still failed him.

The pastor's jowly face wore a patient smile. He waited for Tyler to settle and motioned to the corner of the office, where a half-full coffee pot rested on the top of a dorm-sized refrigerator. "The coffee is fresh, but decaf. If you'd prefer, I've got water and a few sodas in the cold box. Feel free to help yourself."

Tyler shook his head. "I'm fine, thanks. I'm not interrupting anything, am I?" His tone was hopeful.

"Not at all. Just trying to arrange my thoughts for

Sunday's sermon." He stared down at the mess of papers on his desk. "Some of them come easier than others. This one can only benefit from a short break while we visit." Pastor Gordon leaned forward on crossed arms. "What brings you to my office?"

Tyler crossed his legs. The leather of his wide black utility belt and holster ground against the leather of the chair, filling the room with muted squeaks as he shifted uncomfortably under the pastor's stare.

The old pastor grinned at his obvious discomfort. He took his glasses off, fished a handkerchief from his pocket, and polished the lenses. "Tyler, how many times have you reassured someone that you aren't the enemy, that you're there to help them?"

He stilled in the seat. "Too many to count."

"Exactly. The clergy and the police both tend to get a bad rap. We're the bad guys pretending to be the good guys. People think they have to walk around on eggshells, always on their best behavior when we're around because all we really want is to catch someone in a wrong. Nothing could be further from the truth. So relax and talk to me. What's up?"

Tyler pulled in a deep breath and exhaled it slowly. "I need to talk to you about Melanie, my wife. She left me a few days ago. I guess...I mean...I need..." He swallowed hard. "Nicolas told me I should talk to you about it."

"Nicolas Black?"

Tyler nodded. "We're partners, but you probably knew that."

"That boy always did have a level head on his shoulders. It was wonderful to see him rededicate his life to the Lord last Sunday. But"—he sat up in his chair—"we aren't here to talk about Nicolas. Tell me what's happening between you and your wife."

"She moved out."

The pastor's eyes crinkled in a smile. "So you said, but that's the result of the problem, not the problem. You guys fighting?"

Tyler shrugged. "Not as much as you might think, given the circumstances. We've been married for almost twelve years, and she's just never understood that I need to be a guy."

Brother Gordon titled his head, clearly puzzled. "You need to be a guy in what way?"

Tyler pursed his lips and thought about his answer. "I'm a man. I work long hours at a challenging job. When I get home, I don't need to be greeted at the door with questions and demands on my time. I deserve a chance to unwind, but she wants to talk about my day. Well, she used to, anyway. I don't want to talk about my day. A lot of my day is spent dealing with ugly people doing ugly things. I don't want to share those things with Melanie. She's a lady. I don't want that ugliness brought into our home more than it has to be."

The older man unearthed a clean sheet of paper from the pile on his desk and made a quick note. "OK, what else?"

"She keeps trying to make me into something I'm not." Tyler sat up, warming to his subject. "I watched my dad slave his life away, never taking time for himself. I'm not my dad. When I'm not working, I keep the yard up, I keep up with home repairs, I make sure the bills are paid. When those things are done, I don't want to go for a walk by the lake, play a game of cards, or go visit the family. I certainly don't want to traipse all over the world and back looking at mountains and oceans I can see just fine on the TV."

"Does Melanie enjoy those things?"

"Yes, and I respect that. I try not to get in her way. I wish she'd return the favor."

The old pastor studied him in silence for a few seconds. "So you want someone to come home to, someone to cook you a nice meal, someone to be...intimate...with on occasion. And the rest of the time?"

"The rest of the time is mine."

"Don't you think that's a little selfish?""I'll give you selfish, but you only get one life, and I want to live it the way I want to live it. Like I said, I don't get in her way. I can't understand what more she wants from me."

"Maybe she wants a friend. Maybe she wants some companionship and conversation."

Tyler raised his hands in a helpless gesture. "I'm home every night watching TV with her."

"Tyler, I think you're smarter than that. Sitting in the same room together isn't companionship, and it certainly isn't a marriage. How about communication, how about building some memories?" He studied Tyler from across the desk. "You guys don't have kids, do you?"

Tyler shook his head. "We tried. Wasted a lot of time and money going to doctors, trying fertility drugs. Having sex on a schedule." He ducked his head in embarrassment. "Nothing worked. The doctors all said the same thing. We're both healthy, and there's no clinical reason we couldn't have kids. It just never happened. We finally gave up." He raised his head and looked Pastor Gordon in the eye. "Not having kids isn't part of our problem, but I have wondered if things would have been different with a kid or two to focus on." He shrugged. "We're both on the downhill side of thirty, so it's a moot point now."

The pastor nodded as if conceding the point. "Let me ask you a question, Tyler. One of these days, you're going to retire from your demanding job. What happens then? When it's just you and her twenty-four seven? What happens to the gulf you spent years building between you and your wife? Will you spend your retirement years trying to bridge it?" He shook his head in answer to his own question. "If it's not already too late, it certainly will be by then.

"I don't want you to think I'm taking sides, but I can tell you that my wife would have handed me my ears on a platter by now if I were in your place."

Tyler stared at his pastor. *I knew this was a waste of time. He's taking Melanie's side just like I figured.* He added the pastor's name to the growing list of people who just didn't get it.

"I'd love to talk with Melanie and hear her side of all of this. Do you think she'd be open to that?"

The question pulled Tyler out of his pity party. His response was a mumbled. "I can ask."

"I wish you would." He leaned forward again. "I can tell by the expression on your face that you're disappointed with what I had to say." He paused and rested his hand on the open Bible on his desk. "This is a great how to book on the art of love and marriage. I could quote you scripture all day, but some things are better studied out for yourself. If you'd like, I can work up some reading for you. Can you stop back by tomorrow?"

Tyler nodded.

"In the meantime will you let me pray with you?"

"I think that's a good idea."

The pastor nodded and closed his eyes. "Father, thank You for Tyler and the work that he does. Lord, look into his heart right now. He's Your child, and he's hurt and confused, but You have the answer for all of that. Marriage is the most difficult and the most gratifying relationship two people will ever enter into. It is sacred and ordained by You. Open Tyler's heart to Your voice and direction. Help Melanie hear Your voice as well. Guide them both in Your path. We ask these things in Your name."

Tyler lifted his head and found himself eye-to-eye with the old pastor's stern stare.

"You haven't been saved very long, son. Sometimes we get our signals crossed, and we think salvation will cure our ills and make our lives perfect. We'll never be perfect this side of heaven, and some of those ills take a lot of work, even after we're saved. Talk to your wife, see if she's willing to sit down with me. In the interim, I want you to give some serious thought to being less of a *guy* and more of a husband."

# CHAPTER FOURTEEN

Kate's hand rested on the gearshift under Nicolas's as he took the final corner to her house. He upshifted the gears, and Kate felt the power of the engine radiate up her arm. Her giggle accented the air above the growl of the powerful motor and made them both laugh harder. *High-schoolish?* Kate pushed the thought away. What if it was? Hadn't she decided...hadn't they both decided to see where their business and personal relationship would take them? Shouldn't that exploration be fun?

His red Camaro gathered a bit of speed, and he shifted two more times before roaring to a stop in front of her house. They both surged against the seat belts when he applied the brakes. Her hand, warm beneath his, grew cold when Nicolas reached to turn off the engine. He positioned the gear shift a final time and turned to face her. "I can't believe you never drove a stick shift."

"I can't believe no one ever offered to let me try." She raised her brows at him. "You are offering, right?"

His answer was interrupted by the roar of the dual exhaust of the blue Chevy four-by-four approaching from the opposite corner. The truck turned into the drive and nosed up to the back bumper of her car. Kate climbed out and met her son on the curb beside the Camaro.

Patrick gave her a quick squeeze and bussed her cheek with his lips before stepping away to walk around the shiny sports car. He whistled as he completed his inspection. "That is a mag set of wheels! 350?"

"396."

Patrick took a step back, both hands on his hips, eyebrows lowered in concentration. "1970, right?"

Nicolas stiffened at Kate's side. She frowned as he stared at Patrick in a lengthy silence. Kate touched his arm. "Nicolas?"

Nicolas actually shook under her hand. He blinked. "What?"

"Are you OK? You're white as a sheet."

He blinked and took a couple of deep breaths. When he faced Patrick again, he'd regained most of his color.

"I'm sorry, what did you say?"

"I asked if it was a 1970," Patrick repeated

"Close," Nicolas said. "She's one of the last to roll off the line for 1972."

"Sweet. Can I touch it?"

Nicolas turned the keys over in his hands. When he answered Patrick, his tone was pleasant enough, but the smile on his face failed to reach his eyes. "Your mom wants to drive it." He held out his hand. "I don't know if you remember me. Nicolas Black."

Patrick grasped the proffered hand. "I'm not likely to forget anything or anyone involved in Bobbie's kidnapping. Thanks again, Detective, for what you did for my family."

"Just glad we got a happy ending."

That long weekend in December was still a painful

subject for everyone involved. It didn't surprise Kate when Patrick turned back to the car and abruptly changed the subject.

"So, tell me about this beauty. Where on earth did you find her?"

"Dad and I bought her at an auction when I was fifteen. We spent a couple of years restoring it. Then I drove it for a year. It spent the majority of the next twenty years in the garage of my grandmother's house, under a tarp."

Patrick frowned. "Storage, why? Oh"—he snapped his fingers—"while you were in the Air Force. Gotcha. I wouldn't want to drag it around from pillar to post, either. Too much opportunity to damage it." He reached out a hand and stroked the fender. "You guys did an amazing restoration job. She certainly hides her age well."

"Don't be fooled by what you see now," Nicolas told him. "In the last three or four months she's gotten new tires, and a complete tune up—"

"Rotor bug, plugs, new oil and filters, belts, and distributer cap," Patrick interrupted.

"All of that plus a rebuilt carburetor. Not to mention what I had to do to bring the leather interior and the paint job back into shape."

Kate took a few steps away to lean on Patrick's truck while the guys talked. She crossed her arms, tapping the fingers of one hand on the opposite elbow. Patrick was a car guy, and he didn't get a lot of opportunities to indulge that passion. There was an excitement in her son's eyes she hadn't seen in a while. Put there by the car speak of a fellow gear head. She turned back to the men when Patrick sighed.

"This is my dream car. I just bought a house, I'm working on finishing school, and I'm getting married in a few months, but someday...someday I want one of these...and a son to crank the wrenches with."

Nicolas nodded. "She's my baby. I've still got some work to do. She's got a little miss in the engine."

"Can I listen?"

"Sure." Nicolas scooted behind the wheel, and the car roared to life. He climbed back out and released the hood latch. "Can you hear it?"

Patrick stood statue still, his head cocked in concentration. He finally nodded and motioned with his hand. Nicolas reached through his open window and killed the engine. "It's faint, but it's there. Sounds like a flat lifter."

All Kate heard was the uninterrupted rumble of a powerful engine.

"That's what I think, too." Nicolas agreed. "Too much storage time with unequal pressure on the springs. I just need to find the time to tear into her and get a good look-see."

Patrick grinned at the older man. "I wouldn't mind getting my hands dirty when the time comes."

"I'll call you."

Kate shook her head when her son's face lit up like a toddler's on Christmas morning.

"Seriously?"

"Seriously," Nicolas said. "An extra pair of hands is always a good thing."

Kate's stomach rumbled, and she crossed the yard back to the men. "OK, guys. Play time is over. I'm cold, I'm hungry, and I'm feeling neglected."

Patrick looked at Nicolas and grinned. "Mom

doesn't get cars. She can discuss the rules of any ball sport on the planet, but anything mechanical slides right over her blonde head."

"Thanks for the heads up. It's a major character flaw, but I'll do my best to overlook it."

Kate narrowed her eyes at the two men. Patrick was in full pick-on-Mom-mode, and whatever had leached the color from Nicolas's face a few minutes ago seemed to be forgotten beneath the male banter. *Maybe it was just my imagination.* She frowned at both of them. "I'm standing right here."

"Sorry." Nicolas took Kate's hand and gave it a light squeeze. "I've got a feeling we'll be in the mood for a celebration come Friday. Will you go to dinner with me?"

She returned the pressure. "I'd like that."

"Great, see you then." He turned back to Patrick. "Good to see you again. I'll let you know when my schedule opens up for that overhaul party." Nicolas climbed back behind the wheel of the Camaro, turned the key, and pulled the door closed.

Kate and Patrick stood at the curb, waiting for him to pull away. She frowned as Nicolas hesitated. He shook his head, and his lips moved in a silent mutter. *What is he doing?* She jumped back a bit when the door flew open.

Nicolas scrambled out of the car, and sent an apologetic look Patrick's way. With a muffled "Sorry," he pulled Kate into his arms and claimed her lips in a brief, goodbye kiss. He took a step back, rubbed her arms through the sleeves of her jacket, and smiled down into her upturned face. "Turnabout's, fair play. I'll call you tomorrow."

Kate looked into his eyes, stunned and a little gratified at the unexpected heat she saw simmering there. Unable to force words past the pulse beating wildly in her constricted throat, she nodded, lifting her hand for a small wave as the car pulled from the curb. She looked up when she felt Patrick's eyes on her.

Her son took a step away, crossed his arms, and studied her much the same way he'd studied the Camaro a few minutes earlier. "Business partners?"

Kate struggled to pull her scattered thoughts back to the here and now. "Yes...with a recently added contingency clause for more...personal possibilities." She lowered her eyes, brought her hands together at her waist, and picked at a rough cuticle. *How could I have failed to take Patrick's feelings into consideration?* The only father he'd ever known had barely been gone a year. *Time for some damage control.*

"Patrick, I know how much you loved Alan. You two had a very special relationship. I loved him too, more than I have words to express, but...I...I mean..." She looked up, unable to decipher her son's expression. "I was done. I told God I was done, but there's a part of my heart that's so stinking lonely. I don't know that Nicolas can fill that spot, but...I won't know if I don't give him a chance. I hope you aren't angry with me. I—"

"Angry?"

She recognized the confusion in his single word. "Well, OK. Maybe not angry...but disappointed. I know Alan hasn't been gone very long, and I don't want you to think that I'd..." She searched for a word. "Dishonor his memory by getting involved with someone else so soon." Kate chanced a glance at Patrick, hesitating at his puzzled expression.

"Have you lost your mind?"

"You are angry." Kate sighed and looked away. This whole speech wasn't going well, and she didn't know how to fix it.

"Maybe, but not for the reason's you might think. I only have three words for you and your contingency clause with Detective Black."

Kate met his eyes.

"It's. About. Time."

"What?"

"It's about time. Sheesh, Mom, I'm not a five-year-old. I'm getting ready to have a family of my own. I know how lonely you've been. I never expected you to spend the rest of your life in mourning. I've been praying for God to send someone new into your life. So...I'm not bothered by the possibility of you having a relationship with Nicolas Black, but I am a little upset that you would think I'd be that selfish."

Kate studied the man she'd raised. She could still see the little boy in his face despite his disclaimers. "Can we start this conversation all over again?"

"I'm game."

She nodded, clasped her hands behind her back, and locked eyes with her son. "I think I'm going to go on a few dates with Nicolas Black."

"Works for me. In fact, it could work for me quite well."

Kate raised her brows.

Patrick grinned. "Well, if your relationship should develop into something...permanent, can I assume that a baby brother or sister is not part of the equation?"

"Heaven forbid!"

"Didn't think so. So I could legally be considered Nicolas's son—and heir." Patrick turned his gaze down the road. "I could end up with the sweetest ride in Garfield."

~ * ~

Nicolas smelled the smoke even before the nightmare unfolded behind his closed eyelids. A groan filled the room as colors and shadows coalesced into images he longed to forget. Even in sleep he felt confusion when the familiar shifted and morphed into something new.

The haze in his subconscious cleared, and instead of the destruction wrought by a suicide bomber, his Camaro waited in a shaft of light swirling with fog. The hood stood open and a man in a tattered set of camouflaged BDUs leaned over the engine. The face of the specter remained shrouded, but Nicolas knew who it was just the same.

"What are you...?"

The uniform-clad figure held up a hand to cut him off. "Shh..." He leaned a little further into the motor compartment.

Nicolas became aware of the sound of a running motor.

"Ah...there it is. Hand me those pliers and bring that jar over here."

The haze receded a bit more, revealing a metal table holding a jumble of tools both mechanical and—were those surgical instruments? An empty Mason jar sat in the bottom right corner. Nicolas obeyed, even as his mind struggled to make sense out of the request. He placed the pliers in the outstretched hand, then stared. The hand was sheathed in a blue glove and covered in... He swallowed hard, please let that be grease.

"I need that jar, Lieutenant!"

Nicolas took a step closer and held out the jar.

"This was caught in the carburetor. It'll stop a car's heartbeat just like it'll stop a human's." A spent M16 slug clattered into the jar. "But, I don't have to tell you that, do I?"

The light intensified and became the bright overhead light of a surgical suite, casting everything in harsh angles and bright colors. The figure under the hood began to straighten. The voice had already identified him as C.W., but the hair color was wrong, the way he stood...

"No, you know all about stopping a heartbeat, don't you, pal?"

The shadowy figure stepped into a shaft of light, hands on his hips, brows lowered over blue eyes. Nicolas fell back with a gasp. "What...?"

The body, the posture, the voice belonged to C.W, but the face belonged to Kate's son, Patrick.

Nicolas jerked out of the dream, bedclothes damp and tangled, breath clogged in his lungs, the details of the dream still sharp around the edges. He shook his head. This wasn't right. Even in his worst nightmare C.W. never blamed him for what happened. Nicolas had loaded and carried that guilt all on his own.

He tossed the covers aside, grabbed the Bible from the nightstand with hands that shook, and headed to the kitchen for something cold to drink.

He had enough military experience to recognize an attack when he encountered one. He'd made up his mind to explore the path God seemed to be directing him down. Satan wasn't happy about that decision and wouldn't give up without a fight. Nicolas might not be able to stop the dreams, but he knew how to fight the devil.

He sat at the kitchen table, popped the top on his soda, and bowed his head, praying out loud so the devil would be sure to hear him. "Father, you delivered me from the guilt of the past. Please give me the strength I need to accept that." Nicolas opened his Bible to Psalms. A few chapters would calm him and allow him to get back to sleep. His breathing evened out as he read. The muscles between his shoulders loosened. His hands ceased to tremble. Thirty minutes later, the only thing that remained of the dream was one nagging question. Why had his dead buddy been wearing Patrick's face?

# CHAPTER FIFTEEN

Tyler slid through the door of the bakery at five minutes before one on Friday afternoon. The shop was deserted. With closing time so near, Staci would be long gone, and maybe he could convince Melanie to talk to him for a few minutes. If nothing else, he could use that threatening note as a reason to invade her space. He shook his head. *That feels like an excuse and we've had enough of those.*

In answer to the bell that announced his presence he got a muffled "I'll be right with you," from somewhere in the back of the building. He turned the sign to closed and leaned against the door. This whole thing had gone on long enough. He still had no intention of begging his wife to come home, where, they both knew, she belonged, but maybe Brother Gordon had a point. Maybe they could benefit from some counseling. They certainly hadn't been able to solve their problems on their own. If Melanie could be less demanding, he could work on being less selfish. But nothing could be fixed if they didn't have a conversation. *And boy, does that sound like her line instead of mine.*

"What are you doing here?"

Melanie's abrupt question jerked him out of his introspection. Tyler straightened and drank in the sight of his wife. Smudges of colored frosting decorated her white apron, competing with the patch of flour dusted across one cheek. Her red hair, always neatly bundled into a curly ponytail when she worked, was disheveled after a long day in and out of the hot kitchen. Small damp tendrils curled around her face. Her hands, nails suitably short and unpolished, were delicate but deceptively strong. Right now those hands rested at her waist, fingers tapping impatiently. A wave of loneliness washed over him. *What can I say to make her listen? I love you. I miss you. I'm sorry.* "How do you do it?"

She tilted her head in question.

"You're beautiful. After a day spent in a hot kitchen, you're still so beautiful."

Melanie bit her lip and looked down at the floor. "Tyler, why are you here?"

"Can we sit down? I know I've never been much on conversation, but we need to talk. I thought, once you closed for the day, that this would be a good place."

Melanie shrugged, stepped to a table, and pulled out one of the old-fashioned chairs. She kept her gaze averted and her thoughts to herself. A few seconds of silence passed. She hadn't encouraged him, but she hadn't tossed him out. He decided he'd take that as a good sign.

"We've really messed things up, haven't we?"

That earned him a quick glance before she went back to staring at the table.

"Mel, look at me."

She lifted a shoulder and shook her head.

Tyler bit the inside of his lip. "You know, we've been together for almost twelve years. You don't have to look at me or even speak to me to get your point across. I can almost read your mind. You'll sit here and listen to what I have to say. It won't be too hard since, you've heard it all before, and you're thinking that allowing me to have my say is probably the fastest way to get rid of me. You'll nod and make a few noncommittal noises, and then I'll leave and you can go about your business."

He braced his arms on the table and leaned forward. "I can also read your body language. I know that when you won't look at me, it's because you're afraid you'll cry. And you only cry when your heart is involved. And the only reason your heart would be involved is if you still love me as much as I love you."

A tear splashed on her fisted hands. If he hadn't been so desperate to get her to listen, he would have smiled at the physical confirmation of his words. He reached across the table to Melanie's hands, which were squeezed together in a tense ball, and pried them apart. His thumb stroked her knuckles, trying to release some of the tension. "Am I right, Mel? Do you still love me?" Melanie pulled her hand back, shoved the damp hair off of her forehead, and finally met his eyes.

"What difference does it make if the answer is yes? I didn't leave you because I didn't love you. I left because I was tired of living on my own. Tired of building memories with everyone except..." Her voice broke, but she swallowed back the emotion. "Except the person I most wanted to build them with. Tired of unfulfilled expectations, tired of being last on your list of things to do, tired of carrying on conversations with myself in the bathroom mirror." A tear escaped from the corner of her eye to trace a line through the flour on her cheek. "Just...tired."

"Conversations with yourself?"

Melanie's chuckle carried no humor. "Rehearsing all the pithy remarks I wish I could have said...would have said if you'd listened." She pushed away from the table and crossed her arms. "Tyler, you're a great guy, you've been a wonderful provider, but you're as thick-headed as a loaf of sourdough bread. I never wanted your money." She indicated the shop with a wave of her hand. "I know how to provide for myself. All I ever wanted was your time and attention, the feeling that you needed me in your life as much as I needed you in mine. I wanted to know I mattered. I wanted a friend."

Tyler cringed when his wife repeated some of Pastor Gordon's words. *Can you be lovers without being friends?* A glance at the tears on Melanie's face answered with a resounding yes.

"You know all those expensive vacations you paid for?"

Tyler nodded, at a loss for words.

"I'd trade them all for a weekend at the lake without our phones, computers, and TV. Just a weekend every so often with nothing to interrupt us. Just you and me with nothing to do except sit on the porch with hot coffee, a brilliant sunrise, and birds singing in the trees."

She held out her hands in surrender. "You've gotten everything you wanted out of our marriage. Someone to cook and clean, someone to look pretty on your arm on the rare occasion we go out together. You said you could read me...well let me return the favor."

She tilted her head and studied him for a few seconds. "You're convinced that everything is as good as it needs to be and why am I complaining? Yes, we don't have the relationship I always wanted, but it's good enough."

Tyler closed his eyes when she paused to take in a ragged breath. Her softly delivered words hit him with a force only found in the truth. *I guess all that rehearsing in the mirror finally paid off.* His wife wasn't pulling any punches this time.

"You won't even have a decent argument with me. You just hide your head in the sand of your good-enough world and figure I'll get over it and life will get back to normal."

He opened his eyes, ashamed at just how true her words were.

"Well, I have a news flash for you. I don't want normal, I don't want good enough...not when we had the potential to be great." She lowered her eyes and shook her head, her voice hoarse with suppressed tears. "You aren't willing to work for great...and I can't live with the emptiness of *good enough* any longer."

Tyler heard, for the first time, the despair in her voice. He wanted to reach out to her, wanted to shush her before she had the chance to make their separation permanent.

Her breath shuddered when she continued. "I think it's time to admit that we got it wrong and—"

"I think we should to go to counseling."

"What?"

Tyler took a deep breath. "I'd like to see if someone can help us work through some of this. In fact, I've already started."

Melanie leaned forward, her face a mask of confusion. "You've been to see a counselor?"

"Sort of. I had a long talk with my pastor."

Melanie threw up her hands. "That's perfect. I'm

sure he took your side in this whole thing. I've told you before. I'm not interested in your newest fad."

Tyler inhaled a deep breath and exhaled a silent prayer. *Father, show me how to reach her.* "I know you don't have a lot of reason to believe me, but my conversion to Christianity is not a fad. Christ changed my heart, and now I'm willing to let him change my life. Brother Gordon has fifty years of marriage behind him. And he didn't take my side." Embarrassment heated his face. "In fact, he raked me over the coals pretty good."

She stared at him with narrowed eyes. "Really?"

"Really." Tyler looked at his feet, still trying to figure out a way to take the sting out of the old pastor's remarks. "He told me I had a lot to learn about being a husband...a Christian husband. About loving my wife as much as I love myself. About sacrificing and setting priorities. About being less of a man and more of a couple." His shoulders lifted in a shrug. "A lot of what he said sounded like what you've been saying for a long time. I guess I just needed to hear it from someone else." He looked up in time to see her mouth drop open. "Maybe it's a guy thing."

Melanie rose and took a few steps away from the table. When she faced him again, her smile was sad, her attempt at humor flat. "And even on your best day, you're still just a guy."

"He said he'd be happy to talk with you, if you're willing." Tyler scooted away from the table, crossed the room, and took her hands in his, desperate to make her understand. "Please be willing. Give us...give me...a chance to prove to you that I can change. It's not going to happen overnight. I can't promise you that I won't mess up and make you sad again, but I can promise that I'll keep trying till I get it right."

Melanie lowered her head to his chest. "I'm still not coming home."

He wrapped her in his arms and held on for dear life. "I'm not asking you to, not yet. We both have things to sort through. But can we give this a try? Will you go talk to my pastor?"

She stepped back, pushed him to arm's length, and rested her hand briefly on his cheek before turning away. She crossed to the counter, pulled a napkin from the dispenser, and held it toward him. "Write the number down for me. I'll think about it."

Tyler bent over the counter and scratched out Brother Gordon's office number. He handed the napkin back to Melanie, their hands brushing as she took it. The simple touch renewed the deep longing in his heart to hold her.

Melanie must have read his intent, because she took a few steps away.

*God, please don't let us be too late.*

"You need to leave." Her breath shuddered when she inhaled. "I still have a lot of work to do before I can go home."

Tyler nodded and turned for the door. With his hand on the knob, he looked back and felt a bit of the last week's tension evaporate. Hope had replaced the despair in his wife's eyes.

~ * ~

Kate walked next to Nicolas and shook her hands at her side, trying to relieve the tremors in her fingers. "I'm so nervous I won't be able to hold the pen."

Nicolas pulled her to a stop beside him on the sidewalk in front of what would be, in a matter of minutes, their building. "Second thoughts?"

"Of course not. I know this is where God has been leading me for a long time. It's just..." She paused and looked into her partner's face. His expression was rock-steady. "How can you be so calm at a time like this? We're about to sign paperwork that will change the direction of our lives and, hopefully, thousands of others. Is it just another day in the life of Nicolas Black?"

Nicolas laughed. "Hardly 'just another day.' If it makes you feel better, I'm nervous on the inside, I'm just better trained at hiding it." He slipped his arm around her shoulders and pulled her into a one-armed embrace. "Relax, Kate, enjoy the moment. You've worked hard for it. Me? I'm the newcomer." He released her and took a step back. "Thanks."

"For...?"

"For being willing to share your dream with me." Nicolas broke their eye contact, but not before Kate got a look at the sadness that suddenly clouded the blue depths. "It means more than you know."

Kate took a deep breath of the early spring air, remembering what he'd said about things he might not ever be able to share. *Father, I might not ever know what caused the pain in his eyes, but I'm asking You to heal his heart.* She bumped him hip-to-hip. "Enough. No more sad thoughts or nerves. Let's get this done. Then I'm in the mood for something spicy. I want Mexican for dinner. Chips, cheese, guacamole...the whole shebang!" She smiled when the sadness lifted from his expression.

"I knew you were my kind of woman. Add in some

hot and spicy salsa and—" His cell phone rang, interrupting his dream meal. "Sorry." He took a few steps away, pulled the phone from its belt clip, and swiped open the connection. "Black."

Kate watched his expression change from good-natured-guy to no-nonsense-cop.

"Really? Where?" He nodded then looked at his watch. "OK, keep him on ice for a few minutes. I can be there in an hour or so. Don't start the party without me." Nicolas replaced the phone and looked at Kate. "You remember what I said about my unpredictable schedule?"

She nodded.

"I'm afraid we're going to have to cancel our dinner plans. That was Tyler. The cops in the next county picked up a person of interest in a drug investigation we've been conducting. The drug dogs went crazy when they sniffed out the trunk of the car, then the idiot pulled a knife on the cops."

"Oh no..."

Nicolas waved a hand though the air. "All in a day's work. They took him down with barely a struggle. But, this might be the break in the case we've been looking for. They just delivered him to the station, and he's cooling his heels in a cage until we can interrogate him. I need to be there."

"Of course. Rain check?"

"You bet."

"Then let's get this done so you can get back to your real job. Our celebration can wait until tomorrow. Saturday is a better date night anyway."

Nicolas returned his arm to her shoulders and squeezed. "Thanks for being a good sport."

"All part of dating a cop." Kate allowed him to steer her toward the door while her thoughts ran rampant. *I'm dating again.* She glanced at Nicolas from the corner of her eye. *I'm dating a cop with secrets he can't share, the son of a friend. Someone who thinks facing down an armed bad guy is just a normal part of his day.* The thought that something could happen to a third man she been foolish enough to fall for set her teeth on edge. Her heart lifted a silent prayer. *God, I hope You know what You're doing.*

~ * ~

Nicolas reached for the door to the interrogation room. He looked over his shoulder at Tyler with a grin. "Let's put this guy away."

A scarred wooden table dominated the room. Their suspect sat on the other side, kicked back in his chair, eyes locked on the ceiling, ankles crossed, hands pounding out a beat to some music only he could hear. He finished with a flourish and rocked forward.

"'Bout time you got your bacon butts in here."

Nicolas took a chair and waited for Tyler to do the same. He placed a recorder on the table and switched it on. "Detectives Black and Mason in interview with Lonnie Watts. Mr. Watts, could you please verify, for the record, that you have been read your rights and that you understand them?"

Lonnie waved at the small machine. "Yeah, yeah. I understand my rights. Ask your questions. I've got more important things to do than hang at the hog farm all day."

Nicolas turned to meet Tyler's eyes. He saw his own thoughts mirrored there. Bacon, hog, pig. This could be the person responsible for the note in Tyler's car.

"Interesting choice of words, Lonnie. How about we start with something simple? Can you tell us where you were last Saturday night after...?" Nicolas looked to Tyler.

"Ten-thirty," Tyler provided.

Lonnie smiled, condescension etched in every line of his face. "Snug as a bug in my woman's arms. She'll be happy to verify that for you."

Nicolas nodded. "I'm sure she will." He leaned back and crossed his arms. "Tell us what you know about the abandoned mobile home in lot fifteen of the trailer park out on highway nine."

The punk shrugged. "Never had the pleasure."

"That's a lie." Tyler leaned forward. "Look, Lonnie, the drug dogs went berserk over something in your car. The same car we've seen parked next to the trailer in lot fifteen more than once lately. The lab in the next county is taking it apart as we speak. Be straight with us, and we'll be sure to tell the DA what a nice cooperative crook you are."

Lonnie's insolent grin broadened. "You think I'm a crook?" He laid a hand on his chest. "Me?"

"We think you're a drug dealer," Nicolas answered.

The lowlife across the table shook his head and crossed his arms nonchalantly. "What you think and what you can prove are two different things. Tear the car apart if that makes you and the dogs happy. You'll notice by the dealer tag that I've only had it for a couple of weeks. I can't vouch for who owned it before me or what they did. But I can tell you this about sniffin' around." He leaned forward, the smile gone from his face, his breath heavy with stale cigarette smoke. "Sometimes when you put your noses into places you shouldn't, bad things can happen."

Nicolas braved the odorous fog of the prisoner's breath and leaned in. "Threats, Lonnie?"

"Oh no, sir, Detective, sir. Threatening an officer of the law is illegal. I'm just makin' an observation." He leaned back in the chair. "I think we're done 'til my lawyer gets here."

# CHAPTER SIXTEEN

*Dress nicely.*

Kate smiled at the memory of Nicolas's two-word answer when she'd asked him where they were going tonight. He thought he was being cute, but this was a game she knew how to play. Even with that thought in her mind, she still tried on—and discarded—five outfits. She finally settled on a plain black dress with a flattering hi-lo hem line that skimmed the tops of her knees in the front, but dipped to brush her ankles in the back. The black heels would add a nice bit of height. The sequined scarf looped loosely around her neck matched the amethyst hoops in her ears and added the perfect amount of sparkle to her outfit.

Her hands shook as she fastened the earrings. She was as nervous as a sixteen-year-old preparing for her first date with the high school quarterback. Kate forced a couple of calming breaths and stepped into the bathroom to check out the final effect of earrings, sequins, and her upswept hair under the harsher bathroom lights. *Not too shabby for a used up forty-something.* Her mind flashed back to the heat in Nicolas's eyes right before he pulled from the curb a few days ago. *Maybe not as used up as I wanted to believe.*

Kate bit her lip and then frowned at herself when the nervous habit smeared her lipstick. She backtracked to the vanity, applied a fresh coat of lip color, and dropped the tube into her tiny black handbag. She gave her image a sassy smile. *Gonna get smeared anyway. I'm expecting a healthy good night kiss.* Kate closed her eyes. They'd already shared two quick kisses, and although those had been really nice, she'd decided those quick pecks didn't count in the grand scheme of kissing. But tonight...

How would his lips feel against hers? Would he linger, soft and tender over her mouth, or would their first real kiss be hot and demanding, the product of two adults too long alone?

The thought of kissing Nicolas flushed Kate with heat, and the hoard of butterflies she'd just netted escaped to churn up her stomach once again. "Stop it! You asked Nicolas to take this slowly, and here you are tied up in knots at the thought of kissing the man. Go out, have a nice time, and let the goodbyes at the end of the evening take care of themselves." She nodded at her own good advice.

Merlin, her early warning system for visitors, jumped from his cushion in the corner and made a beeline to the front door.

Kate glanced at the clock on the nightstand just as it ticked over to six-thirty. Nicolas had teased her so unmercifully over the last few days about her penchant for tardiness. She'd been torn when he said he'd pick her up at six-thirty. Did he really mean six-thirty, or was he messing with her head, and he meant seven? She'd determined to be ready at six-thirty even if it killed her, and by some cosmic fluke she was.

Merlin's barking mingled with the sound of the doorbell and drew Kate down the hall. When she reached the door she pointed at the floor. "Sit." The pup's hindquarters hit the tile obediently. She reached for the door, and Merlin scrambled back to his feet. Kate drew her hand back and frowned at the dog. "Merlin. Sit. Stay." Merlin plopped down a second time, but his legs quivered with the effort to be still. Kate grinned. How could she scold him when her insides were doing the same anxious dance?

She pulled the door open. "Sorry Nicolas, I..." Her voice trailed off when she realized it wasn't Nicolas on her porch. "Melanie."

Melanie's shoulders slumped, and a small sigh escaped her pursed lips. "I was going to ask if you were busy..." She waved at the dress. "You don't even have to answer. I should have called." She turned to go, but she twisted around before she reached the top step of the porch. "Would you call me tomorrow? I really need to talk to someone."

Kate took a step out, grabbed Melanie by the shoulders, spun her around, and gave her a gentle shove through the front door. "Oh, no you don't. You can't show up on my doorstep looking like your dog just died and then leave without an explanation. You're not going anywhere just yet. Yes, I'm going out, but Nicolas isn't here yet. You can visit with me until he arrives." She steered her into the living room and pointed to the sofa. "Sit."

"Are you sure?"

"Very sure. Take as long as you need." She held out her hand. "Give me your coat."

Melanie slipped it off her shoulders and passed it to Kate. "I don't want to make you late."

Kate dropped the coat across the back of a chair.

"No worries. I'm ready to walk out the door." She stopped and took in the dark circles underneath her friend's red-rimmed eyes. "You won't make me late, but you are wasting time. Spill it."

"Melanie shrank into the cushions. "I'm so confused. Tyler came to see me yesterday. He didn't beg me to come home, but he made it clear that he isn't giving up on our marriage, either."

"That's a good thing, isn't it?"

Her friend's red head lolled on the back of the couch. "I don't know." She sat up. "I've heard it all before, Kate. Promises to change that never happen. Empty words. We both agree to make an effort, and I work so hard to see my part through. And Tyler...he just makes promises. He doesn't know how to keep them. I get my hopes built up, and we fall on our faces all over again. I don't think he means to disappoint me. I know he loves me. I just don't think he gets the whole *marriage-is-a-partnership* thing. But, now...I'm so tempted to believe him."

Kate shook her head. "He's a man, hon. They leave the womb hard wired for pigheadedness."

Melanie grinned through her tears. "Don't I know it."

"So why are you tempted to believe him now?"

"He says he's willing to get counseling." Melanie's features went soft with hope. "He's already been to talk to your pastor, and he wants me to go as well. He's never done that before."

"You've never left before."

"I know, but there was something in his tone of voice. Something new. I've tried so hard to write this religion thing off as just another one of his fads. What if it isn't?" She met Kate's gaze. "I know you go to this church, too. Could it really have changed him?"

The longing in Melanie's eyes tore at Kate's heart. She moved to sit beside her. "Sweetheart, going to church isn't going to change anyone. But allowing Christ into your heart, developing a living relationship with Him, desiring to be changed and opening up your life to His will—those things can tame the worst of us."

"So, you think I should talk with your pastor?"

Kate patted her hand. "I think you need to do a lot of things, but talking to Pastor Gordon is a great place to start." A car door slammed in the driveway, sending Merlin into a renewed frenzy. "That's Nicolas. I can stall him for a bit it you need me to."

Melanie shook her head. "I'll be OK. I've got a lot to think about. Can I come to church with you again tomorrow? I promise I won't run away this time."

"You know Tyler will be there?"

"Yeah, I know."

Kate stood and pulled Melanie into a hug. "I'll save you a seat." She reached for the discarded jacket and handed it to her friend. A small box tumbled to the carpet, spilling its contents on the floor at Kate's feet.

"I'll get—" Melanie stopped as Merlin grabbed the object and scampered away.

"Merlin!" Kate lunged for the pup as he raced to his favorite corner. He dropped his new prize in a pile of squeaky toys and chew bones, crouching, growling, and wiggling in excitement at the unexpected game.

"Bad boy!" Kate looked up at Melanie. "I'm so sorry. He's going through a puppy-toddler stage. If it hit's the floor, it's his." She rummaged through Merlin's treasures. Her hand finally closed over Melanie's property. "Here it is."

Melanie groaned.

Kate looked up to find her friend ashen-faced and trembling. "Are you OK?"

Melanie collapsed on the sofa, her eyes riveted on the object in Kate's hand.

Kate lowered her gaze. It had been more than twenty years since she'd used one, but she recognized its purpose immediately. "Melanie...?"

Melanie snatched the pregnancy test from Kate's hand and met her unasked question with a shrug. "Like I said, I have a lot to think about."

~ * ~

Kate snuggled back into the leather seat of the Camaro as the car zipped west along I-40 toward Oklahoma City. She glanced at Nicolas. The dash lights cast his face in an array of interesting shadows and planes. The moment would have been perfect, except her mind kept drifting to the secret she now shared with Melanie.

Pregnant and contemplating divorce. Her heart broke anew. There had to be something she could do to help, but not if Melanie wasn't willing to put some effort into it.

"A penny for your thoughts."

Kate shoved Melanie's problems to the back of her mind. She didn't need Nicolas asking questions she couldn't answer. "Oh, trust me, they're worth much more than that."

"OK, can I ask you a question instead? You can refuse to answer if it breaks a confidence."

"Go ahead."

"What was up with Melanie earlier? I don't know her well and...you know Tyler and I are partners, right?"

Kate nodded. "Yes."

"He's so messed up since she moved out. He doesn't say a lot, so I was hoping you might be able to fill in some of the blanks. Not in a gossipy way." Nicolas maneuvered the car into the fast lane to pass a slower vehicle. "I'd love to be able to help him—them—but I don't have a clue about where to start."

Kate stared out her side window, her lip caught between her teeth. The beginnings of an idea took root, but she'd need to tread carefully to keep from revealing Melanie's secret. "Why don't you tell me his side, and I'll tell you hers. Then I have an idea to run by you."

They spent most of the drive comparing notes on the *he-saids* and *she-saids* of Melanie and Tyler's separation.

"Sounds like we've got two stubborn people who love each other but aren't quite sure how to show it. How they've managed to live together for twelve years..."

"Yep," Kate agreed. "It's a miracle and a mystery."

Nicolas chuckled. "So, what's the idea you mentioned?"

"Well, if they've agreed to some counseling, they might finally be on the right track. I think we should arrange some opportunities for them to spend some time together on neutral ground."

"Like..."

"Let's invite them on a double date. I know Melanie has strange hours with the bakery, but the shop is closed on Wednesday. How do you feel about dinner on Tuesday night?"

Nicolas frowned. "I don't know, Kate. That sounds a little...meddlesome. I was thinking about praying for them, encouraging them on the counseling thing, maybe dropping a few hints here and there that we were willing to listen if they needed an ear. Forcing them into spending time together..." He hesitated and glanced her way.

"Oh, forcing." Kate scoffed. "They're grownups. We aren't going to hold them in a headlock until they agree to our nefarious scheme. I just think it would be a nice way to get them to talk to each other about something other than the issues plaguing their relationship. And if they run out of words, they'll have us there to fill in the silences."

Nicolas sighed, and Kate saw by the uncertain look on his face that the battle wasn't won. "I'll tell you what. Mention it to Tyler, and I'll talk to Melanie. If either of them says no, we'll drop it, no harm, no foul, but at least we'll have the satisfaction of knowing we tried. And even if they say no now, they'll know that the invitation is open for later."

"I don't know."

"Come on. You're Karla Black's son. You have matchmaking embedded in your DNA."

"They're married."

"And we want to keep them that way, don't we?"

When he shrugged, Kate took it as a crack in his resistance and hammered the breech wider. "See that wasn't so hard. Melanie is coming to church tomorrow, and I figure Tyler will be there too. Let's watch how they act around each other and go from there."

"Talk about stubborn women." Nicolas took the

next exit. Instead of the upscale establishment she was dressed for, or the Mexican food they'd talked about the day before, he pulled into a brightly-lit strip mall and brought the car to a halt in front of a fast food restaurant ablaze with gaudy lights and neon signs.

"What are we doing here?"

"Having dinner." He faced her with a frown. "You do like burgers, don't you?"

"Well, yeah, but—"

"That's a relief. I couldn't go out with a woman who didn't like a good hamburger."

She looked from him to the crowded dining area. "This is where you come for a good burger...?" Her words trailed off as she glanced down at her dress and allowed her gaze to travel to his suit. "I mean, we're a little overdressed, don't you think?"

Nicolas opened his door, climbed out, and circled the hood of the car to help her out of the low slung seat. "My plans for tonight came together too late to get a reservation someplace nice. If we go somewhere and stand in line for an hour, we'll miss the best part of the evening." He held out a hand. "Come on, it'll be fun. We'll make all those young couples chasing toddlers jealous."

She allowed him to lead her to the front door. "You have a warped sense of humor, Nicolas Black."

He pulled her hand through the bend of his arm. "All part of my charming personality."

Dinner was a blur of harangued adults and noisy kids. She didn't know if the food was good or not, but once they were done, she settled back in the car with a full belly and more questions than answers. "Now where?"

"You'll see." Nicolas pulled into traffic with a satisfied grin on his face and headed into downtown.

Kate straightened with a gasp when he turned into the parking lot of the Civic Center. The marque announced the showing of a production of *My Fair Lady* with a well-known actress in the starring role. Kate had tried for tickets and failed. "How did you know...? I mean, this has been sold out for months."

Nicolas shrugged. "It is sold out, but not for a cop with connections and a few friends in low places."

She unsnapped her seat belt. "I'm not even going to ask. I'm just going to enjoy the show."

"That's probably a good idea."

When the final curtain fell three hours later, Kate slipped her arm around Nicolas and leaned into him. "This has been an amazing evening."

"Even dinner?"

Kate laughed. "Even dinner."

Nicolas raised her hand to his mouth, turned it over, and pressed a kiss into her palm. Kate didn't know if it was the touch of his lips or the intensity of his gaze that routed an electric charge up her spine. The cause was less important than the results. *Wow...*

By the time she restored order to her scattered thoughts, they were across the parking lot and standing next to his car.

Nicolas released her hand and opened the door. "I'm glad you had a good time." He settled her into the passenger seat and took his place beside her. "Would you like to listen to some music on the way home?"

"That's perfect."

Nicolas switched on the stereo, and a Mozart sonata flooded from the speakers.

"Oh, you're just full of surprises, aren't you?"

"What, you think a cop can't appreciate the classics?"

"Oh, I'm learning more and more about cops every day. More than I thought I wanted to know."

"I hope it's mostly good things." His voice was a husky whisper in the dark.

"The best."

The ride home passed in a dreamy blur. Stars in the sky, her hand in his, the music providing a soft romantic background. Kate closed her eyes and surrendered to the ambiance, hardly budging until she felt the car slow down to make the turn into her drive.

"I thought you'd gone to sleep on me. My ego was about to be seriously damaged."

"Just enjoying the ride."

Nicolas walked her up the steps and waited while she searched for her keys. Once she found them, he took them from her, unlocked the door, and took both of her hands in his. "I'm so glad you enjoyed my surprise tonight. Can we do it again?"

"Just say the word, Detective."

"I need to say something else."

The look in his eyes forced the breath from Kate's lungs.

"I know you want to take things slowly, but I've been thinking of kissing you all day."

She stared up into his eyes. *That's makes two of us.*

"May I?"

Kate couldn't speak, so she took a half step toward him, hoping he'd take that as encouragement.

Nicolas raised his eyebrows, backed her up against the closed door, and lowered his forehead to hers. He smiled against her lips. "You're a very special woman, Kate." His mouth came down on hers, and all of the afternoon's musing about what their first real kiss would be like fled her brain in the wonder of reality.

He pulled away and cupped her face in his hands. The words he whispered against her parted lips were a kiss all their own. "May I have another?" When she nodded, he pressed in closer and took a second plunge. Kate was grateful for the door at her back. Without that to lean against, her liquefied knees would not have supported her. She circled her arms around his neck and abandoned herself to feelings she'd promised herself were a thing of the past.

An eternity...a second...later, he raised his head, released her face, and ran the tips of his fingers down the insides of her arms. They drifted down her sides, leaving a trail of fire in their wake, finally coming to rest at the small of her back. "Kate..." His sigh shuddered, and he dipped his head for a quick peck against her lips. "I have to go."

Kate nodded, continuing to use the door for support while she watched him get into his car. He raised his hand in farewell, and she followed suit. His taillights disappeared around the corner, and she opened the door. If her feet touched the floor on the way to her room she never knew it.

# CHAPTER SEVENTEEN

"Thanks, Mr..." Melanie clutched the phone, groping for the man's last name. One of the pamphlets the OB doc had given her talked about "pregnancy fuzz brain." She was learning, first hand, what that meant.

"Pastor, please."

Melanie hesitated over the unfamiliar title as she paced the small pay-by-the-week apartment she'd moved into eight days ago. It was a depressing little place, but at least she could cook a few meals instead of eating out every day. And in addition to the bed, she had a small love seat in the corner. "Sorry. Thanks, Pastor Gordon. I'll see you next Wednesday afternoon at one." She disconnected the call, sat on the edge of the bed, and reached for the calendar lying on the scarred nightstand. Two other appointments stared up at her. Today's consultation with a new lawyer, and tomorrow night's dinner with Kate, Nicolas...and Tyler. She added a note about the meeting on Wednesday and chewed on the end of her pen.

Three meetings...three possible outcomes...three paths for her future. Well, two, if you wanted to be picky, since she was certain Tyler's pastor would urge her toward reconciliation with her husband. That's what dinner tomorrow was ultimately about as well. Her friends meant well, but they weren't fooling her. *I hope Kate hasn't said anything to Nicolas about the baby.* She refused to go there. Kate had promised to keep it between the two of them, and Melanie believed she would.

She turned back to the calendar and considered the appointment with the new lawyer scheduled for later today. *Keep it or reschedule?* The pen tapped the page impatiently. Tyler's pastor had asked her to postpone that meeting until they'd had a chance to talk, but...

Melanie flopped back on the bed. Her free hand came to rest on her stomach. How had the situation come to this? *Am I really prepared to divorce your daddy before I even tell him about you?* Her thoughts trailed into nothingness. She watched dust particles dance in a stream of light, oblivious to the world around them. That had been her twelve years ago. Young, in love, so sure that whatever came down life's road, she and Tyler could handle it together. Tyler Mason and Melanie Hubbard would be an invincible team. She closed her eyes against the late afternoon sunlight, her thoughts boiling up to form a mirthless chuckle. "Some team." *If I could only believe in the change Tyler claims is happening in his life.* Her arm came up to cover her face, and a shuddering sigh echoed through the empty room.

"God, I never doubted Your existence. But You've always been the impersonal *man upstairs.* Someone too distant for me to be concerned with, and someone too big to be concerned with me and what happened in my life. Tyler admits that he's been wrong and claims that You're changing his life for the better. In all the years we've been married, he's never done that before. He wants me to believe him for the umpteenth time, to give him *one more chance* for the four thousandth time.

Everyone seems to think I should. Me? Part of me wants to go home to the man I love, and part of me wants to run while I have the chance. But how can I run when You've finally answered the biggest prayer we ever prayed. Well, not prayed, but You know what I mean."

She lowered her arm and stared at the ceiling, where it felt like her whispered words hovered. "So if You're up there, and if You're listening...if it's Your job to change the direction of our lives, I need to know what to do. I need to know who to believe. I need to know which path to take."

A second sigh followed the first. Melanie rolled to her side, picked up the phone, and selected a number from the recent calls menu, chewing her lip while it rang. *I can't believe I'm doing this.* She sat up when the call connected. "Hi, this is Melanie Mason. I have an appointment with Mr. Wilson at four today. I'm sorry for the short notice, but I need to cancel."

~ * ~

Kate's fork clattered to her plate. She glared across Callie's sunny yellow dining room at Karla. "What?"

Karla braced an elbow on the table and leaned forward. "What, what?"

"Oh, please...what? You've been sending me these little *knowing* glances all evening. Everyone's gone." She motioned around the room. "It's just the five of us—"

"Six." Samantha came back into the room and reclaimed her seat. "I just stepped out to call Iris. I needed to make sure she was OK with watching Bobbie for a little longer."

"Fine...six of us. Now, what's up with you?"

Terri looked up from pouring fresh coffee. "She's probably planning your wedding," she quipped before Karla could answer for herself.

Callie stepped back into the dining room and put a new bottle of chocolate creamer on the table. She gave Terri a high five as she passed. "Yep, she's got that mother-of-the-groom glow all over her face."

"Guys, stop. If Kate has something...unexpected... happening in her life, I'm sure she'll get around to sharing it in due time." Pam mirrored Karla's pose, elbow on the table, chin planted on her fist. "Won't you?"

Kate stared across the large table. Karla, Pam, and Samantha sat across from her, Terri and Callie stood behind them. All eyes were focused expectantly on her. They looked like a board of inquisition. She studied them one by one. Anticipation and gratitude coiled in her stomach. How could she have known, when she'd met them a year ago, that they would each become such an important part of her life?

"So," Karla paused to take a sip of her coffee. "Do you have something you want to share?"

Kate had known that her secrets had a short shelf life, but she had no intention of making the fact-finding phase of the evening easy on any of them. "Oh, not so much," she hedged. "I'm sure Nicolas told you that we've become business partners."

"Oh, yeah. *Business* partners." Sam faced Karla. "Your son kissed her smooth on the mouth, on the sidewalk, in broad daylight, in front of Patrick." She shrugged when Kate sent her a narrow-eyed stare. "Hey, we're almost newlyweds. We don't keep secrets.

He told me, I told Mom, Mom told them. I'm pretty sure that's how it's outlined in the girlfriend code of conduct manual." Her grin was almost contagious.

Kate bit her lip to keep the answering smile at bay and shook her head. "Sam, I love you, so I hope you won't be insulted when I tell you you're a brat." She looked at the four older women. "You guys are...well, I don't have a good word for what you guys are." She returned her focus to Karla. "And you have no idea how much it pains me to tell you that you were right." She shrugged. "What can I say? You and Mitch raised an amazing son."

Karla straightened with a broad smile. The jarring smack she gave the tabletop had the coffee sloshing in the cups. "I knew it." She looked at the women seated on either side of her. "Haven't I been telling you all for a couple of months that my Nicolas and Kate would hit it off if they just gave each other a chance?"

Callie rounded the table to take her seat on Kate's left. "Yes you have, and if you'll stop crowing about your insight, Kate might have a chance to tell us about it."

Karla sputtered to a stop, but her expression was good-natured as she threw a balled up napkin in Callie's direction. "I'm all ears."

Kate drew designs in the top of her cheesecake with her fork as a few seconds of silence ticked by. It wasn't that she didn't want to share. It was just hard to know where to start. *All the way back to the beginning, I guess.*

"I have a sophomoric confession to make. I'm a hopeless romantic." Her shoulders lifted in a small shrug. "There have been times in my life when I've embraced that knowledge, times when I struggled against it, and times when I've denied it. But it's something I've always known."

The admission raised goose flesh on her arms. She scooted away from the table, leaned back in her chair, and tried to rub the bumps away. "When I met Chad Wheeler, he quite simply melted me in my tennis shoes. Love at first sight doesn't even begin to describe the hold he had on my heart. He was so handsome." Kate reached for the purse hanging from the back of her chair. She fished for a moment, digging through receipts, makeup, and to-do lists before unearthing her wallet. She thumbed through a stack of photos, found what she wanted, and handed it to Callie.

"Oh, wow!" Callie passed it around the table where her comment was met with murmurs of agreement. "We've been to your house. How come we've never seen a picture until now?"

Kate shrugged. "I keep pictures of Chad and Alan on my desk in my office." Her voice dropped to a whisper, and her face heated in embarrassment. "I talk to them about my day, about Patrick and Samantha's wedding plans, about the center." She dropped her gaze to her bare left hand. *Oh, I miss you guys.* "And that makes me sound more than a little crazy."

"Oh, sweetheart." Callie reached across the back of Kate's chair and gave her shoulders a tight squeeze. "Not crazy, just lonely."

Kate accepted the photo back after everyone saw it, pausing for a moment to study the face of her first love. She traced the sturdy chin with an unsteady finger before tucking it back into its hiding place. "I fell so hard. It wasn't those gorgeous eyes, or the lashes any woman would kill for, or even that reckless-looking dark stubble he could never quite get rid of. Well, not just those things. As handsome as he was on the outside, he was just as beautiful on the inside. When I was in his arms, I knew I was the center of his world, protected and treasured. He had my heart with the first smile." There were tears in her eyes when she looked up. "Patrick tells people that I shunned the attention of other men to concentrate on raising him after his dad died. Truth is, it took me twenty years to get over the senseless loss of Chad and all the dreams and plans we had together. I just couldn't see another man fulfilling any of those promises. So I held the grief close, tried to make sense of the pointless way he died, and raised our son."

Her gaze flicked to Pam for a second. "Then I met Alan." She picked up her cup, frowning when she realized it was empty.

"Let me get you some," Callie offered.

"Thanks."

"I'll get it," Samantha offered. The youngest of the group scurried into the kitchen. When she came back, she brought the carafe with her. She filled Kate's cup, topped off everyone else's, and set the pot on the hot plate Callie kept on her side bar. She took her seat and prompted Kate to continue. "You met Alan when Patrick first went away to college, right?"

Kate nodded. "I had some investments that needed juggling once Patrick went to school. I'm not good with that sort of thing, and a friend recommended Alan's accounting firm. He was the opposite of Chad in every way. Fair where Chad was dark. Brisk where Chad was laid back and patient. A nonbeliever at the time where Chad was a dedicated Christian from the day I met him. My heart still fell straight to my toes."

This time when she looked at Pam, it was with a full on smile, grateful that she could talk freely in front of Alan's ex-wife. "You know how charming he could be when he wanted something."

Pam raised her cup in a silent salute. "Been there, done that."

"He called me two days after our initial appointment and asked me out. Scared me to death. Not because I hadn't been asked out in all the years since Chad died, but because it was the first time I was tempted to accept. I blamed my hesitation on the whole unequally yoked thing. I had no intention of dating anyone, certainly not an unbeliever. I tried to be polite when I explained that to him. Then he turned up in my church a few Sunday's later and rededicated his life to Christ. The next time he called to ask me out, I didn't have a legitimate reason to say no. That's when I realized the hold fear had on my heart. God and I had a long talk, and I made up my mind to embrace a future I'd denied myself. That sounds easy when I say it, but taking that leap was one of the hardest things I've ever done." The deep breath she pulled in shuddered in her lungs and echoed through the room. "We all know how that turned out."

Karla reached across the table to lay a hand on Kate's.

Kate shook her head. "No regrets. I loved Alan, and I'm grateful for the short time we had, but I'm done with men. Well, at least I thought I was." Her shoulders slumped. "I really, really wanted to be." She turned her hand in Karla's and gave it a squeeze before pushing away from the table.

"As much as I've denied it to you guys, and Patrick, and myself, I'm so incredibly lonely. There's this huge void in my life that"—her gaze swept the table— "friends"—and landed on Samantha—"the promise of grandchildren, volunteer work, and the foundation I plan on building can't fill. I've tried to fill it with God, but He keeps whispering that He has more than that for me."

She met Karla's green-eyed stare. "I don't know what God has in store for me or Nicolas. I'm terrified of opening my heart to a new love—and to the opportunity to have it snatched away a third time. But I have this soul-deep feeling that our futures are linked together."

Karla's eyes went bright with unshed tears. "You're both so wounded."

"Yes, we are, and as unrelated as those old wounds must be, maybe there's a way we can help each other move beyond them."

# CHAPTER EIGHTEEN

Kate frowned. "What did you just say?"

Melanie crossed her arms and stared at her friend. "I don't need a new dress to have dinner with my husband."

Kate shook her head, hooked a hand around Melanie's elbow, and dragged her through the automatic doors of the department store. She sent a furtive glance at the other shoppers. "Will you hush? You're breaking the code. You're gonna lose your girl card."

Melanie shook her arm loose, planted her feet on the tile floor, and frowned. "My what?"

"Your girl card. You know, that thing that makes you a woman." She brushed a hand across Melanie's stomach. "We love all babies, shoes run a close second. We love pretty things, soft things, and shopping. We never, ever admit, out loud, that we don't need a new dress. We *always* need a new dress. You're going to be a mother. Is this the sort of example you plan to set for a daughter?"

It was Melanie's turn to motion for quiet, batting Kate's hands away from her midsection. "Can we be a little more discreet about my impending need for mothering skills?" Melanie shook her head. "I don't need a new dress, but I think you need serious help."

"No, I need a new dress. Now that I'm officially dating Nicolas, I need to jazz up my wardrobe a little. Unlike you, my girly instincts go all the way to my bones."

Melanie rolled her eyes. "Fine, I'll help you look for something, but just for you. There's no sense in me buying new clothes right now. I'll need new soon enough. Besides, dressing up for Tyler is a waste. He never pays any attention to what I wear."

Kate stopped and pulled Melanie out of the main flow of shoppers and into a quiet corner. "Look, you need to put some effort into this reconciliation thing. I know you're hurt, and I know you feel like tonight is a waste of time, but hon, if you do things the way you've always done them, you can't be disappointed when you get the results you always got." She cocked her head and studied her red-headed friend. "I thought you wanted to give this a shot."

Melanie turned away and studied a rack of colorful silk blouses. "I don't know what I want." She turned back to Kate and crossed her arms. "Do you think he's really changed?"

Kate shrugged. "I've met him exactly one time, and I got the distinct impression he wanted me to disappear. But I do know that God is in the business of changing lives. What would it hurt to give them both a chance to prove it to you?"

Kate waited for a response while Melanie stared off into space. A plethora of emotions paraded across her friend's face. *Father, I don't know why trying to fix Tyler and Melanie's marriage has become so important to me. I have to believe You've placed this whole thing in my heart—and Nicolas's. Please soften her heart just a little bit.* Kate took a few steps away in order to give Melanie some space to make up her mind.

"You're right."

Kate hurried back to Melanie's side. "Yay! I knew there was a full-fledged girl in there somewhere."

With a small nod Melanie turned back to the rack. "Maybe I could use something new, but just a blouse. Remember, I'm a struggling small-business owner."

Kate exhaled. "Dresses, my treat."

"No, Kate—"

"My treat," she repeated. "It's your turn to remember—I'm a rich widow." Kate sucked in a sharp breath and pressed her hand to her own stomach.

"What's wrong?"

She met Melanie's eyes. "Nothing. Absolutely nothing."

"Then what...?"

"This is the first time since Alan died that remembering I'm a widow didn't flood my heart with loneliness." She pulled Melanie into a joyous hug, released her, and turned her toward the aisle where a discreet sign pointed the way to ladies' dresses. "Come on, we need to hurry with those dresses. We need time for new shoes and pedicures, too. We both have hot dates with seriously gorgeous men tonight, and I intend to relish every single moment of girly preparation."

~ * ~

Melanie raised her arms and allowed the emerald green dress to slither down the length of her body. The soft jersey material felt like water from a warm summer rain as it settled against her skin. She turned to look in the mirror, concerned that the clingy fabric would reveal more than she wanted. There wasn't a thing to worry about. Her breasts might be a bit fuller, but her stomach remained flat. She studied her reflection critically and brushed at nonexistent wrinkles.

The dress hugged her curves in all the right places, accenting her still-narrow waist, and flowing gracefully around her calves when she moved. Next, she retrieved the strappy silver shoes with the slender heels and bent to slip them on. Melanie shook her head when her eyes met her reflected image. Kate had been spot on about both purchases.

Yes, she'd tried the dress on in the store, but barefoot, standing in the harsh light of the fitting room, the dress had not looked anywhere near this flattering. Likewise, the shoes had not been a good fit with the jeans she'd worn shopping, but together... If Tyler didn't pay attention to her tonight, there was no hope for either of them. She crossed to the tiny night stand and picked up their final purchase of the afternoon.

When she upended the bag, sparkling emeralds and silver cascaded into her hand. Costume, of course. Kate might have money to burn, but the woman wasn't stupid. The thought spread a grin over Melanie's face. Kate was so determined to see this evening succeed as a turning point for Melanie and Tyler, she probably would have spent the money for the real thing.

Melanie clasped the necklace around her neck, then returned to the mirror to fasten the matching earrings. She took a step back and studied the whole picture, turning from side to side, watching the light play on the stones and watching the delicate sway of the dress's hem.

Butterflies danced in her stomach, and she pressed a hand against her middle. "Get a grip," she cautioned herself. It was stupid to be so excited about spending the evening with Tyler. They'd been married for nearly twelve years, for pity sake, and here she was acting like a schoolgirl going to the prom.

"No." She spoke the word into the empty room. "I promised to give this a chance. If I leave here with a negative mindset, the evening is doomed from the get-go." Melanie put the finishing touches on her hair, twisting it into a knot high on her head. She fastened it with silver combs and pulled a few tendrils loose to curl around her face and neck.

She rummaged in a jewelry box, looking for a ring to wear on her right hand. "Oh..." She plucked out the emerald ring she'd bought onboard the ship during her first cruise to the Caribbean. "I almost forgot about you, and you're the perfect final accent." The ring slipped onto her finger, and Melanie twisted her hand back and forth in the light, watching as the white sapphires surrounding the large, square green stone flashed with fire.

The ring brought back memories of crystal blue water, white sand, arching green palm trees, and pampered luxury. "Maybe I should check into an Australian cruise instead of just flying in. I'll bet I could see a lot more of the country that way." The idea pleased her. Cruises were always so tranquil and romantic. A very unladylike snort filled the room. "And you'd know about the romance part how?" Her answer was bitter. "From being a lonely observer, that's how." She looked back at the ring and the butterflies in her stomach died a cruel and untimely death, smothered under a blanket of disappointment. "And what difference does it make where I go, or how I get there? It all boils down to another trip alone."

She reached to remove the ring and hesitated. It really did look great with the outfit. "Fine, I'll wear the confounded thing." Her earlier intentions of a positive attitude joined the stink of the dead butterflies. *This is just another futile attempt to make things right that will always be wrong.* "I'll let the ring be my hogwash detector. Every time I'm tempted to believe in Tyler's professed change of heart, I'll look at my ring. It'll keep me focused." She grabbed her bag, slammed out the door, and went to *enjoy* dinner with her husband.

~ * ~

Kate toyed with her salad and glanced at Melanie from beneath her lashes. Her friend looked stunning, but something was definitely wrong on the other side of the table. Melanie's answers bordered on abrupt, her posture was stiff, and her movements seemed forced as she picked at the food on her plate. *Late day morning sickness?* She discarded the thought. That wouldn't explain the tension hovering over their table like a San Francisco fog. Kate had no idea where it was coming from, but Tyler wasn't helping, sitting next to his wife, silent as a stone. Something had made a drastic change to Melanie's mood over the last couple of hours. This was not her shopping buddy from just a few hours ago.

Their trip to the mall had been a spontaneous good time. They'd tried on clothes and shoes, had their fingernails and toenails done, laughing and whispering like a couple of teenagers the whole time. Everything had been fine when they'd gone their separate ways to get ready for the evening. *What happened between then and now?*

"Is your salad OK?" Nicolas asked.

"What? Oh..." Kate smiled at her date, realizing that her fork had been poised between her plate and her mouth for several seconds. "It's delicious." She took a deep breath. The scent of freshly baked bread, garlic, rosemary, and tomatoes permeated the air. "This was the perfect choice. I love the smell of Italian food. Even if you aren't hungry, you will be if you sit here long enough."

Nicolas nodded. "It does whet the appetite." He leaned closer. "And so do you. You're beautiful tonight, Kate. Dressed in all that purple and silver you look almost...regal."

Kate saw an opening for some conversation and ran with it. "Aww...that's the second nicest thing I've heard all day."

"Second nicest?" Nicolas leaned back in his chair and crossed his arms. "What was the first?"

Kate tapped her chin with a fingertip and grinned. "Well, I'd have to say that the clerk at the mall wins first place hands down. When Melanie and I paid for our dresses this afternoon, they rang up at half the ticket price. When I asked him about it, he told us that they had just gone on sale this morning, but he hadn't had a chance to change the sign or the tags, I pretty much wanted to drag him across the counter and kiss him right on the mouth." She looked across the table and waited until Melanie met her stare. "That was pretty special, wasn't it?"

Melanie nodded. "I suppose."

While Kate frowned over her friend's two-word answer, Nicolas picked up the conversational ball.

"I thought you ladies had a fresh retail glow about you this evening. I don't know of anything that perks up a woman like a day at the mall. You both got new dresses?"

"New dresses, new shoes," Kate wiggled her fingers under Nicolas's nose, "new polish, top and bottom."

Nicolas looked at Tyler. "We are two lucky men, partner. Melanie looks wonderful, doesn't she?"

Tyler glanced up at his wife and smiled. "She always does." He surrendered his empty salad plate to the waiter and nodded his thanks when a bowl of minestrone took its place. "But she already knows that I think she's the loveliest woman in the room." He spooned up a bite of the fragrant broth.

Kate stared at him. *Of all the... We like to hear the words, you dolt! I can't believe...* Kate paused her internal tirade and watched Tyler watch his wife. She saw affection on his face and tenderness in his eyes. Enough that she began to reassess her opinion. Melanie complained that he didn't talk to her, but maybe he just took it for granted that she could see the same things Kate saw. Maybe Tyler expressed his feelings more by doing and less by saying.

*Father, they really are just dancing around each other. Please help them see what I see.*

Conversation, such as it was, lagged again while everyone sampled their soups. Kate had the minestrone as well, but Nicolas had selected something heavy with pasta, tomatoes, and sliced sausage. Melanie's, creamy and full of bits of diced chicken, looked equally delicious. Kate took a few bites, trying to decide where to go next. She touched the amethyst hoops that dangled from her ears and looked at Melanie.

"Melanie, did I tell you about the mystery Nicolas helped me solve a few days ago?"

Melanie's gaze flickered in her direction before returning to her barely-touched soup. She pushed her bowl aside and fingered the stem of her water glass. "I don't think so," she mumbled.

"It was amazing," Kate continued, undaunted. "The day we agreed to become partners, we went to dinner to celebrate, and somewhere along the way I lost one of these earrings. I was devastated, because they were a wedding gift." She laid a hand on Nicolas's arm. "Nicolas wouldn't let me panic. He took complete charge of the situation and had the earring back to me the next day, along with a beautiful bouquet of flowers." She turned from Melanie and rested her gaze on Nicolas. "It was amazing."

Nicolas shook his head. "I wouldn't call it amazing. I found it in the floorboard of my car." He laughed. "Not the most difficult case I've ever cracked."

"Maybe not, but it was important to me." Kate turned back to her friend. "That's when I knew I'd made the right decision about my new partner. If he could be so diligent over something so small and insignificant, I knew he'd give his all to make our business work. It's funny how God brings things together when you let Him. Now we're partners and business owners, all nice and legal. We're going over to our new building tomorrow to start making some plans on how to divide the space."

Melanie never even looked up. "I think you did mention the missing earring. Nice to know it worked out."

*Well, strike two.* Was there no way to break up the glacier on the other side of the table?

Melanie lifted her hand to swipe a curl from her eyes, and Kate noticed the emerald ring for the first time.

"Ohh..." She reached across the table, captured Melanie's hand, and drew it into the light. "What a beautiful ring. No wonder you went for the green dress. I would have too if I'd had something this stunning to wear with it. Was it a gift from Tyler?"

Melanie pulled her hand from Kate's grasp, finally looking up to meet her gaze. Kate saw tears even in the dim light.

"A gift from Tyler?" Her breath came out in a huff. "Hardly." She held the ring up as if seeing it for the first time. "No, I bought it for myself on one of the many vacations Tyler sent me on to get me out of his hair for a few days. A romantic cruise, all by myself."

Tyler finally found his tongue. "I never sent you on vacation to get you out of my hair. I sent you on vacation because I love you."

Melanie scooted her chair away from the table and stared into Tyler's face. "Uh-huh. You love me so much, you've not spoken a dozen words to me since we got here."

"I could tell you were in a mood. I didn't know why, and I didn't want to make things worse by saying the wrong thing."

Melanie narrowed her eyes. "I'm in a *mood*?"

Tyler apparently lost his voice under the heat of her temper. He answered her with a shrug.

"Fine." Melanie snatched the napkin from her lap

and tossed it on the table. "I'm in a mood." She stood. "I'm in the mood to go home." She turned and marched toward the front of the restaurant as fast as the spiky silver heels would allow.

Tyler mumbled an apology and hurried out behind her. "Melanie...Mel..."

Kate looked at Nicolas, who watched his friend rush from the catastrophe their dinner had become. When he finally faced Kate, she read the same regret she was feeling on his face. They'd meddled and failed...miserably.

"I told you this wasn't a good idea."

Kate put her head in her hands. *I told you so* was not the dessert she'd planned to enjoy.

# CHAPTER NINETEEN

Kate retracted the tape measure bright and early Wednesday morning, typed a note into her iPad, and turned just in time to see Nicolas blow a warm breath into his cupped hands.

"If you're freezing, we can do this another day."

"No." He crossed the room and handed her his stack of notes. "I'm just glad we stopped in today. If that cold front the weather gurus are predicting comes through tonight, we'd have had more than just a faulty thermostat and no heat to deal with. We'd have busted water pipes as well."

Kate bundled her jacket closer and motioned to the boots hugging her feet and ankles. "Yep, gotta love Oklahoma weather. And to think, I wore new spring shoes to dinner last night."

Nicolas held up a hand. "Please, let's not go there. As beautiful as you were last night, I'm trying to forget the evening ever happened."

"How's that workin' for you?"

"Not as well as I'd like, thanks."

Kate shook her head and ignored his request to let it drop. "It's sad. Did you see the way they looked at each other when the other wasn't paying attention? It's so easy to see that they still love each other, even if they've forgotten how to get the point across."

"Listening to Tyler talk, I'm not sure they ever knew."

"Yeah, I get that from Melanie, too. Shouldn't it be easier if you care for someone?"

He took a step closer and gathered her into his arms. "Probably, but I'm not an expert in the romance department." He leaned in to nuzzle her neck. "I'm just a lowly beginner."

Her heart fluttered as his lips trailed tiny kisses from her jaw to her hairline. Kisses that revived a level of desire that wasn't safe for either of them in the solitude of an unoccupied building. A shiver swam through her bloodstream that had nothing to do with the broken heater. She took a deep breath and wiggled out of his arms. "Beginner? I think you're a prodigy."

He grinned. "Practice makes perfect. Hey," he said when she took two more steps away. "Where are you going? I was just getting started."

Kate fanned her flushed face. "Someplace where you aren't." He advanced with a mischievous smile. Kate took another step back and shoved her tablet into his gut. "I need to look at some things upstairs. Take this. I bookmarked some office furniture sites. See if there's a theme or color scheme that appeals to your manly tastes."

She escaped up the stairs before Nicolas had a chance to reply. The man was way too tempting for his, or her, own good. Her feet clomped on the bare wood. She turned midway and stared down at Nicolas from a safer distance. "Did they say when the carpet would go down on these stairs?"

Nicolas answered without looking up from the tablet. "Monday. They want that to be the last thing on the renovation agenda. It'll stay cleaner that way."

Kate lifted a hand from the banister and frowned at the combination of dust and grit. "Good idea." She continued up the stairs, wiping her hand on the seat of her jeans as she climbed. Once she reached the landing, she considered her options. Of the five rooms on this level, the two largest were on the street side of the building. Equal in size, they both featured a bank of windows that overlooked the street and would keep the rooms well lit with natural light. Perfect, nearly identical office space for her and her partner. Kate turned to the room in the north east corner and threw open the door. "Identical except for these divine built-in bookcases."

She stepped through and ran her hand over the rich blond oak. *They're smooth as a baby's tushy.* Moving to the windows, she looked down on the view of Garfield's main thoroughfare. The winter bare branches of the trees lining the street swayed with the increased wind of the approaching cold front. People, bundled in coats and jackets, hurried about their business without any of the sidewalk gossip and friendly conversations that were so much a normal part of small-town living. From up here she could watch the seasons change while she pursued the dream she'd had ever since Chad's death. She turned and envisioned the room as it would look once the furniture was arranged. *My office.* Her eyes went back to the beautiful old shelves. *My bookcases.*

Kate moved across the hall into the other corner office to peer out those windows. The view was the same, the dimensions were the same, but the mental image of the finished product left her feeling flat. The office across the hall had her name written all over it.

"Yep, I'm staking my claim."

"On what?"

Kate jumped, and a guilty yelp escaped her throat. Her hand jerked up to clutch her chest. She spun. "What are you doing?"

Nicolas waved the tablet. "You told me to take a look and let you know what I thought."

She dropped her hand as her heartbeat returned to normal. "How did you get up those creaky old steps without me hearing you?"

"You couldn't hear me because you were too busy talking to yourself. Staking your claim on what?"

"Oh. Right. On my personal office space. I—"

"Stop right there. If you're even thinking of sticking me across the hall, think again. I've already picked out my office furniture and it clashes with those silly bookcases." He pointed to the floor at his feet. "This one's mine."

Kate raised her eyebrows. "Well, that's a little selfish, don't you think? Making that sort of decision without even consulting your partner?" She turned to hide a grin. "I mean really..." She gave an exaggerated sigh. "If that's the way you plan to do business, we're going to have to set some boundaries."

Nicolas was silent for a few seconds. Kate was just about to turn around to let him know he'd been had when he spoke again. "I'll tell you what. You give me first choice of office space, and I'll give you full control over the downstairs decorations."

*Oh, honey, you are way too easy.* "Deal." She faced him and held out her hand. "I'll take the other room and figure out a way to make the bookcases work, but only because I don't want to start things off on the wrong foot." She narrowed her eyes at him and struggled to keep the triumph out of her voice. *I know I'm going to pay for this somewhere down the road.* "But, lets agree to discuss these things from here on out."

Nicolas studied her face. "I'm missing something here, but my mama didn't raise no fool. I know enough to stop when I'm getting my way." He took her hand, but instead of shaking, he pulled her into his arms and met her startled mouth with his. "Let's seal it with a kiss."

His lips were slow and thorough on hers, and the feelings they ignited had nothing to do with a cliché'. Kate backed away and pressed her fingers to his lips. "Wow. With moves like that you could have your way in just about any argument." The sound of a banjo strumming floated up the stairs. She felt of her pockets and grunted in frustration.

"What?"

"That's my phone. I left a message for Melanie this morning. I thought maybe she'd want to talk." She sprinted for the stairs. "I left the phone in my purse by the front door."

"You can call her back."

She glanced at him from the landing. "Her business comes in waves. If she has time to talk now, I don't want to ignore her." Kate raced down the stairs.

"Kate, it's her day off," he reminded her. "Be careful of—"

Kate gasped when the toe of her shoe caught the same loose board she'd tripped on a few days earlier. She struggled to turn and grab the banister. Her fingers closed on air. She had just enough time to dread the landing that raced to meet her. The last things she heard was Nicolas as he pounded down behind her. Noisy feet accompanied by his raised voice.

"Kate!"

~ * ~

Nicolas crouched next to where Kate lay, facedown, at the bottom of the stairs. "Kate?" He touched her shoulder, patting gently, afraid to shake her. Only the good Lord above knew what she might have injured or broken in her fall.

She groaned and shifted just enough for him to see blood pooling beneath her head, but not enough to see where it was coming from.

"What...?" Her words trailed away as what little consciousness she might have regained faded.

The blood unnerved him, but he reminded himself that head wounds, even minor ones bled like the dickens. Nicolas kept one hand firmly on her back and fumbled his cell phone out of his pocket with the other. "Lie still. I'm getting you some help." If she heard him, she didn't fight him, and that only intensified his certainly that something was seriously wrong.

"9-1-1, please state the nature of your emergency."

Nicolas rattled of his official title and the address to the building. "I've got a white female, mid-forties, who just took a fall down a set of stairs."

"Is she conscious?"

"In and out, and she's got some moderate bleeding from an undetermined head wound."

"I've got an ambulance dispatched, ETA seven minutes. Unless you judge the bleeding to be life threatening, do not move her or allow her to move herself. There could be spinal injuries. Just keep the line open until help gets there."

Nicolas nodded as the operator talked. *I just told you that I'm a cop.* He refused to growl at her, though. She had a set of scripted instructions, and most of the time they were necessary to the well-being of the victim. The steady rise and fall of Kate's lungs under his hand gave him some comfort. He laid the phone aside, stood, and slipped off his jacket. He knelt back down and tucked it around her shoulders. The added warmth would help stave off shock. "Kate, can you hear me?"

Silence.

He retrieved the phone. "She's been out for a few minutes. How much longer?"

"Any second now."

And on the tail of her words he heard the siren. "They're here. Thanks for your help." He disconnected the call and rushed to open the door for the rescue personnel.

There were two of them. Mutt and Jeff in blue scrubs. The first, tall, fair, and clean-shaven. He looked young enough to still be in high school. Next through the door, a thirty something guy. He was more portly in build, with dark hair. A thick black mustache, waxed to handlebar perfection, covered his upper lip.

The medical techs took a few seconds to access the situation and then made quick work of getting Kate ready for transport to the hospital twenty miles away. They stabilized her neck with a thick yellow collar, placed a backboard on the floor next to her, and gently rolled her over on it. Once they had Kate loaded onto a gurney, the shorter of the two produced a clipboard while the taller proceeded to take her vital signs. He called off Kate's temperature and blood pressure to his partner and then looked into Kate's eyes with a small flashlight.

Nicolas stood aside and let them work. An unaccustomed feeling of helplessness swamped him. His fingers itched to clean the blood from her face. He wanted to soothe the goose egg on her forehead. He wanted to hold her hand. He wanted...

"How long has she been unconscious?"

The question pulled him back to the present. "Um...sorry." He glanced at his phone. Twelve minutes had elapsed since he called 911. "She was groggy but awake right after it happened, but she hasn't made a sound in the last ten minutes."

"OK. We're going to transport her to the ER. You can follow us if you'd like. Do you know if she's allergic to any medications?"

"No, but her son..." He pinched the bridge of his nose. *I should have called Patrick the minute I got off the phone with the 911 operator.* "Her son will know. I'll call him, and I'll have some answers for you by the time we get to the hospital."

"Good enough." He took the foot end of the gurney while his partner guided the front.

Nicolas winced when the whole shebang jarred as the legs folded up. The doors of the ambulance slammed shut.

He locked the door to the building, and sprinted to his car, pulling out his phone while he ran. He still had Patrick's number from the kidnapping case three months earlier.

"Patrick, your mother had an accident this

morning."

"What? Where?"

"She fell down the stairs while we were taking some measurements in the new building. She's got a good bump on her head, and she wasn't conscious when they left in the ambulance, but her color was good, and the EMT's are with her. They have some questions about her medical history that I can't answer. Can you meet us at the Med Center ER?"

"I'm on my way!"

The phone went dead in his hand. Nicolas tossed it aside and gave his full attention to staying behind the ambulance transporting the only woman he'd ever allowed himself to love.

# CHAPTER TWENTY

Kate's world lurched. She struggled to get her bearings and failed. She tried to raise her head, confused to find herself restrained. *What the...?* When her eyes squinted open, the lurching transitioned to spinning. The spinning took her stomach with it. Her eyes snapped shut against the sudden nausea, and she took a few deep breaths.

"Welcome back."

The unfamiliar voice only added to her confusion. "What...?"

"You're in an ambulance, and we're almost to the hospital. Do you remember what happened?"

Memory flooded back. "I tripped on the stairs." She tried to turn her head in the direction of the voice, but something was holding her head in place. Her heart threatened to pound out of her chest. *I can't turn my head...what if...?* Kate's breathing accelerated, coming in gulps.

A strange man leaned into her field of vision. "Easy there. What's wrong?"

"I can't move my head. Am I...?"

"We've got you on a back board as a precaution. Can you wiggle your fingers and toes for me?"

Kate forced her breathing to slow and focused on the simple request. Tears of relief stung her eyes when her body obeyed.

"Good job. Can you tell me your name and what day it is?"

A noise buzzed in her ear, and something tightened on her upper arm, squeezing the muscle in a vice. A hand took hold of her wrist and held it in gentle fingers. *Vital signs.* The thought managed to work its way through the fog surrounding her brain. She swallowed. "Kate Archer. It's Wednesday."

The tech nodded. "Perfect. Your blood pressure is a little elevated, but that's normal under the circumstances. How do you feel?"

"Like my head's about to explode."

"Also normal. You've got quite a bump on your forehead. Dizziness, nausea?"

"Yes to both."

"I'm betting concussion."

Kate groaned at his words. "Can I please sit up? I think I'd feel better if I weren't tied down."

"Not a good idea. Something might be broken. Once we get to the hospital, they'll get you checked out."

His words trailed off as she felt the ambulance slow. Her world tilted on its axis as the boxy vehicle made a slow turn. Panic welled up along with the contents of her stomach. "I'm going to throw up!"

"Hang in there. Take some slow deep breaths for me. There a couple of speed bumps ahead, my partner's going to take them real slow, but you're gonna feel a little shake."

His "little shake" felt more like a nine-point-oh on the Richter scale. Her breakfast clawed at her stomach for release. Kate closed her eyes and forced herself to breathe. *I won't be sick, I won't be sick...* With a final rock, the motion of the vehicle stopped.

"How ya doing?"

Kate didn't trust her heaving stomach enough to speak. She lifted her hand and gave the EMT a shaky thumbs up.

His thick, dark mustache twitched when he grinned down at her. "That bad, huh? Let's get you inside so they can check you out. It wouldn't surprise me if there weren't some really good drugs in your future."

She scrunched her eyes closed and bit her lip as they juggled the gurney out of the ambulance. The promise of *really good drugs* became more appealing with each thud of her head. She felt a hand brush her hair.

"Kate?"

She opened her eyes and found Nicolas leaning over her. Worry etched his face in the straight line of his mouth and the vertical creases between his brows.

"Hey."

"Hey yourself." He glanced away from her and fixed his gaze on the EMT. "Is she OK?"

The mustache twitched again. "If you'll let us get her inside, I'm sure someone can answer that for you."

Nicolas nodded and took a step back. Kate kept hold of his hand as the gurney began to move. "Call Patrick."

"He's on his way. I'll wait here for him. You worry about you for now."

~ * ~

Nicolas watched them push her into a room and close the door. Helplessness settled on his shoulders, intensifying when a nurse with a handful of paperwork approached him.

"She's in good hands." She led him to a chair and held out the stack of forms. "I need you to fill these out for me."

He sank into the seat. "I'm not...I mean, I don't..." *Where is Patrick?*

The glass doors swished open and Kate's son raced through. His sudden stop made his tennis shoes squeak on the tile floor. He looked around, spotted Nicolas, and hurried in his direction.

"Where's my mom?"

"They just took her back to an exam room."

Patrick turned to look at the line of closed doors. "Which one?"

Before Nicolas could answer the nurse obviously decided which man she needed to be talking to. She turned to Patrick and offered him the stack of paperwork. "I need you to fill out these forms for me. I'll also need an insurance card."

"I need to see my mom."

"I understand." She nodded at the stack of forms. "I'll fix that for you just as soon as you get these filled out. We need this info to get her the proper treatment."

Patrick ran his fingers through his hair. "Whatever." He took the forms in one hand and pulled out his wallet with the other. He jammed the papers under his arm while he searched through a stack of plastic. "Where..." On the third shuffle through he held up a card. "Here you go."

"Thanks," the nurse answered. "I'll get started with this." She handed him a pen. "You work on these, and I'll get you back with your mom in no time."

She hurried away, and Patrick lowered himself into a chair and scribbled out bits and pieces of information. He signed the final form, and Nicolas trailed him back to the nurse's desk. "Here you go. Which room?"

"They just took her back to X-ray."

"You said..."

"Five more minutes, I promise."

Nicolas placed a hand on the younger man's shoulder. "Let's sit down and give them time to do their jobs. I don't like the wait any more than you do, but—"

Patrick rounded on Nicolas. "What in blue blazes happened?"

"She tripped on the stairs."

Patrick fisted his hands on his hips and leaned into Nicolas's space. "The same stairs she said she tripped on last week? If you knew they hadn't been fixed, why would you let her—"

"Whoa, son, throttle back, will you?" Nicolas took a step back and studied the younger man. Beneath the sheen of sweat on Patrick's face his features were stiff with concern. *Not just worry, the kid is scared to death.* Nicolas gentled his tone. "I understand that you're anxious and impatient, so am I. Let's sit down. I'm sure they'll call us back in no time."

Patrick squeezed his eyes shut, pinched the bridge of his nose, and drew in a ragged breath. "Sorry. It's not your fault." He looked around the room. "It's this place. I haven't been back here since Dad..." He swallowed hard. "I don't have the greatest memories of this place, and Mom's all I have. It's...unnerving." He looked at the nurse's desk. "Especially when they won't tell you anything."

"She was awake and talking when they took her back. She didn't look like she was in a lot of pain. I don't know your mother as well as I'd like, but I think we'll both have our hands full trying to keep her down for a couple of days."

A small smile returned to Patrick's face. "You don't know the half of it."

~ * ~

After the many ER visits with Alan before he died, Kate was more familiar with the process than she would have liked. Vital signs, waiting, discussions, waiting, questions, waiting, X-rays, more waiting.

They'd allowed Nicolas and Patrick to join her in the small room. They spent their time pacing, fretting, and whispering to each other. She wondered, briefly what was up with the two men in her life, but the headache pounding in her forehead didn't leave a lot of room for speculation.

Finally, *thank You, Jesus*, they removed the restraints while a doctor stood to the side making notes on a clipboard. Once Kate was freed, she struggled to sit up. That effort ended in a fresh wave of dizziness and aches in places she'd never expected. She eased back down with a groan.

"Let that be a lesson to you, Ms. Archer. Slow and steady is the name of the game for you for the next week or so. You took an ugly fall, and people our age don't bounce as well as we used to." He stopped to consult the chart in his hand, flipping through the pages with practiced ease. "Nothing is broken, but you do have a mild concussion and some ugly contusions."

The doctor stepped to her side. Freckles dusted his cheeks and copper-colored peach fuzz accented his chin. *This kid was a doctor?* Kate raised her hand to the throbbing lump on her forehead. She touched the gauze and winced.

"Not to mention a bump the size of a golf ball with a small laceration on top. Even though we closed it with butterfly strips instead of stitches, it's going to be pretty tender for a few days."

*Yes, yes, I know all of this.* She forced a single deep breath. Doctors got paid to be repetitive and cautious. "When can I go home?"

He crossed his arms and held the clipboard to his chest. "We won't keep you too much longer. I'd like to order you a light lunch to make sure the nausea is under control. The nurse will have a couple of prescriptions for you." He looked across the room at Patrick and Nicolas. "She can't be alone tonight. She's going to want to sleep a lot, but sleep is not her friend with this sort of injury. Someone needs to be there to wake her up every couple of hours."

"You're kidding right?" Kate asked.

"I don't get paid to kid. I want you awake every two hours." He focused his attention back on the men. "If you can't wake her up, or if she seems overly confused once she is, I want her back in here immediately."

The men huddled in the corner for a quick conference. Glances in her direction, grunts, nods, and gestures followed. Kate frowned at their backs. You could cut the testosterone in the room with a knife. Instinct told her that she was about to be steamrolled. The guys broke from their huddle and Nicolas took a step forward. *Here it comes.*

He addressed the doctor. "I'll take her home when she's ready. Patrick will take the prescriptions and get them filled. I'll stay with her until he gets back to the house with his things. He's gonna stay with her for a few days."

"He absolutely will not." Kate objected and cut her eyes to her son. "You have class—"

"And I have a Mom who needs me." He crossed the room and put on his stern face. "Remember all those days of work you missed when I was a kid? Colds, strep throat, chicken pox? Too sick to go to school or the sitters. Who stayed home with me, took care of me with chicken soup and ice cream in bed?"

Kate's narrowed eyes had little to do with the pain in her head.

"Now it's my turn," Patrick continued. "Let's see if I can remember the rules." He grinned. "No TV, no phone conversations, and you have to stay in bed. If you're too sick to go to school, you are too sick to leave your room."

"Patrick."

"Mom..." he mimicked before his expression turned serious. "I'll miss class Thursday and Friday. It's nothing I can't make up online while you rest. If you're feeling better by the weekend, I promise I'll be back in my own house and back in school by Monday morning."

"It's either that," Nicolas interjected, "or I call Mom. She won't move in with you, but she'll insist that you stay with her and Pop for the weekend, and when you try to refuse, she'll play every guilt card in the deck. We both know you'll cave." He shrugged. "Wouldn't you be happier in your own home?"

Kate closed her eyes, too exhausted to fight this battle to her own advantage. "You guys make my head hurt." *But it's nice to be so loved.* She looked at the doctor. "What's for lunch?"

~ * ~

Nicolas parked in Kate's drive and turned off his ignition. "Stay put." He got out, circled the nose of the car, and opened Kate's door. "Hand me your keys and take my hand."

Kate accepted the offer with a frustrated growl. "I'm not helpless." And then, because God had a great sense of humor, she stumbled.

"Whoa!" Nicolas bent and scooped her off her feet. He silenced her with a look. "I'm going to reserve judgment on helpless, but stubborn...will you give me stubborn?"

She frowned, and he bundled her closer, placing a quick kiss on her lips. "You're cute when you frown like that."

Kate met his eyes with a fiery green stare.

"Will you give me a smile?" When she answered with an obviously forced smirk, he tucked her head between his chin and his shoulder, careful of the gauze-covered lump, and headed for her front door. The feel of her in his arms warmed something in his heart. *I could get used to this.* "You scared the life out of me this morning."

"Can't say it did much for me, either. Do you know how many things can pass through your head in that second when you're suspended in midair and you know you're going to fall? I have a whole new appreciation for the whole my-life-flashed-before-my-eyes thing."

"I'll bet." He shifted her while he fumbled with her keys.

"You might have better luck if you put me down."

"Shh!"

The key finally slid home. He turned the knob, nudging the door open with his foot. Kate's little black Cocker Spaniel launched himself at his knee caps, a blur of fur and bared teeth, raising a ruckus that he figured could be heard all the way downtown. Nicolas spun out of the way, eliciting a moan from Kate.

She raised a hand to her head, frowning in pain. "Merlin, inside voice! Nicolas stop going in circles!"

Man and dog both froze in place.

Nicolas studied her face. "Sweetheart, I'm sorry. Are you OK?"

The breath that shuddered against his shoulder had him bundling her closer.

"I just need to lie down on something that isn't moving."

Nicolas dropped a kiss on her hair. "Gotcha." He paused. "I've never been past the entryway. Point me in the right direction."

"Left, last door on the right."

With the dog on his heels he followed her directions, opening the door on a room decorated in yellows and greens. A floral scent teased his nostrils as he crossed the room and laid her on the daisy-patterned comforter. Merlin jumped up on the bed and sniffed at his mistress from head to toe. Obviously satisfied that all was well, he snuggled by her side, glaring at Nicolas when he sat on the edge of the mattress.

"It's good to know that you're well protected."

Kate raised a hand to stroke the silky black head. "Yep, he thinks he's a German Sheppard."

"Do I need to let him out?"

"Nope, I had a doggy door installed just for him." She looked up at him with a grimace. "Sorry."

"For what?"

"Oh, let's see. For being a clumsy blonde, for all the trouble that followed, for my dog trying to attack you, and for being such a lousy patient." Her shoulders moved in a small shrug. "I'm used to being the caregiver, not the receiver. I don't like being on the receiving end very much."

Nicolas leaned forward and tucked a stray strand of blonde hair behind Kate's ear. "You don't need to apologize. The accident could have happened to anyone. As far as I'm concerned, the building is off-limits until that staircase gets fixed." He stopped to scratch Merlin behind the ears. "Merlin was just doing his job, and as for being a bad patient, everyone needs to be babied on occasion. Now that I know you're going to be all right, I'm sort of enjoying it." He took her hand in his. *So fragile.* "It won't hurt you to let Patrick and me pamper you for a few days."

"Speaking of. What's up with you and my son? You two were awfully cozy in the ER."

Nicolas grinned at her choice of words and the memory of tense moments. "Let's just say we bonded over your injury, and we have a mutual desire to keep you healthy."

Kate smiled and closed her eyes. "Yeah, well I guess I can deal with a little bit of TLC."

*TLC?* He studied her in the silence and felt the

jumbled emotions of the day settle into a single certainty. *I'm falling in love with her.* The logical part of his brain rejected that thought. *How can you be in love with someone you've only known for nineteen days?* He chuckled. Something was going on if he was numbering the days.

"But you won't enjoy it when I'm lazy and spoiled."

Her words startled him out of his daydream. He'd thought she'd fallen asleep. "You'll never be lazy. I'm going to let you rest. I'll make myself at home in your living room while we wait on Patrick. Is there anything you need?"

She rubbed her arms. "I'm a little chilly." She started to roll to her feet and the color drained from her face.

Nicolas raised his brows.

"I was going to get up and slide under the covers, but I think I'll just stay where I am. I left a throw on the back of my chair next door. Would you get it for me?"

"You got it." He released her hand and stood. "Be back in just a second."

Nicolas exited one room and entered another, this one obviously a spare bedroom transformed into office space. Overflowing bookcases, a dog bed under the window, and a desk cluttered with computer equipment and paperwork. He spotted the throw draped over the back of the desk chair and pulled it free. Turning, his gaze fell on a couple of framed eight-by-ten pictures on the back corner of the desk. Curiosity drew him forward. *My predecessors?*

The picture on the left drew his attention. His ears filled with the sound of explosions, his nose with the scent of smoke and blood. His knees went weak, and he groped for the chair with one hand as he pulled the picture of the uniformed man toward him with the other. His pulse raced out of control. His mind refused to process what his eyes told him to be the truth.

"C.W?"

# CHAPTER TWENTY-ONE

Nicolas Black collapsed into the chair and stared at the picture of the man he'd killed more than twenty years before. An accident, certainly, but his friend was still dead, his family still deprived of a husband and a father. He would carry that innocent blood on his hands until the day he died.

Grief sent his thoughts reeling.

*This can't be happening!*

He bent his head over the desk and rested it on the cold glass housed within the frame. His words were a harsh whisper that bounced back to him from the walls of the room. "Oh, C. W. I found them." Nicolas lifted his head and stared at the wall that separated him from Kate. Invisible bands circled his chest and drove the air from his lungs at the thought of the woman resting in the next room.

The woman expecting him to return in just a moment.

His dead buddy's wife.

The woman he loved.

Nicolas struggled to breathe past the pressure in his chest. He turned back to the picture, barley able to focus on the image because of the way it shook in his hands. "After all these years I found Blondie and Little Man. And after all the tall tales we used to tell each other for entertainment, you'd never believe..."

He closed his eyes. So many things made sense now. That vague feeling of familiarity whenever he was around Patrick. The odd moments of déjà vu some of Patrick's expressions and gestures produced. Nicolas shuddered at the memory of his most recent nightmare, finally understanding why the specter in his dream had worn Patrick's face. *I knew his last name was Wheeler, but why would I ever think...?*

"Nicolas?"

He cringed at the sound of Kate's voice. How could he go back in there and pretend the last five minutes hadn't happened? If he went back in the room, he'd have to confess. Maybe he should just leave. Patrick was on his way, she'd be OK for a few minutes.

*Let it go. She doesn't ever need to know. It's ancient history.* Nicolas shook the thought away. He didn't have a lot of experience with relationships, but he knew better than to try to build one on a lie. *Would it be a lie if I just kept my mouth shut?* He'd considered their future a lot lately. Now he tried to picture their life together with this unspoken truth lurking between them. He failed.

The air shuddered out of his lungs when he exhaled. "I'm coming, Kate." His stride, so filled with confidence and enthusiasm just a few minutes ago, felt weighted with lead on the return trip. He entered the bedroom to find Kate struggling to rearrange her pillows. She wasn't having much luck.

"Here, let me do that."

"I want to lie back, but not down."

"I understand." Maybe if he could keep her occupied she wouldn't notice the guilt on his face. He dropped the throw and positioned the pillows behind her. "Better?"

"Perfect."

Her smile lit up his world.

"I thought you got lost."

"No, just sidetracked." Nicolas picked up the blanket and draped it over her legs. He sat on the side of the bed and reclaimed her hand.

"How are you feeling?"

"Better. I still have a headache, and my head feels a little...fuzzy. Does that even make sense?"

Nicolas nodded.

"But I think being home, resting in my own bed, makes a big difference."

He found it impossible to meet her eyes. He traced a finger over the delicate blue veins in her hand. You have to tell her. *No, I don't. Not now.*

Kate tugged at his hand. "Are you OK? You look like you did the other day when you were talking to Patrick, like you've seen a ghost or something."

His ragged breath echoed in his ears. *She deserves the truth.*

"Kate, I love you." Not the best way to start, not the best time to declare his feelings, but he needed her to know what his heart had finally accepted.

The fingers in his hand tightened and tugged until he looked up. Kate tilted her head on the pillow and studied him, a confused frown etched between her green eyes. "You...what? Is something wrong?"

Wrong didn't even begin to cover it. He lifted her hand and brushed her knuckles with his lips. "Tell me about your first husband. You don't say a lot about him. I don't even know"—he stopped to clear his throat—"his name."

"Nicolas, you're scaring me."

"I'm sorry. I know it probably seems like an unusual request after the morning we've had, but humor me, OK?"

Her shoulders lifted in a small gesture of surrender. "His name was Chad Wheeler."

Nicolas hadn't needed confirmation, but the name struck his heart like a dagger. *Chad Wheeler...C.W.* He nodded. "Tell me about him."

He watched her expression soften with memories. The look on her face drove the dagger deeper.

"I met him when my dad's job transferred him to Kansas City the summer between my sophomore and junior years of high school. I was so angry. How could my parents force me to change schools two years before graduation? I barely spoke to either of them for a month, certain my life would never be the same. Once we got settled in the new house, my parents started looking for a church to attend. I wasn't having any of that either. I can still remember thinking that if they knew how unhappy I was, they'd find a way to move back to Iowa and my friends." Her lips lifted at the memory. "I pouted, I cried, I wheedled, and the day we were going to attend the new church for the first time, I pretended to be sick. Mom and Dad weren't buying it. Sunday was for worship, and my teenaged snit didn't classify as an excuse to skip service."

"They sound a little like my mom and dad."

Kate raised her eyebrows. "I can see that. Anyway, I slouched in behind them that first morning, determined to make everyone's life miserable, and there was Chad. Six foot three, black wavy hair, and a smile that threatened to melt me into a puddle at his feet. And his eyes..." Kate closed her eyes and sighed with the memory. "Those eyes...he had the most beautiful blue eyes, fringed in the longest black lashes I'd ever seen on a guy. I fell in puppy love with him on the spot. He asked me out two weeks later, and we were married three years after that. The Air Force made me a widow before my second anniversary." She pulled the corner of the throw free and dabbed at her eyes.

"The Air Force sent him to the desert and shipped him home a few months later in a flag-draped box with a purple heart and a letter saying that he'd died in the line of duty, a victim of friendly fire."

*Friendly fire.* Every muscle in his body went taut with memory. Those words would haunt him to his grave. *Why couldn't it have been me in that box?*

She stopped, obviously trying to reign in her emotions. "I've never understood that term—friendly fire. What does that mean exactly? Were they on the firing range and someone got stupid? Were they cleaning their guns in their tent and a weapon discharged?"

Her questions ripped the heart from his chest. The lost look on her face ground the fragments to dust.

"All I've ever had are questions with no answers." Kate shook her head, and a single tear streaked down her cheek. "I mean, I lost Alan and it hurt, but there was some sense to that. He had a heart condition and he died, but Chad...I guess I'm no different than any other military widow. I want to know what those last weeks of his life were like. Who were his friends, how did he spend his days? Did he get my letters? Was he proud of his son? They don't give you a lot of information to fill in those blanks. If he'd died in battle, maybe I wouldn't have felt so lost, but as it is..." Her words trailed off and she looked him square in the eyes. "I don't talk about him much because it's still such a raw wound. Ripping the bandage free just keeps it from healing. Maybe if I had some answers..." She frowned at him, her tone uncertain. "I don't understand how this is important to you."

Nicolas studied her and fought with emotions he couldn't begin to put a name to. He'd considered his relationship with Kate a gift from God. As gifts went, this one ranked right up there with finding an empty candy bar wrapper in his Christmas stocking. He took a deep breath and a quick glance toward heaven. *Thanks a lot, God.* He closed his eyes and squeezed Kate's hand. "He called you guys Blondie and Little Man."

~ * ~

The bottom dropped out of Kate's stomach, and it had nothing to do with her concussion. She yanked her hand out of Nicolas's grip. "How do you...how could you possibly...?"

Nicolas moved like a ninety-year-old man as he rose to pace beside her bed, his breathing harsh and ragged as he moved back and forth. Kate read anxiety in every line of his body, from the shuffling gait, to his clenched hands, to the way he avoided her eyes.

The pounding in her head increased with each step he took, each second he remained silent. *Blondie and Little Man.* "Nicolas, what's going on? How in the world could you possibly know the nicknames Chad used for Patrick and me?"

Nicolas paused and raised his face to the ceiling. "I

was there, Kate." He drew his hands down the length of his face, his voice rough when he continued. "God help me, I was there."

Kate stared at him, trying to process what she heard. She knew he'd been in the Air Force for twenty-plus years. He was certainly the right age to have crossed paths with Chad. She raised her own hands and pressed her fingers against her throbbing temples. *Father, please take this pain away so I can focus on what Nicolas is telling me.* She pulled in a deep breath. "Talk to me, Nicolas. If you can tell me anything about Chad's last days and the incident that took his life, I need to know."

Nicolas sat on the edge of the mattress. His every movement contained a weariness Kate had never seen before. She wanted to reach out to him, to comfort him, but something on his face scared her. He wouldn't look at her, instead he stared at the far wall, his eyes focused on something she couldn't see.

"C.W. wrote to you almost every day. Did he ever mention anyone he called Snick?"

Kate straightened until she was sitting instead of leaning. Balance eluded her, but she was determined to remain upright, fighting to keep her world steady while her head pounded. Her narrowed eyes had nothing to do with the headache. "I sent him a care package every few weeks. He told me about a buddy who always swiped his Snickers bars." She tilted her head. "Chad had a nickname for everyone. Snickers...Snick...that was you." A statement, not a question.

Nicolas nodded. "We were two kids, thousands of miles away from home and everyone we loved for the first time. Both SPs, in the same unit, we ended up in the same ten-man tent. There was so little to do when we weren't on duty. We were in sight of the ocean but not allowed to explore the beach or the water." His smile was sad. "We used to watch the supply helos, belly slings budging, bringing our provisions in from the Navy ships. We'd stand beside the landing pads and hold up big score cards to let the pilots know what we thought of their flying." The sound that escaped his throat might have been a laugh on a different day. "Some of the pilots didn't appreciate our scoring system. C.W. and I got dusted on more than one occasion."

"He never—"

"I'm not surprised. As fun goes, it was pretty pathetic. You just had to be there. He probably thought it wouldn't make much sense to you. Anyway, we sort of gravitated to each other. We had Bible studies together, and we shared stories about our families."

He finally faced her. She drew back from the pain she saw in his eyes. *He must have endured horrible things to put that look on his face.*

"Kate, that man loved you and Patrick so much. You were all he talked about. Never by name though, you were always Blondie and Little Man. We all had our little phobias over there. For me, it was the New Testament I carried, zipped into the lining of my duffle bag. Mom and Dad prayed over it, and me, the day I left. I knew I'd be safe as long as I had that little Bible with me. For C.W., he didn't speak of you guys by name, because he felt like it would jinx his chances of getting home. Pretty silly for Christian guys, but in that environment, you hold onto whatever makes you feel safe. I swear, if I had ever known your names, I would have tracked you down before now. I would have shared this story with you sooner."

"I'm found now. I'm listening now." Kate used the throw, again, on her streaming eyes. She was almost afraid to move. *I have so many questions. I can't believe I'm getting some answers after twenty years, and from someone who actually knew him.* "Please, Nicolas, if you can tell me what happened, I need to know."

"It's ugly, Kate."

"I don't care."

Nicolas nodded, his breath a loud shudder in the quiet room.

Kate saw tears in his eyes before he closed them. *He must have loved him, too.* She laid a hand on his arm in silent encouragement. He covered it with his own for a second before getting up to pace.

"Like I said, we were living in a big tent-city out in the middle of the desert. Not a lot for the security police to do other than break up the occasional fight between men too lonely for their own good. There wasn't a lot of danger when you were inside the fence."

He faced her and ran a hand through his hair. His hand shook. Kate saw it tremble and couldn't keep her heart for doing likewise.

"It wasn't like it is today, where we're the enemy in an enemy country and everyone wants to kill you. Twenty years ago, Americans were the good guys as far as most of the Arab countries were concerned." He shrugged. "We didn't even carry weapons unless we were on guard duty at the exterior gates and check points." He stopped and focused on the floor.

Kate wanted to urge him on, but she waited.

"One day C.W. and I pulled joint duty patrolling the perimeter barrier a short distance from one of the back gates. Off in the distance, we could see a handful of people coming our way, herding some cattle. Rare, but not unheard of. The natives were always around, but they knew not to approach too close to the compound.

"It was lunch time, and they stopped a couple hundred feet from us, made a small camp, and prepared a meal over an open fire. C.W. and I watched them. It looked like a family. They were eating and laughing. I don't know what they were cooking, but it smelled heavenly. One of the men broke away from the group and approached the gate. He had a platter in his hand, holding it out like he meant to offer us some of their food." Nicolas had ceased to wipe the moisture from his face. He told his story while tears tracked down his cheeks.

"I told that man to stop, and he just kept coming. I thought maybe he couldn't understand me, or hear me, but there was something about the way he carried himself that had alarms going off in my head. I told C.W. to call for some support, and I took a few steps away and raised my weapon, hoping that my M16 would bridge the language barrier." Nicolas finally raised his arm and swiped at his streaming eyes with the sleeve of his shirt before delving back into his memories.

"He was close enough now for me to see that he was just a kid, younger than me or C.W. I guess the raised weapon got my point across. He stopped, dropped the platter, and started fumbling with something under his shirt. I don't know how I knew, but I did. Before I could shout a warning, the earth shook with an explosion, and the kid disintegrated right before our eyes. The concussion of the bomb knocked

C.W. and me to the ground, but the bomber hadn't gotten close enough to cause any real damage." Nicolas swallowed hard and bowed his head.

"Two more of the guys in the group started running our way, yelling at the top of their lungs. C.W. and I both got a couple of shots off before the next bomb knocked us both to the ground."

He raised his eyes and Kate could see the horror of the day reflected there.

"We weren't prepared, Kate. For battle, yes, but not an attack on the compound, not from an enemy that didn't care any more for their own lives than they cared for ours." He bit his lip. "I still don't remember what happened after that second bomb exploded. C.W. and I were both on the ground, I could barely hear the vehicles screaming to a stop at the gate behind us. The rest of the insurgents fled once help arrived. I got up, I had a few lacerations from flying shrapnel, but C.W....He wasn't moving."

Kate couldn't breathe. All the years she'd hungered for answers and now she just wanted him to stop. *No, God, No. Please don't take this where I think it's going.*

"I turned him over. The explosion hadn't killed him. Somewhere in the confusion of being knocked off my feet...my weapon discharged." Nicolas closed his eyes. "The bullet struck C.W. in the chest."

The room became a vacuum. All Kate could hear was the pounding of her head and the ringing in her ears. She had answers. They didn't help. Nicolas faced her with spread hands and haunted eyes.

Kate wanted to put her hands over her ears like a five-year-old. If she couldn't hear what came next, it couldn't shred her heart. *Don't say it...don't say it...please don't say it.*

"I killed your husband, Kate."

# CHAPTER TWENTY-TWO

*I love you.*

Her hands covered her eyes instead of her ears.

*I killed your husband.*

Kate struggled to bring those two random statements into some sort of logical pattern. Against her eyelids, Chad's face floated. Sweet, noble, beloved. In the corner of her heart reserved for the pain of his death, some of the twenty-year-old hurt fell away. The answers she'd always wanted hadn't been good ones, but knowing the details helped, would likely help more in the days ahead once she had time to process everything Nicolas had told her.

And Nicolas?

Where did he fit into her future?

Did he still fit?

Her head continued to pound. *Injury or emotion?*

Nicolas approached the bed, hand outstretched, but not touching her. "Kate, I know you must hate me. I'd give anything if I could change what happened all those years ago. Once the dust settled, they hauled me off to the medical unit and treated my wounds. They kept me pretty sedated for a couple of days, and by the time I woke up C.W. was gone, his stuff cleared out of our tent. I had no way to find you then and, if I had known who you were now, I would have kept my distance.

There's no way I would have suggested a business partnership between us, much less a personal one. That's not a heartbreak I'd have allowed either of us to risk. I'll go tomorrow and talk to the lawyer. I'll foot the bill for breaking our contract. I'll—"

She cut him off with a gesture. "Just shut up, would you?" Kate raised her eyes, her voice weary. "I really...I just need you to stop." An uncomfortable silence filled the room. Even Merlin, in the astute way of dogs, had grown still at her side as if waiting to see what would happen next.

*I need to think. If my head would just quit hurting, I could think.* Kate took a few deep breaths and tried to make sense of her scattered thoughts. "I don't hate you. I don't know what I feel, OK? My head hurts, and the more I try to concentrate, the more it hurts. I can't think straight, and I refuse to make any decisions until I can." Her eyes narrowed against the relentless pounding in her skull. She pressed two fingers to her forehead and rubbed the spot between brow and goose egg, searching for relief, finding none. "All I want you to do right now is leave."

"But Patrick isn't—"

"He must be on his way. I'll be fine by myself until he gets here. But you have to go." She lowered her hand and looked him in the eye. "Just promise me that you won't do anything about our partnership until you hear from me."

"I promise."

Nicolas moved to the door, his shoulders slumped, his feet dragging. He turned with his hand on the knob. "I loved Chad like a brother, Kate. I've spent twenty years wishing our positions were reversed, that I'd died that day instead of him. Except I wouldn't wish the last twenty years of guilt on anyone." He faced the floor. "I love you." He stepped through the door, his voice echoing with the click of the latch.

His whispered words ground the broken pieces of her heart into shards and drove the sharp pieces into her skull. She rolled to her side and let the tears come, hot and bitter. She wept for the past she never had the chance to share with Chad and for the future she'd begun to believe she could enjoy with Nicolas.

She tried again to isolate the strongest of those feelings. All her search yielded was a soul-deep weariness.

"Oh, God, I can't bear this again. You made me think this time would be different. At least I thought it was You. But how can we be together with this huge hurt between us?" Kate allowed her prayerful question to stand for a few moments before she hugged Merlin close, buried her face in his silky fur, and let the tears sweep her away again. She was still crying when Patrick entered her room.

"Mom?" Patrick hurried across the room, pried the dog from her arms, and gathered her to his chest. "What's wrong? Are you in pain?"

Kate clung to her son and babbled into the front of his shirt. His arms felt like a haven. *Just like his father's.* The thought carried a new torrent of tears.

Patrick rubbed her back. "Mom, where's Nicolas? I can't believe he left you alone after the doctor told us to stay with you. I'm so going to give him a piece of my mind." He inched her away so that he could look into her face. "Do you need to go back to the hospital?"

Kate sniffed back the tears. Her hand shook when

she reached up to stoke her son's hair. For just a second, he wore his father's face. It was her undoing. She collapsed against him a second time. "He didn't leave by choice. I sent him away."

"What...why would you do that?"

Her exhale vibrated against his chest. "Patrick, he killed your father."

~ * ~

Nicolas drove in circles, unaware of the passing time. He wanted to lose himself, but getting lost in Garfield was an impossible task for someone who'd grown up pedaling every street in town on a ten-speed bike.

*You're a real piece of work, you know?* Nicolas turned a familiar corner. He hadn't meant to tell Kate he loved her the first time, much less the second. The words had simply overflowed from his heart and fallen out of his mouth before his brain could stop them. And when he left? If he never spoke to Kate again, he wanted those words to be the ones she remembered. He shrugged. Of all the things he had to be sorry for, speaking the truth took a really low place on the list.

He drew the car to the curb and stared at his parent's house. Telling his story a second time today was the last thing he wanted to do, but they needed to hear it. Nicolas had no doubt that Kate was sharing it with Patrick. Patrick had a fiancé', the fiancé had a mother, the mother was a friend of the family. It was just a matter of time before they heard the story, and he wanted it to come from him.

He lowered his head to the steering wheel, his

shoulders slumped, suddenly unable to bear the weight of the day's events. Why...why...why had he allowed himself to fall into the trap of thinking he finally deserved a life beyond penance? He'd had plenty of opportunities to pursue a future with a beautiful woman over the years. Why now, and why Kate? Part of his heart ached with the need to pray, to run into the comforting arms he'd so recently reacquainted himself with. He raised his head with a snort. *Yeah, that works!*

Nicolas considered the God of the universe with a pessimistic shake of his head. "I bore the guilt for Chad's death, but I blamed You." His memory produced a vivid picture of Kate's face as his story unfolded. "I'll take the guilt for breaking Kate's heart as well. I knew better than to get involved. But the blame? All Yours—Master of the cosmos, King of the heavens. You are the only one I know capable of orchestrating such a huge disaster. Well I'm done being a pawn on Your galactic chess board."

He slammed out of the car. The vehicle shook with the force, the noise of the closing door rang through the peaceful neighborhood like a gunshot. The violence pleased him. It matched his mood. His displeasure carried him up the walk and through the front door of his parents' home. A long ingrained discipline had him catching the front door before it slammed into the facing.

"Mom?"

"In the kitchen, son."

His mother's voice carried from the rear of the house. Nicolas followed the voice and his nose. The kitchen had always been his favorite room in any house they'd lived in. Mom always had something interesting in the cookie jar or hidden in a pan under a piece of plastic wrap. Even during her thirty-plus years of federal employment, she always managed to keep her family supplied in homemade treats. He stepped through the door just in time to see a cake come out of the oven. Leaning in the doorway, he took a deep breath of home. It should have soothed him, instead it reminded him of all he'd just lost.

"Nicolas." His mother stood up and placed a cake pan on hot pads lining the counter. "I wasn't expecting to see you today. I'm almost done with dinner. Can you stay?"

"We'll see. I need to talk to you and Dad. Can dinner wait a bit?"

Karla stopped what she was doing and turned to study her son. "Dad should be home any second. I've got chicken and dumplings in the crock pot, nothing that can't be put on hold." The anxieties of the day pressed on his shoulders like a physical weight. His canny mother saw through every effort to hide his feelings. She crossed the room, arms outstretched. "What's wrong, baby?"

Nicolas stepped into the embrace, drawing in the comfort her arms offered. What was it about Mama's hugs in Mama's kitchen? "Everything, but nothing you can kiss and make better, even though I know you would if you could. Can we wait on Dad? I've had this conversation once today. I'd really like to tell you both at the same time."

The front door slammed from down the hall. "Karla, come kiss your husband and tell me what's for dinner. Benton was a slave driver today, and I'm hungry enough to eat a moose!"

Karla reached up and patted Nicolas on the cheek. "Right on time." She took glasses down from the cabinet and filled them with ice and sweet tea. "Let's head him off. If he gets in here with a fresh cake and a crock pot full of food, you'll never have his full attention." She handed Nicolas a drink, picked up the other two, and led the way back to the living room.

"Look who came for a visit."

Mitch took the glass she offered and leaned down to kiss his wife's cheek. "Sort of hard to miss that flashy car parked in front of the house." He grinned at his son. "Come to mooch some home cooking?"

"Not exactly."

"Sit down, Mitch. Nicolas has something he needs to talk to us about. Dinner is almost done. We'll eat after."

His mother wasn't the only shrewd parent in the house. Raising their four children had been a team effort. Nicolas relied on their support and love and had always had their combined attention when he needed it.

His mind went back to the conversation with his dad a couple of weeks ago. Would it have been easier to tell the story then? *Why have I waited so long to share this with them?* The question rattled around in his brain while he searched for a place to start. His parents sat and sipped their tea, willing to give him as much time as he needed. The magnitude of what he had to say drove him to his feet with a groan. He paced in front of them, finally facing the sofa where they sat.

"Kate and I were over at the building today. While we were there, she took a header down the stairs."

Karla leaned forward, her hand to her chest. "Is she OK?"

"She has a nice goose egg on her forehead and a mild concussion. The ER doc says she'll be fine." Nicolas wrestled with the rest of what he had to say. "I took her home, and while I was there, I happened to see a picture of her first husband—"

"Chad Wheeler," his mother supplied. "Quite a handsome young man. Except for his mother's coloring, Patrick favors him in a lot of ways."

Nicolas took the chair across the room and swallowed a deep drink of his tea to wet his suddenly dry throat. "I see that now."

"You see..." Karla's expression reflected her confusion. "How could you...?"

"Hush, Karla, and let the boy talk."

Nicolas leaned forward, bracing his elbows on his knees. "Once I saw the picture, I saw the resemblance as well. I should have seen it months ago." His gaze roamed the room, finally settling on his parents. "I served with Chad Wheeler during my first desert deployment. I—"

"What a nice coincidence." Karla took a sip of her tea, her face wreathed in smiles. "It's amazing how God always brings us full circle once we put our lives in his hands. I'll bet Kate feels the same way."

"Karla." His dad's tone was cautionary. Dad set his glass aside, and Nicolas found himself staring into the no-nonsense eyes of the father of his youth. "Son, you need to tell us what's going on. No more sidestepping or games."

Nicolas sat back and studied his parents. They were both silent now, returning the scrutiny. He took a deep breath and focused on his mother. "Yeah well, it's not as nice as you think, Mom." He took a deep breath. "I killed him."

His admission hung in the room like a heavy fog for several seconds. His mom took hold of his dad's hand. They looked at each other, exchanging some sort of silent communication.

Dad covered Mom's hand with his free one and leaned forward. "We've always been here for you. Tell us what happened."

His father's words brought stability and comfort back into the room. Twenty years of fear dissolved. These two people would understand. These two people would never hold him nearly as accountable as he'd held himself.

The story poured out. It wasn't any easier to tell the second time around, but he didn't have as much to lose. Kate probably hated him. His parents never would. By the time Nicolas finished, his mother's eyes streamed tears, and his father's face held a sympathy that almost broke him. Nicolas sat back, exhausted, waiting for one of his parents to speak.

His mom snatched a handful of tissues from the side table and swiped her face dry. "Finally."

"Finally?"

She rose to cross the room, sat on the arm of his chair, and drew him to her side.

Nicolas allowed himself to be held, grateful that he could depend on the love of his parents, even when he didn't think he deserved it.

"Yes, finally. We knew something horrible happened during that first deployment. You withdrew from everyone who loved you, and from God. It's been hard to watch you struggle, not knowing what caused the pain festering inside your heart. Now that you've rededicated your life to Christ and you've cleared the air with Kate, maybe you can move beyond this."

Her hopeful assessment brought his anger boiling back to the surface. Bitterness pumped through his heart along with his blood. *How could she think...?* He shrugged out of her embrace and lurched to his feet. "Oh yeah, God's been a big help." His words were scornful. "I gave my life back to him and what did I get in return? I got my heart handed to me on a silver platter, crushed and burned, with a dagger jabbed into it for good measure. God didn't care what happened in my life, or Chad's, twenty years ago and He certainly doesn't give a rats..." Nicolas caught the swear word before it could leave his mouth. "...*backside* now."

"Son." The word came from his father in a low growl. "I know you're hurting, but I'll ask you to remember where you are."

Nicolas sucked back some of the vinegar threatening to spew from his mouth. This was a Christian home. Nothing he said or felt would ever change that. He paced in silence.

"How did Kate take all of this?" his mother asked.

The noise that escaped his throat contained no humor. "How do you think she took it? I'll be lucky if she ever speaks to me again. I don't know what's going to happen with our partnership. I offered to have it dissolved. She asked me to wait." He stopped and ran his hands through his hair. "I'm waiting, but if you can see this working out for us, romantically or professionally, I want to borrow your glasses."

"I'll talk to her—"

He silenced his mother with a look. "That's the one thing I don't want you to do. Kate knows how I feel about her. She needs the time and space to process this in her own way. If it makes you feel better, pray about it, and for her, all you want. I know you're going to anyway." *For all the good that does.* "But I want you to promise me that you'll leave it at that for now."

She exhaled a tired breath. "I promise."

"Good." Nicolas crossed to where she sat and bent down to kiss her cheek. "I know I'm asking a lot, but I'm not a five-year-old anymore. I need to get myself out of this mess."

With the story still fresh in the air he turned for the door. "I need to go." Outside, he unlocked the Camaro and slid behind the wheel. Grief and anger still pounded through his blood stream with every beat of his heart. His parents didn't hate him, and despite Mom's promises, she'd keep an eye on Kate for him, even if she did it from a distance. He looked through the windshield. The late winter sky had faded to a dusky blue, speckled with early evening stars. Nicolas shook his head, his irreverent thought becoming a whispered challenge. "Check. Your move."

~ * ~

Across town Kate burrowed under her covers in a room gone dark with an early sunset. Beat up from the fall, exhausted from conversations, tears, and explanations, her heart and nerves twisted into a quivering mess, she did the only thing she had left to do. She prayed. "Father, if You have a plan in all of this, please show me."

# CHAPTER TWENTY-THREE

Nicolas sat in the passenger seat of one of Garfield's three unmarked patrol cars Friday morning. An unscheduled personal day off the day before had not improved his mood. He'd spent the day acting like a love sick adolescent. Not venturing too far from the phone, hoping against all his expectations to hear from Kate, but that call never came. He hated that his life would spend another day in limbo. *Just one more day? Optimistic aren't you?* He shook his head. As far as he could tell, there were no solutions for the problems looming in his life. Despite his refusal to unburden himself over the last twenty years, there'd been a part of him that had hoped the action might make him feel better.

He buckled his seat belt, intercepting a look from his partner. "What?"

Tyler made an exaggerated face at Nicolas's growled response and faced the windshield of the vehicle with a smirk. "I didn't say a word, buddy. Not a word."

"You don't have to say a word to get your point across. I can read you like the top line of an eye chart. If you have something to say, spit it out. I'm not sitting on a stake-out all morning with you staring at me like I'm some monkey in a circus."

Tyler maneuvered the car out of the parking lot and

onto the street. He turned for Garfield's northern city limits and gave his attention to the road. Their interrogation earlier in the week had ended in a dead end. Lonnie Watts spent the night in a cell, leaving captivity behind in less than forty-eight hours, thanks to a slick lawyer and no solid evidence. All they had left was a cryptic text message retrieved from Watts's cell phone, leading them to believe that there was a major drug buy scheduled to go down sometime today. Garfield's uniformed officers stood by, ready to offer assistance, but the long hours of watching the comings and goings of the old trailer park fell to Tyler and Nicolas.

Tyler pulled into an abandoned driveway across from the run-down community. He positioned the car behind some bushes. They had a clear line of sight to the home in question, but they were shielded from direct view. Nicolas angled in the seat and looked out the window. He swept the area with binoculars to satisfy himself that all was quiet, then he crossed his arms and continued to stare out the window. It was going to be a tedious morning if his partner didn't take the hint and let him be.

"You don't look sick."

And there it was. "Never said I was."

"Well, I'm just thinking out loud. Silence from the passenger seat does that to me. It's not like you to take an unplanned day off work without saying something to me. Dispatch said you called in sick. I figured you must be on your deathbed."

"No such luck."

Tyler drummed his fingers on the wheel and tainted the air with an off tune whistle.

Nicolas pinched the bridge of his nose and turned up the service radio. Static-filled chatter between Garfield's patrol cars was better than the torturous noise coming from the driver's seat.

Tyler turned it down. "OK...You aren't sick, we've a decent handle on this case, so that shouldn't be troubling you. Seems to me the only option left to explain your sour mood is woman trouble. Something wrong in your newfound paradise?"

Nicolas reached under his seat and extracted a dog-eared book of crossword puzzles left over from their last all-nighter. He opened the glove box and rummaged for a couple of pencils. He ripped a page free and shoved it and a pencil across the seat. "Take this, occupy yourself, and leave me alone. You don't want to push it today." Nicolas angled away in his seat and focused on his own puzzle. *Five letter word for a series of changes in the moon, ends in E...* He licked the tip of the pencil. P.H.A.S...

"Sure I do."

The pencil point skittered across Nicolas's page and snapped off."We've got nothing to do except sit here and wait for our bad guys to show up. The only way in and out of this place is right in front of us. Let's talk."

Nicolas closed his eyes and drew in a deep breath, accepting the inevitable. They were partners after all. "I'm not going into the gory details, but yes, Kate and I are having issues. Suffice it to say we're pretty much done."

Tyler frowned. "After two weeks? That's got to be a busted relationship record, even for you."

"Tyler, you don't want to go there." He narrowed his eyes at the smile on his partner's face and the gleam in his eyes. "And why are you so chipper this morning? Last I checked you were still batching it because your wife walked out on you. Shouldn't you be just as hacked off at the world as I am?"

"Probably, but I spoke to Pastor last night. Melanie has an appointment to talk with him Wednesday afternoon. I'm taking that as a positive sign, an indication that we might be moving in right direction. You really should tell me what's going on between you and Kate. I've got lots of experience with a stubborn woman. I might be able to help."

Nicolas snorted and narrowed his eyes. *I'd give anything to have what you have.* "What you have is a beautiful woman who loves you and wants to spend time with you." He frowned at his partner. "Frankly, the appeal escapes me."

"Hey."

"What you don't have is sense enough to appreciate it. You can both talk to Pastor Gordon 'til you're blue in the face. Talking can't fix stupid." Nicolas faced the window again, determined to put an end to the discussion. "You want to help me today? Sit on your side of the car and think about ways to solve your own woman problems before you dig any deeper into mine."

~ * ~

Melanie carried a fresh tray of treats from the kitchen and stacked them into the glass-fronted display cases. Fridays tended to be busy, and today was no exception. Plenty of free cookies walked out the door, but the ratio of paid to free remained high and continued to climb every week. *I can't wait to talk to Staci's granddaughter. The busier we get, the more appealing and extra set of hands sounds. That, and if I'm going to see Australia, I need to do more than just think about it.* Her hand rested briefly against her stomach. It wasn't just her vacation plans that factored into that decision. Raising a child on her own would mandate some career changes.

She worked on autopilot while she considered her situation, present and future. The disastrous Tuesday night dinner with Tyler only reinforced her need to make some decisions about her marriage, which left her needing to decide about a more permanent living arrangement. She'd need something with at least two bedrooms, something with a nice nursery space. She wouldn't have her child's crib jammed into a corner like an afterthought. She'd waited too long for this, and she planned to go all out. Her thoughts were bitter-sweet. In all her wildest dreams she'd never imagined making these kinds of plans on her own. Despite her upcoming talk with Tyler's pastor, she didn't see things getting better where her busted marriage was concerned.

The bell over the door announced new customers and drew Melanie back to the here and now. Two women waved at a few of the existing patrons before stopping to browse the selection of goodies "Welcome to Sweet Moments. What can I get for you today?"

The women grinned at each other and turned to Melanie with matching shrugs. "That's a difficult question," the older of the two answered. "How does anyone choose just one thing?"

Melanie smiled. "Take your time." While she waited for them to make a choice she assembled a large box and loaded it with aqua iced cupcakes. A special order for a baby shower later this evening. She sent a thought down to the baby nestled in her womb. *What color would you like your room to be?*

A burst of coarse laughter erupted from the table in the back corner. Three young men she'd never seen before today occupied the table. She'd been watching them on and off for almost an hour.

They'd initially ordered coffee to go with their free cookies. Once their cups were empty, they'd refilled their drinks, purchased a dozen chocolate chip cookies, and retreated to their table. Dressed in plain black hoodies with unmarked ball caps pulled low over their eyes, the trio huddled around the table, and their snack, like a pack of dogs over a bone. They weren't causing any trouble, and Melanie knew she couldn't judge her clientele on appearance, but something about the way their eyes roamed the shop and lingered on her customers raised tiny bumps of alarm on the back of her neck. *You've been married to a cop too long. It's got you seeing trouble where there isn't any.* Maybe so, but she looked forward to their departure.

Work provided a distraction from worry. Coffee pots needed refilling, cups and plastic ware ran out and needed to be restocked. Melanie lost track of the boxes of cookies and other treats that departed the bakery with happy shoppers. *Good grief, I need roller skates!*

Melanie straightened from the lower shelf of a display. She pushed one hand into the small of her aching back and with the other, shoved a loose strand of hair out of her face. She glanced at the clock. *Noon.* Just sixty more minutes, and she could lock the door and prop up her tired feet. She was just a few weeks pregnant, the baby no bigger than a lima bean. How could something so small tie her back in knots and sap so much of her energy? She needed a comfortable chair in the back room, something with an ottoman. That, and a portable crib. With more help in the shop, she could keep the baby here for the first couple of months. Her imagination painted a fanciful picture of her, comfortable in a cushy chair, a baby nestled to her breast, while her help ran the bakery for thirty minutes. Mind made up, she promised herself a shopping trip on her next day off.

The bell tinkled as the door closed behind another customer, leaving the store empty except for the three boys still clustered around the back table. Melanie felt a tingle of relief when they rose as well and headed for the door. Instead of leaving, the smallest of the three turned her open sign to closed and flipped the lock. The hair on the back of her neck came to attention, and a sweat that had nothing to do with the heat of the store soaked the underarms of her shirt. He leaned against the door as the two burlier ones approached the counter.

Melanie backed up until she met the solid resistance of the wall. With no place to go, she waited. Some of her cop's wife training kicked in, and she studied each of them for identifying traits. The one by the door would be easy to remember, young and slight, his blond hair hung dirty with the ends tinted red beneath the edge of his cap. Of the two moving toward her, one had brilliant green eyes that had to be contacts, and the other had a strand of barbed wire tattooed across the backs of both hands.

Green eyes took the lead. "Hey there, Mama,

business is good in this hick town."

*Mama?* Melanie shuddered. It had to be a figure of speech, not a threat to her child. No way could they know about the baby. She planned to keep it that way. She did her best to stare him down.

He grinned in response. "What? I'm not worth talkin' to? You shore been running your mouth at everyone else all mornin'."

Melanie bit her lip and waited. She'd give them whatever they wanted. Tyler had taught her that. *Cooperate, don't anticipate. Money can be replaced.*

The green eyes narrowed, and any trace of good humor faded. "No matter." He paused and lifted the hem of his hoodie just enough for her to see the gun tucked into his waistband.

Melanie felt the blood drain from her brain.

The thug nodded and gave the weapon a pat. "We're gonna keep these out of sight as much as possible. No need for you to panic or cause a stir on the street. Now, you've been real busy today, and if you want to be around to be real busy tomorrow, you're going to let us help you with all that nice money you been rakin' in." He stopped and snapped his fingers. Tattoo guy tossed a cloth bag on the counter. "Be a good victim now and load that bag up for us nice and fast. You do that and we disappear. You get any heroic ideas..." He motioned to the bulge at his waist and winked. "Won't be pretty."

The room grew quiet on the heels of his threat. Melanie urged her paralyzed limbs to comply with his demands. Her whole body remained frozen in place.

"Move!"

She moved, grabbing bills from the register,

including the one on the bottom rigged to sound a silent alarm.

~ * ~

*All units, we have a silent alarm at 231 South Main.*

Tyler bolted upright in his seat. *Melanie.* He twisted the key in the ignition with enough force to snap it off in the switch.

Nicolas looked up from his puzzle as the engine roared to life and the car lurched into gear. "What...?"

"Get your seat belt on." Tyler backed out of their hiding place, pointed the car toward town, and tromped the gas petal. Tire smoke billowed around the car as it launched forward.

"Why—?"

"That's the address for the bakery." The car fishtailed, tires searching for purchase in the gravel as they left the side road for the main road into town. Tyler fought the wheel for control and won a narrow victory.

"Tyler, slow down. Killing us before we get there won't help Melanie. They said silent alarm. If this is the real deal and you go in there hot, you're likely to spook someone."

"And if I take my time, Melanie might get hurt. Not a great selection of options, partner. Hold on."

Tyler careened into the oncoming lane to dodge a slower vehicle.

Nicolas planted a hand on the dash and braced himself as the car whipped back into the proper lane.

"Tyler, it's Garfield. There hasn't been a store robbery here in at least two years. Someone probably tripped the alarm by mistake."

"I hope so, but think about it. A note of warning in my floor board, Lonnie's veiled threats in interview." Tyler swerved out of the path of a biker. "Then we just *happen* to find a text on his phone that has us staked out all morning. My gut says we've been suckered, and I think Melanie's about to pay the price for our persistence."

Nicolas grabbed the mic of the two way radio. "Detective's Black and Mason responding to silent alarm at 231 Main."

"Roger that."

Tyler reduced his speed two blocks from Melanie's shop. He ignored the patrol cars in position around the front of the building and zipped into the alley that ran behind the row of businesses. The car rocked to a sudden stop.

"What...?"

Tyler shut off the engine. "I have a key to the back entrance. I'm going in that way."

Nicolas grabbed his arm. "No, you aren't. I know you're worried, but there are protocols in place for situations like this for a reason."

Tyler shook him off and opened the door. "What would you do if that were Kate in there?" He didn't wait for an answer. With his service revolver in one hand and the key in the other, Tyler approached the door, crouched beside it, and inserted the key.

He took a deep breath when the lock whispered open. *Father, protect us both.* The door swung open, and Tyler edged through the narrow opening, leading with his gun supported in both hands. His eyes roamed to the four corners. The back room was empty. He stared at the door leading into the shop. Panicked voices filtered through.

"What are we gonna do man? The cops are here. She musta' called them."

"Shut up. Let me think!"

"But—"

"Shut your pie hole before I shut it for you."

Tyler inched his way toward the open doorway. He stopped at the door frame and risked a single glance. Melanie stood behind the counter facing three punks pressed against the far wall. One of the thugs had a gun. The weapon shook in a dangerous arc between the cops visible through the plate glass window of the shop and Melanie.

The sight pushed Tyler over the edge of caution. He swung into the doorway, gun raised. "Police!"

# CHAPTER TWENTY-FOUR

For a split second Nicolas found himself paralyzed, overwhelmed by a sense of déjà vu caused by another partner facing a life or death situation on his watch. He shook it off and reached for the radio mic. "We're in place in the back of the building. Is the front secure?"

"10-4. Three visible suspects. At least one of them has a weapon."

Nicolas nodded. "Detective Mason is attempting entry through the back door. Get a second unit back here. Let us know if you see anything that indicates the perps are aware of his presence." He dropped the mic and went to back up his partner. Before Nicolas could reach the door, Tyler slipped through the small opening. Nicolas's heart plummeted to his feet when three shots rang into the silence.

Nicolas charged the door. His own safety of no concern in the face of history repeating itself. With stealth no longer an issue, he shoved through the door, the force of his entry slammed the heavy metal against the concrete wall of the bakery. The sight spread before him brought Nicolas skidding to a stop. Tyler lay crumpled on the floor, Melanie on her knees at his side. Blood poured from a wound in his partner's chest.

Nicolas sucked in a breath, searching for the protocols he'd reminded Tyler of seconds earlier. Panic would accomplish nothing. Panic could get them all killed. He crossed the room and crouched next to the doorway into the shop. He lurched into the bakery, leading with his weapon. "Police." The room was empty. He holstered his gun and left the bad guys to the uniforms waiting outside the front of the building.

He knelt next to his fallen partner, shouldered Melanie out of the way, and tried to staunch the flow of blood with his bare hands. "Melanie, I need towels."

Melanie's low moan bore no resemblance to words.

"Melanie, are you hurt?"

"I... He... No."

He spoke slowly, hoping to penetrate the cloud of shock she seemed lost in. "Do you have any clean towels?"

"I...yes!" She scrambled to her feet and raced, her feet slipping in her husband's blood, to a cabinet in the far corner. She pulled it open, filled her arms with clean, white towels, and hurried back to his side. "Nicolas...is he...?"

"He's alive, but it's not good."

"Don't let him die."

*If only it were up to me.* Nicolas stacked towels on the wound and applied pressure. The walkie-talkie at his side crackled to life. "We have three suspects in custody, two with minor wounds." Nicolas lifted a shaky hand and toggled the broadcast button. "I need an ambulance back here, now. I have an officer down." He ignored the rest of the chatter and focused on his partner.

Tyler's eyes fluttered open on a breathless groan.

Melanie took his hand and smoothed his hair from his forehead. "Tyler, sweetheart, I'm here. Hang on."

"I love you, Mel." The words came out as barely a whisper.

"I love you, too." She shook his shoulder when his eyes fluttered shut. "Tyler, don't close your eyes. Look at me! We're having a baby. Do you hear me? A baby!"

His gaze fixed on her face for just a second before his eyelids closed again. Bubbles, formed by blood and spit, clung to the corners of his mouth.

Nicolas increased the pressure on his chest. "Tyler, open your eyes. Come on, buddy, you open your eyes and stay with me. Help is coming." Tyler remained unresponsive, and Nicolas felt panic welling in his chest. "Tyler! Don't you dare die on me!"

~ * ~

Kate's eyes snapped open when Patrick burst into her room. Groggy from a forty-eight hour headache, two days of pain medication, and the early afternoon nap they'd induced, she struggled to sit up and get her bearings.

"Mom, wake up." Patrick snatched the remote from the bedside table, aimed it at the TV, and clicked it on. "You have to see this." The picture flickered to life at the same instant her phone rang.

Kate stared at the screen and swiped the phone connection open. "Hello."

"Kate, it's Karla. You need to turn on your TV."

"Karla, what's going on? Patrick just—"

"Turn it to channel five."

Patrick was pushing buttons before Kate had a chance to acknowledge her friend's instructions. He cranked the volume up and sat on the side of Kate's bed.

"We're reporting live from Garfield, where a police detective was shot and critically wounded in a robbery attempt gone horribly wrong this afternoon."

"Nicolas."

"Not Nicolas," Karla assured her. "Tyler."

The dark-headed reporter shook her hair away from her face and allowed her eyes to grow suitably empathic before she continued.

"According to early reports, Melanie Mason, owner of"—she paused to look at her notes—"the Sweet Moments Bakery, was held at gunpoint by three unidentified assailants. Her husband, Tyler Mason, a detective with the Garfield Police Department, heard the emergency radio call and rushed to his wife's rescue. Two of the suspects were wounded in the gunfire that followed." The camera panned across the front of the bakery, lingering for a second on the yellow crime scene tape, before moving on to picture the police vehicles, lights flashing, parked in disarray before the building.

"Detective Mason has been medevac'd to a nearby trauma center. Stay tuned for updates as this tragic story unfolds. This is Hailey Wolfe reporting."

Kate ignored the rest of the report as she rolled to her feet. She blinked at Patrick, standing like he was ready to catch her if she fell, then spoke into the phone. "Melanie?"

"I don't know anything, Kate," Karla said. "I can't reach Nicolas, and the station isn't releasing any info. All they'd tell me was that Nicolas was fine and they'd taken Tyler to Brighton Park Trauma. I'm headed that way now. I can pick you up if you'd like."

"I'll be ready in fifteen minutes." Kate tossed the phone on the bed and yanked a pair of jeans from her closet.

"Mom?"

"You know what I know at this point. Karla's on her way, I'm going to the hospital with her. I..." She turned too quickly, and a wave of dizziness forced her to sit on the edge of her mattress. She held out a hand to her son. It took all her effort to stem the tears of helplessness that threatened to overwhelm her. Patrick took her hand and sat next to her.

"Would it do me any good to tell you that you need to stay in bed?"

"We don't always get to do what we need. I'm going to be with Melanie."

"Fine, but Melanie won't be the only one there. You're going to have to face Nicolas Black as well. Are you ready for that? Have you given any thought to how that conversation will go?"

Kate shook her head. Love, confusion, and hurt warred in her heart. There were no clear winners. She leaned into her son. "It's only been two days. I haven't given it a lot of thought. And I haven't thought of anything else." Her sigh filled the room. "I don't know any more than I knew forty-eight hours ago."

Patrick squeezed her hand, and his baritone voice filled the room. "Jesus, if we ever needed Your direction and wisdom, we need them now. Cover Detective Mason with Your protection. Calm Mom's spirit and help her find Your will in all of this. I know she's been praying for her friend, Melanie. Help her know that she can lean on you."

Kate turned and placed a kiss on Patrick's cheek. "I

wish I could have had four more, just like you."

"That's not what you said when I was fifteen." He chuckled before pulling away to look her in the eye. "Mom, I don't mean to meddle in your business, but I've been doing a lot of thinking and praying while you've been sleeping off your concussion. I want you to know that I don't blame Nicolas for what happened to Dad. I want you to be happy, and I think this is a chance for you to have something you've never had. If you can look into his face and not see how much he cares for you...you're goofy...and my mom isn't known for her goofiness."

He shrugged. "However you decide to handle it, I love you, and I've got your back." Patrick stood before Kate could acknowledge his words. "Now get dressed. Karla will be here any minute."

~ * ~

Kate followed Karla through the swinging doors of Brighton Park's family waiting area. She stopped just inside the room, her muddled brain still a couple of seconds behind processing the details.

Bathed in bright lights and the ever-present smell of antiseptics, the room was supposed to look homey, but the decorators hadn't quite hit the mark. Nicolas, the cuffs of his shirt stained with a dark substance, prowled the room from one wall to the next, phone to his ear, mumbling quietly. Kate's pulse edged higher as her gaze skirted over him and landed on Melanie.

Her friend sat in a corner chair, eyes wide and staring, her arms wrapped around her torso. She rocked back and forth.

Karla hurried to take her son in her arms, no doubt relieved to confirm that none of the blood spilled that morning belonged to him. Kate crossed to Melanie, pried one of her hands free, and said a silent prayer for wisdom.

Melanie blinked and turned to Kate as if just now registering her presence. "He just has to be OK. We've both been so stubborn and foolish the last few weeks...years." A tear escaped the corner of her eye and rolled down her cheek. "He has to be OK."

Kate squeezed her hand. "What happened?"

"They wanted money."

"They?"

Nicolas disentangled himself from his mother. "Three punk junkies from the city. Tyler and I have been working a drug case. Our drug dealers sent in three of their flunkies to try and scare us off by threatening Melanie." He paused and knelt in front of Melanie. "They weren't supposed to hurt you, but they had orders to give you a good scare. They didn't consider Garfield's police force much of a threat. So they got greedy and turned the warning into a robbery." He stopped, his gaze went to the far wall and bored a hole in the plaster. "But they didn't count on my partner. He got two of them before they took him down. Third one is in lock up, singing like a bird in a cage."

Melanie leaned forward, rested her head on his shoulder, and dissolved into a round of fresh tears. Nicolas held her while she cried and patted her back. "He'll be OK." He looked up at Kate and Karla. "The doc said it looked worse than it was."

Melanie shook herself free. "Oh, they probably say

that to everyone. They can't very well tell you to sit here and worry because he doesn't have a chance. What if the doctor's wrong? What if I don't get another chance to tell him that I'm sorry and that I love him? What if...?" Her words trailed off as tears streaked down her face. "This whole thing is my fault."

Kate frowned at her friend. "How is this your fault?"

Melanie pulled tissues from the box sitting on the table next to her chair and swiped at her face. Her expression was woeful when she continued. "I'm a stubborn, hateful, unreasonable shrew of a wife. I've never done anything except make demands that Tyler couldn't fulfill. Why couldn't I just accept what he had to give and be happy?" She jerked out of her seat to pace in the tracks Nicolas had worn into the carpet. "I'll tell you why. I wanted the fairy tale, the whole happily-ever-after package."

Kate settled into her chair and waited for Melanie's rant to wind down. There were valid reasons for the separation, but getting this out of her system might help her friend find the solution she was looking for.

"Someone to be at my beck and call, someone to share every minute of my day. Someone who couldn't breathe if they were away from me for too long." She turned and her shoulders slumped. "How realistic is that? I left my husband because the ways he loved me weren't good enough for me, and now I may never get the chance to tell him I was wrong. To make sure he knows that I love him. To make a family with our baby." She sat back in her seat and bounced her fisted hand off her forehead. "Stupid...stupid...stupid."

Kate opened her mouth to speak, but Nicolas stepped into the gap.

He shook his head. "None of this is your fault, Melanie. I should have stopped him from going through that door, even if I had to sit on him. I'm his partner. It's my job to have his back, and I screwed it up..."

His eyes held on Kate's, and the sorrow reflected in his gaze broke her heart.

Nicolas shook his head. "I failed my partner. It's what I do."

Kate looked from Nicolas to Melanie. She felt a nudge in her heart and prayed for God to direct her words. "You two both need to stop. What about God's place in all of this?"

Nicolas snorted and turned away.

Kate focused her attention on Melanie, knowing that Nicolas heard every word. "Sweetheart, if the worst happens and Tyler doesn't pull through this, it's not because of anything you, or Nicolas, did or didn't do. You both love him. Neither of you ever wanted to see him hurt, and neither of you pulled the trigger this morning." She sat back and scanned the room, seeing what she wanted on an end table by the door. She nodded in that direction. "Karla, hand me that Bible, will you?"

Karla placed the book in her hands, and Kate caressed the cover. *Father, please give me the words they need to hear.* "There's so much in here about God's plan for our lives. We have all the free will we want, but God knows from the day we're born how much time we have on this earth. The manner of our coming and going" She opened the Bible and flipped through several pages. "Here it is, Matthew 6:27. 'Which of you by taking thought can add one cubit to his stature?' It says the same thing in Luke. Stature isn't referring to how tall we are, guys. Most translations render that as adding one moment to our lives. All the worry in the world, the guilt, the blame, the second guessing—they can't give any of us one more second of life than we had when we started."

Kate took a deep breath as the words hit a bull's eye in her own heart. *Not one more second.* She closed her eyes and pictured Chad's sweet face. *Oh. Chad. You were gone before you left.* "Psalms 139:16 tells us that God knew our days and had them written in His book before they ever were. Daniel tells us that God holds our breath in His hands and owns our days."

She looked at Nicolas, and the doubt melted from her heart. *Not his fault. Not now and not then.* Tears battered at the backs of her eyes. *He loved Chad, would have taken his place if he could. Now he loves me.* "Life happens, and we can't control it, but the rest of the story is that we can be ready when life throws us a curve if we chose to be."

"I wish I had your faith," Melanie said.

Kate smiled. "I've been trying to share it with you, so has Tyler. It's yours for the asking, just a prayer away."

Melanie bit her lip and looked toward the doorway leading to the hall and the surgery suites beyond. Unabashed hope filled her face.

Kate tilted her head and refused to give into the sudden dizziness that washed over her. She studied Melanie's expression. *Time for a reality check.* She tugged her friend's hand until Melanie turned back to face her. She shook her head. "Girlfriend, I can almost read your mind. If you don't hear anything else I say, hear this.

Salvation is a life changer, but it's not a magic pill. Being a committed Christian is hard work. It doesn't guarantee you a life of roses. It doesn't mean that Tyler pulls through. It isn't a cure all for your marriage problems." She shrugged. "I'm not trying to talk you out of it, I'm just being honest. It's not a magic pill," she repeated. "But, it's a great step in the right direction. Are you ready to ask?"

Melanie nodded. "I think so."

Kate motioned to Karla, and both women gathered around their friend in prayer as she asked Jesus into her life and prayed for the well-being of her husband. Kate couldn't help but notice the frown on Nicolas's face as he watched them from across the room.

# CHAPTER TWENTY-FIVE

Kate was wide awake as the sun began to filter through the blinds of her bedroom windows the next morning. The light increased with each breath, turning the items in her room from vague shadows to clearly defined furnishings. She tried to blame her sleeplessness on the constant napping of the last two days, but that didn't ring true. When the clock glowed seven-thirty, she gave up, tossed the covers aside, and went in search of her morning cup of caffeine. Patrick's voice filtered from his old room as she tiptoed past his door.

"Mom?"

"I'm OK, sweetheart. Just going to make some coffee. Go back to sleep for a while." She continued to the kitchen, briefly debated her choice of flavors, and decided on the hazelnut. Kate sat at the table with a weary sigh. Yesterday had been a never-ending day. The robbery, the time at the hospital, Melanie's tearful conversion, the unending wait for word on Tyler's condition, and finally, the golden moment when the doctor came though the double doors with word that Tyler was in recovery and doing well. Through it all, Nicolas kept to himself, a man apart, guilt evident in the slump of his shoulders and down-turned corners of his mouth.

Karla had driven everyone except Melanie home at

ten. Nicolas slumped out of his mother's car without a word or a backwards glance.

Kate cradled her cup and breathed a prayer. "He's so hurt, Father. Please hold him up today. He needs you."

*He's awake, go talk to him.*

She frowned at the words that took shape in her heart. *Wishful thinking or heavenly instruction?* He'd been so distant yesterday. He probably wouldn't welcome her presence on his doorstep now or any other time. Kate tapped the rim of her cup. *We do have business to resolve. I haven't changed my mind about our partnership at the center, I don't want him thinking I have.* She grinned and pushed the half empty cup away. *That's my story, and I'm sticking to it.*

"In fact..." Kate crossed to the cabinet, removed two large, insulated travel mugs, and filled them from the pot. Her smile brightened as she took a box of cookie dough from the freezer, turned the oven on, and placed a dozen mounds of dough on a pan, enough for her, Nicolas, and Patrick. A sweet breakfast peace offering to Nicolas and an apology to Patrick for sneaking out of the house when he was supposed to be watching her.

While the cookies baked, Kate crept back to her bedroom to get dressed. She returned to the kitchen before the timer rang, boxed up eight cookies, left four on a plate along with a note, for her son, and stepped out into a beautiful spring morning.

The drive to Nicolas's house didn't give her nearly enough time to organize her thoughts. But when she pulled to his curb an hour after rising, she was relieved to see that his front door stood open, allowing the morning sunshine to filter through the glass storm door. Retrieving her peace offering, she navigated the walk with a determined stride and rang the bell.

Nicolas answered the door, barefoot, dressed in blue jeans and a wrinkled USAF sweatshirt. His expression remained guarded as he held the door open for her.

Kate shook her head at his unspoken invitation. "I brought us a treat, but the morning is too beautiful to waste it inside." She handed him the cookies. "I'll wait out here while you put these in the kitchen. Grab your shoes. Let's go for a walk."

He left her where she stood without saying a word. Nerves zinged up her spine. *What if I've read him wrong?* She shoved the thought aside. Two days ago he'd told her twice that he loved her. The last forty-eight hours had been torturous for both of them, but nothing had changed. With her back to the door, she lifted her gaze to the blue sky. *Please guide my words.*

The door creaked behind her, and Nicolas joined her on the porch. Kate smiled up at him and handed him a mug of coffee, proud that her hands didn't betray the nerves rolling in her stomach. She started off down the sidewalk. Nicolas fell into step beside her, still silent, obviously waiting for her to take the lead.

Kate took in her surroundings. The neighborhood was one of the older ones in Garfield. Old-fashioned two-story houses stretched on either side of the walk. Pristine paint, shining windows flanked with contrasting shutters. Tall, naked trees towered over brown lawns littered with brittle leaves. Large porches, many decorated with rockers and porch swings. Birds chirped and squirrels played tag. It was beautiful and peaceful. The only thing marring the scene was the frown on Nicolas's face.

Kate pulled in a deep breath and reached out to take his hand.

The contact stopped Nicolas in his tracks. He stared at their joined hands. "What's going on, Kate?"

Kate turned to face him. "I came by to talk about our partnership."

The expression on his face would have been more fitting for a death row inmate. "I figured." He shrugged. "I told you I'd take care of the expense of breaking our contract, and I will. I'll call the lawyer first thing Monday morning."

Kate studied him with her head tilted to the side. "Not so fast. I have no intention of breaking our agreement."

"But—"

"No buts. I don't see any reason why we can't work together." She turned away and noticed a small park on the other side of the street. "Let's check out the park." Kate pulled Nicolas across the street and onto one of the winding paths that cut through the evergreen shrubbery.

She meandered, taking her time, looking for the right words. Through it all she clung to his hand while he walked silently by her side.

Once away from the street and the prying eyes of neighbors, Kate faced Nicolas, but he refused to meet her gaze. *Father, give me words.* She took the cup from his hand and placed both of them on the bench that skirted the path, then she took both of his hands in hers. "Did you mean what you said when you left on Wednesday?"

Nicolas closed his eyes and groaned. "Look, Kate, I was out of line. I just..." He leaned his forehead against hers. "Things just moved so fast. I fell for you...hard. I had no business saying what I said, especially after...I promise, if you're still willing to work with me, I'll try to keep my feelings to myself. I won't let them interfere with our business."

"That would be a real shame."

Nicolas backed up, reopening the distance between them. "What?"

Kate shook her head. "Do I have to spell it out for you?"

"I think you'd better."

Kate grabbed a handful of his jacket and pulled him close to her. She wrapped her arms around his waist and jumped from a cliff she'd promised never to leap from again. "I love you, too." Kate felt the muscles in Nicolas's back relax beneath her hands, almost like he'd been holding his breath. His arms came around her in a powerful embrace.

"Kate, I'm so sorry."

Kate shook her head and looked up into his eyes. "I want you to listen to me, because this is the last time we'll speak of this. You don't have anything to be sorry for, but I'll accept your apology if it brings you some comfort." She released him and placed her hands on his beard-stubbled cheeks. "Did you love Chad?"

"Like a brother."

"Then that's everything I need to know. You were there for him, Nicolas, when I couldn't be. You were his friend in a situation I'll never really understand. I know that if there had been a way to save him from what happened, you would have." Kate used a finger to trace the deeply embedded worry lines around his mouth.

"Chad's death was a grief I never quite got over. I know you've felt the same. We've had our faith tested over the last few days. I honestly believe that everything that's happened was God-ordained as an opportunity for us to heal and move beyond those old feelings."

She returned her hands to his waist and leaned her head against his chest. "There's always going to be a spot in my heart reserved for Chad Wheeler, just like there's a spot reserved for Alan Archer. I loved both of those men with all my heart. But there's a new spot in my heart right now. It has your name on it, if you'd like to take up residence."

Nicolas nudged her face up. He swiped away a tear she hadn't been aware of. She looked into his eyes and saw moisture reflected there as well. It didn't matter. For both of them, these were the tears of a twenty-year-old pain finally being healed by the God who loved them both.

He leaned down and joined his lips to hers. The kiss spun Kate's world onto a new path. She couldn't wait to see where God would lead them.

Nicolas lifted his lips, brushing them along her jaw, and up to her forehead as he straightened. "You up for a ride?"

"What did you have in mind?"

"Melanie called just before you got here. Tyler's awake."

~ * ~

Nicolas knocked on the hospital door and shoved it open without waiting for a response. With Kate right behind him, he entered the room and stopped short on the threshold. Tyler was sitting up in bed with a breakfast tray in front of him and a beaming wife at his side. If ever twelve hours had made a difference in a situation, this was it.

Tyler grinned and motioned them forward, his voice hearty when he spoke. "Hey, you two, come join the party."

Nicolas took a few steps forward. "Party? You got shot, and we almost lost you. I don't call that a party."

"Well, not my best day on a normal scale of one to ten, but all things considered." He stopped to smile at Melanie. "I'll take it." His gaze turned serious when he focused on Nicolas. "They tell me you saved my life yesterday." He shook his head. "I was way more than rash, and I probably deserve to be dead. Thanks to you—and God—I'm not."

"You scared the life out of me. I'm your partner, but I gotta tell ya, if you ever try a bonehead stunt like that again, I'll shoot you myself."

Tyler's answering laugh turned into a groan of pain. "Please don't make me laugh."

Melanie moved his tray out of the way and took his hand. "Can I tell them?"

Tyler nodded, a sparkle in his eye that had been missing for weeks. "Be my guest. They need to know, since I'm pretty sure we have plans for both of them down the road."

Melanie's face split in a beaming smile. "We're having a baby!"

Kate grinned and clapped her hands. "Oh, yay!"

Melanie shook her head. "He knows you knew, so you don't have to act surprised."

Kate wiped imaginary sweat from her forehead. "Double yay, I'm a lousy pretender."

Melanie took Tyler's hand, but she looked at Nicolas. "He heard me yesterday. I was so afraid he hadn't...that he would die not knowing about our miracle."

Tyler had eyes only for his wife. "I woke up thinking I'd dreamed it and afraid to ask her if she'd actually said it."

Melanie smiled when Tyler raised her hand to his lips for a kiss. "Tyler and I have been talking since last night. We've both been sort of dumb where our relationship is concerned. But we've decided it's too valuable to give up on, especially with the baby coming. If we can find a middle ground between my fairy tale expectations and his raging independence, we want to start over." She glanced at her husband and received an encouraging nod.

"All the way over," Melanie continued. "We've decided not to move back in together until we've had some counseling. Our anniversary is in two months. If we can work things out, we want to renew our vows on our wedding night. When we got married the first time, it was a quickie ceremony at the courthouse. I don't even have a wedding picture. This time we want the whole production. Flowers, music, a cake, and if I'm not a balloon by then, a real wedding dress." She smiled. "We'd like you guys to stand up for us."

"Oh..." Kate rushed forward and pulled Melanie into a hug. "What a beautiful idea. I'd love that. You have to let me help with the plans. And I have an offer for you. Why don't you ditch that tiny apartment and move in to Patrick's empty room for the next two months? I've got plenty of room, and frankly, I've been going a little crazy since Patrick moved out again." Kate leaned forward and whispered loudly in Melanie's ear. "With the hunky men in our lives, I think we're both going to need help staying on the straight and narrow. We can be accountability partners for each other."

Nicolas grinned when she looked into his eyes, and his heart went a bit wonky in his chest. *Wonky?* He examined the feeling and decided the word fit. *Father, I don't know how You did it, but I know You did it. I'm sorry I questioned You. I'm sorry I challenged You. I'm sorry it took me twenty years to see Your plan for my life. Thanks for not giving up on me.*

~ \* ~

*Two months later*

Pastor Gordon cleared his throat. "I now re-pronounce you husband and wife."

Kate's eyebrows swept up her forehead as Tyler pulled Melanie into his arms and dove, lips first, into a passionate kiss. She made a football time out signal with her hands. "Hold up there you two. This is only the rehearsal. I need to see some light between the two of you...now."

The couple broke apart. Melanie faced her friend. "You do understand that we're still married."

Kate frowned at her. "You told me that you wanted this to be a completely new beginning. If you want to ruin two months' worth of effort on the eve of success"—she waved a hand—"go for it. But if you do, I'm canceling your plane tickets. You can find a way to get to Sydney to catch that Australian cruise under your own steam."

"You wouldn't."

Kate stared her down.

Melanie shook her head and turned to pat her groom's cheek. "Sorry, Tyler. She knows how to hurt me. Sex with my *husband.*" She empathized the word. "Or transportation out of the country. You lose!" The bride danced out of the grooms reach and bent to talk to four-year-old Bobbie Evans about her flower girl duties.

Nicolas stepped up behind Kate, slipped his arms around her, and pulled her back against his chest. He spoke softly into her ear. "I think they're going to be OK now."

"I hope so. It's going to be a beautiful ceremony tomorrow."

"You've put a lot of work into it. Melanie and Tyler tomorrow, Sam and Patrick in June. You must enjoy planning weddings."

She sighed and nestled against him, content in the moment and the happiness of her friends. "It has its moments. I'll admit, putting two weddings together in two months has been a bit of a challenge. Mostly in a good way though."

"I'm relieved to hear you say that."

He shifted, one arm releasing her to dig in a pocket. When he raised his hand in front of her face, she gasped. He held a small black velvet box. "I was hoping I could talk you into a third."

# ABOUT THE AUTHOR

Sharon Srock went from science fiction to Christian fiction at slightly less than warp speed. Twenty five years ago, she cut her writer's teeth on Star Trek fiction. Today, she writes inspirational stories that focus on ordinary women and their extraordinary faith. Sharon lives in the middle of nowhere Oklahoma with her husband and three very large dogs. When she isn't writing you can find her cuddled up with a good book, baking something interesting in the kitchen, or exploring a beach on vacation. She hasn't quite figured out how to do all three at the same time.

Connect with her here:

Blog: www.sharonsrock.com

Facebook: www.facebook.com/SharonSrock#!/SharonSrock

Goodreads: www.goodreads.com/author/show/6448789.Sharon_Srock

Sign up for her quarterly newsletter from the blog or Facebook page.